Honored Oaths

&

Tangled Truths

B. Lynn Hedge

To anyone going through grief, know you're not alone. A large part of this book was written during a time that I was dealing with grief over losing my sweet Pebbles, who was my soul dog and best friend for 16 years. The pain never leaves; it just gets easier to carry as time goes on.

Rest easy, Pebbles.

I can go anywhere I want, just not home.
- Taylor Swift

Foreword

This is an interesting new story for me to write, and if you've taken the time to give it a chance, I first want to say THANK YOU.

There will be a lot of emotions in this story, and with it, some trigger warnings to keep in mind before reading.

This book is a reverse harem romance, meaning that the FMC will end up in a relationship with multiple men. It will contain mentions of suicidal thoughts, self-harm, flashbacks of self-harm, domestic abuse, substance abuse, death of a family member, violence, breath play, light bdsm, knife play, arranged marriage, mafia/crime family activities, and mentions of human auctions and skin trading.

If you have made it through that list and you are good with all of the above, then come and join me on this roller coaster that is Camilla Russo's story.

Contents

Foreword

Preface

Acknowledgments

Prologue   1

Camilla   8

Camilla   22

Camilla   38

Lev   54

Camilla   64

Camilla   76

Dima   87

Camilla   99

Roman   110

Camilla   119

Roman   127

Camilla   136

Camilla   151

Lev   173

Camilla	189
Roman	208
Camilla	221
Abram	241
Camilla	254
Camilla	267
Dima	278
Camilla	287
Camilla	297
Camilla	307
Camilla	322
Abram	333
Camilla	350
Epilogue	355

1

Prologue

~ *Camilla* ~

*M*y heart won't start anymore.

That was the goal on my mind when I pulled the blade across the fragile skin of my wrists. Drowning in grief, I ignore the voice in my head telling me it was a bad idea. That voice sounded too much like Dante, my brother.

Knowing I'd never hear him again made me try to push that voice away and fade into nothing.

Let the grief swallow me whole, pull me under its dark and churning waves in my mind as the last breath gets sucked out of me.

As I lay in the tub, letting blood flow around me, the voice in my mind gets quieter, taking me back to a different place.

Sitting in the booth of Mel's diner, I pick at the crumpled edges of the menu falling apart in front of me.

"Come on, Cami. Don't be angry at me," Dante pleads, lying over the table, trying to meet my gaze.

I stay still, refusing to give in. He's leaving tomorrow to go halfway around the world to some fancy school, leaving me with our father.

I wasn't taking it well.

Dante is my best friend, the best brother anyone could have. He always looks after me and makes me feel safe.

Now he's leaving, taking my safety with him.

I may only be 12, but I know our family differs significantly from others.

Mom ran off after having me, and my father has only ever looked at me with disgust and anger. Dante has been the one who has taken care of me all my life. Impressive considering he's only 16. He never got to have a childhood because of me; that thought alone almost makes me feel guilty for giving him the silent treatment.

Almost.

"Come on, Cami. You know if I could, I would take you with me. You're too young to go to the Academy, and father would never allow you to leave and go that far." He's right, but I still don't want to release my anger.

"I don't see why he'd care. He hates me anyway." I spit out petulantly.

He sits up, with relief flashing in his eyes when I speak to him again, quickly replaced by a guarded expression.

"Father is complicated. He doesn't hate you; he just doesn't have any use for you that he can benefit from. Trust me, that's a good thing."

I raise a brow at him, trying to come across as intimidating.

"What makes you think he won't find a use for me now that you won't be here?" I ask.

Dante's brow raises much higher than mine as he leans forward again.

"Father and I have talked. I'm doing what I need to do, and we have an agreement. He will not bother you; if he does, you call me immediately."

His tone offers no room for argument. I've seen him serious before when I've done something to get into trouble, but this is different. It gives me chills, like when I watch scary movies.

I don't like this.

"I still don't see why you have to go so far away." I pout, thinking about the distance that would soon be between us.

Reaching out, he holds my hands in his, rubbing circles on the backs.

"The academy will teach me things I can't learn here. I'll learn what I need; before you know it, I'll be back. I'll take you somewhere pretty when I'm back, somewhere with a beach, where we can have our own house. You'll be able to do whatever you want. We will have a happy life, far away from here and father."

He paints such a pretty picture for us and for our future.

"I still don't like it," I tell him half-heartedly.

His gaze softens, love shining in his eyes now.

"I know, Cam bam," He tells me tenderly, "But this is going to be good for us. You can call me whenever you want. I may be gone for a little while, but I will never leave you," He promises as he reaches into his pocket, pulling out a chain with a small silver and gold pendant on it. "And here, this way I'll always be with you, even while I'm away."

He passes the chain to me. The small pendant features a crescent moon bordering a sunflower, with small vines snaking up the chain. Flipping it over, I see a small script engraving: 'Always by your side. Love you lots. ~Dante'.

I smile, thinking about when I was little and told Dante that "love you" seemed too simple and that I needed something else to express how much I loved him. Given that I was 6, my only idea at the time was to make it "Love you lots," and over the years, it has stuck.

I thumb the pendant for a moment before peering at him.

"You promise you're coming back soon?" I ask.

He squeezes both my hands in his, "I promise Cami. I will come back to get you as soon as I can," he vows, not breaking eye contact. "Love you lots, Cam bam."

"Love you lots," I tell him, slipping the chain around my neck.

That was the last truly peaceful moment I'd had with him.

Since that day, I'd only seen him a couple of times when he came to visit, but Father always kept him busy while he was here. We talked a lot on the phone, but I tried not to bother him too much, knowing he had made good friends and was living his own life at the academy.

He was always my protector. I knew I could tell him anything, but I never did tell him how cruel Father had become when he left. I couldn't bring myself to ruin his newfound freedom.

Once he left, my father became invested in my life for the first time. He controlled how I dressed, behaved, who I could be friends with, and what I ate. Everything was his decision. What he said was what I was expected to do; his rules were the law in our household.

I told myself that it wouldn't last forever. I just had to stick it out until Dante came back home. All of this would be a memory that we could leave behind.

I told myself that I could make it another year.

But my plan was shattered like a broken window as soon as my father callously delivered the news to me.

Dante was dead. He wasn't coming back for me.

I didn't believe him at first. He was such a sick man that, even as twisted as it was, he could have been lying to me. After all, what kind of father can look so pleased with himself while getting to tell his daughter that her older brother, his only son, was dead?

It wasn't until Father threw the academy report at me that I was forced to face the facts.

A night of drinking with friends gone wrong, it said. My brother's body was found in the lake, having drowned sometime in the night.

Father left me alone after that. Leaving me at war with myself, my emotions raging inside me.

Grief for my brother, who I would never see again, disbelief at him actually being gone, fear of my father and being left here alone with him, and anger. Anger at the promise my brother made to me being broken. Guilt slammed into me again at feeling angry when Dante was dead, but I couldn't stop it. All the emotions kept warring to see which would come out on top. It left me feeling like a hollow shell of a person, like I was outside of my body watching myself shut down.

I waited three days for the hollow feeling to subside, reliving memories and conversations with Dante. Dwelling on the things I never told him and berating myself for not calling him enough.

I felt useless. Dante had always taken care of me, yet I could never offer him anything in return. And then he died before I ever got the chance to repay him.

I didn't know how to live without him—three days alone in my room with nothing but my thoughts offered me no insight on moving past this.

So, this morning I made my choice. I was going to end it all. I can take my own life, leave father to his miserable existence, and maybe, if I'm lucky, then I'll get to be with Dante again.

I'm not scared. I feel peace.

Peace in knowing that I made this decision, no one else, just me. It's the only way I can stop feeling all this pain.

Without Dante, I have no one. So, I'm not sad, I'm not leaving anyone behind who can't get over it.

My story will end here. No one will even notice.

Lying here, surrounded by blood, I let my mind drift. Eager to welcome the peace with open arms.

My pulse slows down, silently slipping away.

I let the darkness creep in, knowing my heart won't start anymore.

As I drift away, a loud crash and shouting fill the small space around me.

I'm too far gone to open my heavy eyelids and see what it is.

I let myself continue to slip. Just waiting to see my brother.

2

Camilla

Three years in this God forsaken place, with its stark white walls, plastic furniture, and grippy socks, yet each day sucked just as much as the one before it.

Life sucks.

Every day, after a cocktail of pills to start the morning, I get to meet with a therapist who usually wants to revisit me trying to kill myself, for no other reason than to rub it in my face that I failed at trying to kill myself.

If I were unsure if I wanted to die before, this place would leave no doubt in my mind.

My father truly was a sadistic man. Finding this place had to involve a special skill set I'm not sure many possessed.

Not only was this *asylum* completely remote, buried deep in the Wisconsin wilderness, but it also came with sadistic guards who loved to fuck with the patients for sport.

Making us fight each other, threatening to withhold food, or strapping us to our beds for psych evaluations, and they were always ready to step in at any movement to dole out their punishments.

Punishments usually meant the typical beating, manual labor, or solitary confinement, but if you got an irate guard, then they'd use the trench. The trench sounded about as lovely as it was, a hole dug in the ground with a metal grate on top. Just deep enough that you couldn't climb out, but still shallow enough that the sun burned your skin after being left out there all day with nothing to shade you.

It was by far one of the worst punishments to endure, exposed to the elements and truly miserable.

The 'doctors' and 'therapists' turned a blind eye to the treatment we endured from the guards, ignoring any physical signs during our mandatory sessions. I'd only known of one girl who tried to tell her therapist about the abuse; she was taken to isolation "for her safety" and hasn't been seen since.

Most of my first year here was spent getting repeatedly punished; my body is now littered with scars, each telling the tale of a different transgression. I tried my hardest to resist being medicated or fighting other patients, and even went on a hunger strike after a guard demanded that I steal another patient's food.

I'd been beaten, strapped down, and force-fed through a tube for that one.

I've faced many punishments, but that one was brutal. Being strapped to a bed for three weeks fucked with my mind more than I care to admit. I was so weak when they let me out, which only made me the target of attacks and fights when the guards were bored.

When I was admitted, I was a scrawny 16-year-old who had just tried to slit her wrists, but I'm almost sure that I'm smaller and weaker now at 19.

Between the drugs and these stupid sessions with Dr. Watson - my appointed therapist, my mind was hanging on by a thread, straddling the line between sanity and the deep spiraling void of insanity.

"So, can you acknowledge what you did in that bathtub?" Dr. Watson's voice pulls me from my thoughts.

"I tried to kill myself," I respond, the words tasting like ash in my mouth.

His usual line of questioning scratches a part of my brain that says we should jump into that spiraling void of the insane.

"And what was the mistake that you made?" he asks, his beady eyes studying me.

"I failed to kill myself." My voice is flat, having repeated the same thing every day for years, which means I can fulfill my end of the conversation with no thought.

It's not as if this was actual therapy, meant to help us. It was just another stupid game.

"Why is that?"

"Because I'm weak." It had taken me three weeks and daily punishments before I'd first repeated those words. I tried to resist, not wanting to give in to what he was making me say. But this place has a way of crushing spirits and dismantling a person's free will.

"Yes, you are weak. You showed poor judgment. That's why you need structure; someone else to make decisions for you." I block out the rest of his tired lecture, instead envisioning ways I could stab him with the pen he twirls around his fingers during every session.

"And I helped your father set up a counselor at your new school to keep up your regular appointments once he gets you settled."

What?

All of my visions of violence and blood come to a screeching halt.

"What school?" I interrupt, not paying any mind to his disapproving look.

With a heavy exhale, he reaches up to adjust his glasses.

"Your father felt that you had had enough treatment and has decided that you will attend college to get acclimated back into everyday life."

"But I never even finished high school." I have so many questions, but my lack of a diploma seems to be what my brain is focusing on.

Dr. Watson starts to twirl his pen, looking very bored with the conversation.

"Yes, well, with your father's money and many connections, it seems that he was able to write off your time here as some sort of academic study program." his words come out clipped, irritation lacing through as he works to keep his face impassive.

He's probably just mad about losing a patient, especially considering how much trouble I get into. I unintentionally give him plenty of opportunities to dish out whatever extra 'therapy' he wants to try out.

When my father dumped me here, he didn't seem to have any intention of ever coming back to get me. So, I'm sure the good doctor is just pouting about his time getting cut short.

Wait, my father.

Why is my father suddenly interested in making sure I have an education? He hasn't cared for three years that I've lost out on my schooling, so what's changed?

"Why now?" I wonder aloud.

Watson tucks his pen into his notebook, exhaling sharply.

"Now, because your father decided it's time. As we've established, you cannot be trusted to make decisions." His beady eyes lock onto me, keeping me rooted in my seat, "Your father is making the decision *he* feels is best for *you*. One would say that you should show some gratitude that he still has the patience to even spare you a second thought."

Gratitude? For the man who showed me no sympathy for my dead brother, and who wasted no time in locking me away?

How does one even respond to such bullshit?

Watson stands and opens the door behind him, leading back into the main hallway.

"Your father will be here to collect you tomorrow morning. You're dismissed." His voice is clipped as he avoids looking at me, picking invisible lint from his suit jacket.

I want to feel some gratitude about getting to leave his office unscathed, but the anger rolling off of him keeps it at bay.

Keeping my head down, I slip past him and make my way back to my room.

Father left me with nothing when he dumped me here, so it's not like I have to spend time packing anything to go home. Given the circumstances of the living conditions in this hellhole, I don't exactly have any friends to say goodbye to.

With nothing better to do, I decide to take a nap before dinner.

Lying on the prison-grade cot and plastic bedframe, I can't even feel optimistic at the thought of getting to sleep in a real bed again. A real bed might be nice, but I can only think about what it's going to cost me.

The most crucial thing Dante ever taught me was that Father doesn't do anything unless it's for his own benefit. I dread to find out how bringing me home benefits him.

***

I'm woken by the presence of two massive figures looming over me. Two guards are now occupying my room.

Immediately, I move to sit up, but a burly hand snaps out to hold me down.

"What-"

"Morning, Princess," One of their voices spits out, cutting me off.

Morning? I must've slept through dinner.

"We were sad to see your name on the discharge notice today, princess." The second guard drawls out, standing to the side of the bed, hovering over me. As the sleep clears from my eyes, I can see his eyes raking over the thin potato sack of a gown I'm wearing, making my skin crawl. It feels like every inch of me is on display for them.

"We wanted to give you a parting gift, but dear old *daddy* advised against it." The first tells me, annoyance clear in his tone.

His words offer me no relief. If they can't do whatever they want to, then why the fuck are they in here?

"Yes, very disappointing." The second guard agrees, "But your father did give us the chance to collect you and give you your medicine."

My stomach immediately rolls with disgust at the predatory sound of his voice. My mind is trying not to think about the implications of what he just said.

Before I can start to panic, he draws his hand from behind his back, revealing a syringe. A new sense of dread washes over me.

14

Over the last couple of months, I mindlessly followed orders, meaning I haven't needed to be sedated. The syringes the guards carried had an elaborate cocktail of sedatives and drugs that left the recipient a zombie. Able to still walk and move as a normal person, it completely douses your mind with a dense fog that was almost impossible to break through.

I hate it.

I hate feeling like a prisoner in my own body.

I could hear everyone around me, but I did not have the strength to respond.

"Dear old daddy doesn't want you acting up just because you're getting out of here. This should keep you nice and calm. We even have spare time to say goodbye properly." The guard's hand slides from my shoulder to my breast, roughly squeezing as he whispers in my ear.

I try to struggle, but his weight is crushing me, keeping me trapped.

"Shh. Just stay still, and you'll be out of here in no time." He tells me just as he jabs the syringe in my arm, quickly pushing the drugs into me.

The effects are instant. The heavy fog washes over me and weighs me down. The guard's hands aren't even holding me down anymore, but it doesn't matter, as I don't have the strength to move.

Any panic that should be consuming me in this situation is smothered by the drugs, like a fire being smothered by a blanket; it smothers me.

I welcome the hazy thoughts as the guards move me around like a ragdoll, knowing that being numb to their actions is probably better for me.

My disjointed observations are like a puzzle; if I put all the pieces together, I could get the complete picture of what's happening.

But I'd rather not know.

My gown is removed.

I try not to think. Try not to feel. But some things burn through the haze.

A painful squeeze on my breast.

Heavy breaths brush the back of my neck.

Something sticky and warm splashes on my stomach.

Before I realize it, I'm wearing new clothes. A pair of sweatpants and a plain white t-shirt, I even have a pair of shoes snugly hugging my feet.

The guards half lead, half drag me into the building's main lobby, which is warm and inviting, unlike the halls that I've become so accustomed to. Plush leather couches sit opposite the reception desk, boxed in by vending machines and a coffee corner. This place looks amazing; so peaceful and relaxing. No one would ever know what lies beyond the door.

"Camilla, dear!" A voice startles me from the front door. "Oh, how I've missed you, my darling girl." The sickly sweet voice doesn't register in my muddled brain. It isn't until I focus my attention on the figure standing before me.

Here in the flesh, my father. The 'great' Aurelio Russo.

He's certainly aged since the last time I saw him, his once dark hair now peppered with grey on the sides. He's gained weight as well. Once trim and muscular, now his gut slightly protrudes, and his face shows deep wrinkles around his eyes.

The most unsettling difference is that he's smiling. His smile makes my skin crawl. I could probably count on one hand how many times I've seen my father smile, but here he is, and he's trying to hug me?

The guards must have given me the good drugs, and they're causing me to hallucinate.

"My darling girl, it's been so long. I'm so ready to have you home." My father tells me as his arms band tightly around me, just shy of crushing my weakened body.

I stand limply in his embrace, trying to catch up with his new personality. Letting me go, he steps back, straightening his suit.

"You should show some appreciation for your dad coming to get you; lots of girls in there would kill to be in your shoes, I'm sure." The guard to my right hisses, reminding me of their presence.

"I'm sure it's just a bit overwhelming. The thought of getting to come home, isn't it, Camilla?" Father asks.

My mind is swimming, too many thoughts fighting against the drugs. I think I somehow manage to nod.

"Good girl." My stomach immediately protests my father's words of praise, "Now, it's been too long, and I'm eager to get you home. We have a lot of matters to attend to." He reaches out, wrapping a hand around my arm and pulling me to stand beside him before addressing the guards. "Gentlemen, thank you for your assistance and for looking out for my sweet Camilla during her stay."

A devious smile takes over their faces, seemingly innocent, but the darkness in their eyes shows that they're thinking back on all the time I've endured with them over the years.

"It was our pleasure, Mr. Russo. And please be sure to call us if you ever need any *assistance*."

Smiling, Father pulls me towards the door.

"Thank you, gentlemen, but I have it under control. I'm sure Camilla here won't be giving me any issues." He calls over his shoulder.

It takes my eyes a few moments to adjust to the blinding light once we step through the doors. The sun was beating down, warming every inch of my skin.

I try to take a moment to bask in its warmth and breathe in the fresh air, but Father's grip tightens as he drags me towards an idling SUV.

He's anything but gentle as he wrenches open the back door and shoves me inside, following closely after me.

A grey-haired driver sits in the front seat, next to him a mountain of a man, wearing a suit that threatens to split at the seams from his impressively large muscles. His buzzed hair and tattoos crawling up his neck don't do him any favors when it comes to looking inviting.

We sit in silence for a few minutes as the driver takes us away from Briarwood Asylum, only to be disrupted by my father's sharp tone.

"Buckle up, Camilla. You've already tried to kill yourself once; I won't have you testing your luck in the off chance that we crash."

Numbly, I do what he says.

"As I'm sure Dr. Watson informed you, you were removed from the facility under my decision so that you can attend school and re-acclimate to the real world."

Questions swirl around my brain, but I'm not able to grasp onto any long enough to voice them.

Father continues, blissfully unaware of my mental gymnastics.

"You will be going to the school tomorrow, you'll be attending Hill Crest University in Michigan. You will also be joining me tonight for a friendly gala so that the families can see you alive and well before you go."

Michigan. That gives me some peace of mind, knowing that I wouldn't be stuck in Chicago with my father.

I still don't understand the sudden development of me going to college, but I don't have the energy to look a gift horse in the mouth right now.

"Michael here will accompany you to the school and get you settled," Father gestures to the hulk sitting in the front seat, who doesn't give any acknowledgement that he's listening. "Your rules have not changed." his voice hardens, "You will do as you're told, no questions asked. You will wear what is deemed appropriate, and you will not embarrass the family. You will not discuss your time at Briarwood. If asked, you will say that you decided to study abroad to expand your horizons."

He leaves no room for arguments. Practically, keeping to the same rules means trading one hell for another. I hold on to the sliver of hope that if I can push through, then hopefully I can find a way to slip out from under my father's grasp. I just have to be patient.

"We will discuss more tonight, just do as you're told and refrain from trying to kill yourself," He bitterly ends the conversation.

We stay silent for the rest of the drive, Father tapping away at his phone while I watch the scenery pass by.

I'm not sure how long it takes to get to the airstrip to board Father's jet, then we're on our way back to Illinois.

The flight to Chicago passes quickly, and the haze from my brain is starting to clear by the time we land.

Memories bombard me as we pull up to Father's house. I refuse to think of it as my own, as nothing about it feels welcoming to me.

Father leaves me quickly, barking orders to be ready at 7 o'clock sharp.

I mindlessly find my way to my old bedroom, the emotions hitting me like a brick wall, the memories of the last thing I did in this room. I can still feel the heavy feelings of wanting to end it all sitting heavily in my chest.

Looking around, everything's the same. It's as if no one has been in the space since I left. A glance at the shiny tile in the bathroom tells me that someone at least came in to clean up my mess after Father found me that night.

Sitting on the bed, I'm overwhelmed by its softness. It's almost too comfortable after sleeping on plastic for years.

Nothing about this room feels right. I've never been happy here. The last three years, the life had been sucked out of me, and now, I'm left to feel like this room, empty and hopeless.

3

Camilla

A knock startles me awake, the afternoon sun coming through the windows telling me that I slept for a few hours. The door cracks open, and Maria, my father's housekeeper, pokes her head into the room. A smile breaks out across her face upon seeing me.

"*Dolce ragazza*! I have missed you so much!" Her arms band around me in a crushing hug as she meets me in the middle of the room.

"I missed you, too, Maria. Hopefully, you haven't been too bored here without me." I joke.

Pulling away, Maria looks me over, head to toe.

"Not at all, sunshine. Your father has been having dinners and parties that keep me busy since you left, trying to forge new connections and whatnot."

"Connections with who?" I ask.

I've never been privy to all of the secrets of our family business, but I'd gotten curious over the years after hearing countless rumors. I remember how sick I felt after hearing that our family's shipyard was heavily tied to the Italian crime families and their drug trafficking rings.

I'd asked Dante about it once, but he brushed it off after assuring me that our family was the lowest of the families and acted more like a middleman.

If father is looking to make connections, then the only thing I can think of is that he's trying to move up from being the bottom of the barrel criminal, and that's not good for anyone, least of all me.

She looks anywhere but at me, fiddling with her apron strings.

"A lot of families, but he's been working on the Ivanni's the most." She doesn't make eye contact as she tells me, grabbing a bag from the hall, "Here, I have your dress for tonight and some new makeup. If you like, I can help you get ready, just like when you were little."

"I'd love that." I can't deny the hopeful smile she gives me.

I make a mental note to look up the Ivanni family and see what Father is getting into.

Maria makes the best of what we've got, tying my hair into a pretty braided up-do and making my modest makeup look effortless and stunning. But nothing can really complement the dress Father picked for me. The long sleeves try to make it appear modest, but the mesh-covered deep V that runs down to my navel is trying too hard to show off the assets I don't have. Luckily, the hem is just long enough to cover my ass, but the crimson red makes my pale skin look even more washed out and sickly.

"Ah, you look beautiful." Maria gushes at me in the mirror from over my shoulder.

"I look like a cheap hooker you'd find outside of a Sizzlers." I deadpan right back.

A quick slap to my shoulder makes me laugh. I have to quickly shut down my thoughts as I try to remember the last time I laughed…not today. I push the thoughts down and lock them up tight.

"Don't say that, you have a beautiful soul, and that's what I see when I look at you. That's all that matters."

Warmth fills me at the love and affection that rings through her words. Maria has been the closest thing I've ever had to a mother figure, and I'll always love her, even if she's still under my father's thumb.

"Thank you, Maria." I hug her tightly, wondering if I'll get to see her again after leaving for school. If I'm able to get away from my father, then I'm going to take the opportunity and won't dare to come back, even if that means leaving her behind.

Pulling away, she looks me over one more time.

"I'm just happy to get to see you before you leave. I've packed everything for you, but you can call me anytime. I'll always be here for you, Cami."

"Thank you, I love you." I choke back the tears threatening to spill over. No one has called me Cami since Dante, and hearing it brings back all the memories from before Briarwood. I still remember hearing him affectionately using the name every single day, and the way he would shout it whenever I told him good news, or when he was really excited about something.

"I love you, too, sweet girl. I'm happy you're back. I know Dante would be proud to see you moving on to such great things." Grabbing my hands in hers, I feel the cool touch of metal in my hand.

Looking down, I see the necklace Dante had gifted me when I was younger.

Blinking back tears, I offer her a tight smile, turning around and silently ask her to put it on me.

My chest tightens, and the scars on my wrists burn, begging me to scratch at them.

Before it can consume me, I push it all down, yet again, stomping out the spark before the flame of all the feelings can set me alight inside.

My focus needs to be on getting through tonight; tomorrow, I can go back to the real world.

Ten minutes and five hugs later, Maria leaves me, giving me seven minutes to myself before Father expects me. I scrutinize my appearance in the mirror, cataloging all my flaws.

I'm too thin, sickly looking. My skin's too pale, and my hair is dull, the years of torture having taken the shine away from my once silky-smooth raven colored locks.

If I look hard enough, I can see the silver scars etched into my skin, a roadmap telling the pathetic story of my life.

Nothing about me is appealing. I look as lifeless as I feel, and I wonder if I'll ever get back to feeling like a person again.

Glancing at the clock on the wall, I see that I have two minutes to get downstairs. I quickly slip on the stilettos picked out for me that probably cost more than most people's rent payments and make my way to my father's office.

Michael meets me at the bottom of the stairs, towering over me as I stand on the second step.

"Your father has requested you in his study." He says, giving me a dismissive once-over.

He doesn't spare me a second glance as he stalks off towards the study, leaving me to stumble behind him to keep up.

Real ray of sunshine this guy is.

The constant chatter of guests filters through from the living room and beyond as we walk down the halls. At Father's study, Michael opens the door and gestures for me to go in. The breath is snatched from my lungs as I cross the threshold to find six pairs of eyes leering over every inch of me. Taking a step back, I feel Michael's broad chest blocking my exit as the sound of the lock echoes in my head.

"Camilla, come, sit," Father demands from behind his desk.

An older man stands next to Father like an evil sidekick, his balding head and bulging gut not complementing his Armani suit. But the wicked glint in his eyes tells me that this man is as sinister as my father, and alarm bells ring all around me.

Stiffly sliding into the seat, I look to the man to my right and find a younger version of the man next to Father. He's more attractive than his father, at least; a full head of blonde hair shines in dim office lights, his jawline sharp and defined, his toned body hugged nicely by his fitted charcoal suit. Piercing brown eyes that almost look black as he watches my every move. He looks at me like I'm prey, and he's waiting to strike.

I know I shouldn't take my eyes off of him, but I do, looking to Father with questions in my eyes that I won't dare speak out loud without permission.

"I'd like you to meet the Ivanni's," Father finally breaks the silence. "This is Enzo, and his son, Leonardo," He gestures to each of them as he speaks.

"Leo, please." The younger man next to me interjects.

"Of course, Enzo and Leo." Father amends, "While you've been away, we have gotten fairly close, working together on some business arrangements. Nothing for you to be concerned with."

Fuck.

The Ivanni's.

As in Father's business partners, that's who I'm sitting here looking at right now. Maria mentioned them upstairs, but I didn't exactly have time to look into them before being summoned down here. I curse my lack of knowledge for the monsters sharing this space with me. Even without details, I know that if they're working with Father, they're bad news.

"She doesn't look too thrilled to see us." Enzo sneers from behind the desk.

Father lifts a placating hand, "That's not it, I'm sure. Camilla here has always been timid, and she's still worn out from her trip. She just arrived back today, so I'm sure it's all an adjustment." The lie falls so swiftly from his lips. He truly has no remorse for locking me away in that fucking hell for years while he went on about his life.

Curling my nails into my hand until I feel the familiar bite of pain, I work to control my face, leaving an impassive mask to hide my emotions.

"She could still look grateful to be here, given all that we're offering. It's not like she's that impressive to look at. I'm starting to wonder if this is worth all the hassle." What the fuck is he talking about? What could they be offering Father that involves me being here?

Please, I beg the spirits in my head, don't let my father try to sell sex with me for a fucking business deal.

"Come on, she's not that bad." Leo jumps in, his eyes still boring into the side of my face. "With a little bit of effort and the proper training, I'm sure she'll be just fine."

Training? What am I, a fucking dog?

"She'll be perfect for you, I guarantee it. Besides, we already started telling everyone the good news." Father continues with his vague answers as they all discuss me as if I'm not sitting right in front of them.

"What news?" I venture to ask, bracing myself for Father's backlash.

He shoots me a cold glare that threatens punishment across the desk, his cold, lifeless eyes locked onto me.

"Do not speak without being spoken to, Camilla. It is rude, and I have raised you to know better." He starts to stand from his seat, probably to deliver one of his famous backhands across the desk, but before he can, Leo speaks up, grabbing my hand and uncurling my fingers in the process.

"Aurelio, let's give her a pass. I'm sure I'd be curious in her position too if everyone were speaking about me in this way." Turning to me, he continues, "The good news is that we are officially engaged. We will be married in a year's time, and that will cement our family's bond to ensure good business gets carried out flawlessly with what both sides can bring to the table."

I stop breathing.

Married?

That can't be right. I can't get married. Father just told me today that I was going to school, and now I find out that he's marrying me off to a stranger. Not to mention that I've been held captive for the last three years of my life. I haven't gotten to live, and now I won't even get the chance to get out of here without a ball and chain in the shape of the man in front of me.

This isn't good, this *can't* be good. If Father is giving me away, then that means that whatever he does for his business isn't shady enough for him anymore, but that also means that whatever the Ivanni's are into is much deeper and much darker than I could possibly fathom.

Holy shit.

I'm going to vomit.

I'm going to vomit on someone's overpriced shoes, and then I'm going to pass out. If I pass out, I'll be completely unaware of what's happening around me.

My stomach churns, bile crawling up my throat like a second pulse.

Just breathe.

"Look, the girl is speechless!" Enzo cheers, holding a crystal glass of amber liquid like he's giving a toast. Like, this is some joyous occasion to be celebrated.

"What about school?" I desperately ask my father again, ignoring his rule against speaking without being spoken to.

"While it's not necessary, I actually convinced your father to let you attend school for a year." Leo answers, "Since you've been *away* for so long, we thought it'd be a good way to get you back to socializing with people of your status again. Plus, I figured that you wouldn't be as feisty if you got a chance to say goodbye to your old life before becoming my wife." His words are masked as something sweet. Still, I don't miss the underlying message: my freedom has an expiration date, and once it's up, I'm never getting away.

"Yes, it was a kind gesture. One that you should be thankful for, Camilla." I hear the silent threat in Father's words as well.

"T-thank you," I mutter, not feeling any ounce of gratitude towards these dickheads.

"My pleasure," Leo raises my hand that he holds in his and dusts a kiss on the back, "I'm sure I'll think of a way that you can pay me back, *fiancé*."

I try to pull my hand from his, but he grips it tighter, making the bones rub one another while his eyes stay assessing me, looking for any weakness.

"Right, so you two go roam around the party. Let people see you, congratulate you, and all of that while we discuss business for a bit." Father gestures between himself and Enzo, filling a crystal glass for himself and getting comfortable in his throne.

The last thing I want to do is be paraded around a bunch of strangers like some show pony, but I let Leo pull me up, hoping that soon enough I can slip away and hide out in my room for the rest of the evening. Maybe feign a migraine.

Leo ushers me out of the room, keeping a steely grip around my waist, both ensuring that I don't fall in the ridiculous heels and that I can't escape.

He carries me on his arm as he stops to talk to various people around the room. Even in the midst of conversations, I can still feel the stares from others all across the room. Even if I weren't exhausted from the last few years of torment, these endless conversations and false congratulations would send me into a boredom-induced slumber. I feel dead on my feet.

Finally, the conversation seems to lull, and Leo pulls me away to the back patio. A waiter follows us through the doors with two sparkling drinks on a silver platter.

Releasing me, he grabs both of the glasses, waving the waiter off, and only facing me once we're alone.

His fake smile stays firmly locked in place as he offers me one of the glasses. I take the one closest to his chest, mostly to piss him off, but also in the off chance that the offered glass has something extra in it, a girl could never be too safe.

His eyes crinkle, his amusement only growing as he watches me take the glass, only to hold it close to my chest, not drinking the contents. He takes a hefty swig of his drink, savoring the flavor before zeroing in on me.

"So, *wife*. Tell me about yourself." His lips curl with a smirk, enjoying making a joke of the thought of tying me to him for the rest of my life.

Rolling my eyes, I tear my gaze from his, opting to look out onto the lawn off the porch and beyond. "And why would I do that, *fiancé*?" I make sure to put as much disgust as I can into the word, so that he can't miss my thoughts on the matter.

"Well, because I should know some things about my intended wife, don't you think?" He huffs a laugh, leaning to rest his folded arms against the porch railing, joining me in looking at the lawn. "Like, what if you were allergic to strawberries? And here I've just handed you a glass with a strawberry beverage, I could poison you so easily. All due to a lack of information."

He said it lightly, but I could hear the silent threat that lingered beneath his words. My spine stiffens on instinct, but I try my best to seem unaffected.

"Well, most people *date* the person that they intend to marry, so that seems to be on you," I tell him, glancing at the glass between my fingers as I swirl the liquid around. "And if you did hand me poison, I'd drink it." I smile sweetly, finally throwing back the drink in one gulp, shoving the glass into his chest as I spin to the doors leading inside, intending to retreat to my room and escape this bullshit.

I feel his hand wrap around my arm just before the sound of breaking glass registers in my brain.

Spinning me to face him, he's almost nose to nose with me. He smiles coldly as he leans in to whisper in my ear,

"That was brave. But bravery and stupidity tend to look the same when the consequences come."

His eyes look black this close up, his irises not visible beyond his blown-out pupils. Lifting my chin, I stare defiantly back at him, not cowering in fear.

He squeezes harder, his grip on my arm becoming bruising,

"You might think that your little defiant act is cute, but it's not going to get you anything but my anger. I suggest you get over it quickly while you're away at school. Might I remind you that it was I who convinced your father to give you a year to do what you want before our marriage?" His brow arches high up on his face, as if the reminder makes him seem like the hero in this scenario.

Ripping my arm from his grasp, I don't back down, raising my chin, I stare spitefully back at him.

"Oh yes, you're such a saint." I laugh, humorlessly. "My savior, giving me a year to taste freedom, knowing that you only intend to rip it away. Acting like I'm a commodity that you can what? Purchase me and get yourself a wife? What the fuck do you want me for anyway?"

He rolls his eyes, as if I'm a petulant child throwing a tantrum.

"That's none of your concern. You should just be grateful that I'm giving you a chance to enjoy yourself before we're to be married; others wouldn't be so kind."

"So, I'm just supposed to take your word for it that you're this kind and caring individual? You don't have any other motives for giving me a year away from this?" Waving my hands around us, I emphasize the stupidity of this situation. "That's a little hard when I don't even know you. I just got home today, and now I learn that my father is handing me off to someone with no say in the matter. So apologies if I don't seem as grateful as you had hoped." I spit the words at him, not hiding any of my disgust.

Here stands a typical man, in a typical man's world, thinking that it's completely normal to tell a woman where to go and what to do.

Gross.

"Well, I did ask you to tell me about yourself. I would have returned the favor." He shrugs.

He fucking *shrugs*. This is a joke, right?

Playing his stupid game, I smile sweetly at him, batting my eyes for added effect.

"Oh, Prince Charming, I'm so sorry." I pretend to fix my hair and straighten myself. "I'm nineteen years old, love true crime documentaries and ramen noodles. I'm allergic to peanuts, but love chocolate. I tried to kill myself when I was sixteen, so I guess you could say that I had a bit of a 'rough patch'. I don't like socks because they make my feet feel suffocated. And...oh, my father has always been a complete asshole to me, so naturally, I have daddy issues and hate men who think they can control me." Crossing my arms, I ask, "Is that enough information for you?"

He matches my stance, pondering over all the information I just threw at him, "Well, you should be happy to know that I'll never force you to wear socks."

"Wow, a true gentleman," I respond dryly.

"I know where you've been while your father has told people you've been studying abroad." He admits, his hand reaching down to caress the jagged scar on my wrist. "That's part of the reason I put this stipulation on the agreement. I don't need a socially awkward and mentally unstable wife."

Just when I thought that he could be a decent human being for a moment, he brings me spiraling right back down into reality.

"And how is college going to help with that?" I ask, "Why not go find someone else to play your wife?"

"Going will re-teach you how to socialize with people of your status again." Looking me up and down, I finally see the first flicker of disgust in his expression, "If tonight has told me anything, it's that you could use the practice."

I go to respond, but he holds a hand up to stop me, speaking before I get the chance to.

"Arguing is pointless. You will go to school and have your false sense of freedom, and then you will return and be my wife. You will spend the next year reminding yourself of how a good wife should act and behave. You will answer my calls and follow my directions when they're given. You will not argue, you will not fight."

Each point is emphasized with a step towards me until I'm backed up against the wall just to the side of the patio doors as he towers over me.

"You will fall in line as you're supposed to, or your father will end up with a bullet between his eyes while my father and I take everything that he has." He pauses, letting that sink in.

If that's a threat, then it's a poor one, given that I couldn't care less what happens to the vile man that is my father. "And if that's not enough, then consider that you'll be dropped right back off at Briarwood, with no chance in hell of getting out this time."

There it is.

That's the threat that has my stomach in knots at the sheer thought of it.

Biting my tongue, I fight the tears that are building from the panic of the idea of being thrown back into hell.

"Fine." I avoid his gaze, just wanting this conversation to be over with.

"*Good girl.*" He chuckles, probably seeing the repulsion written all over my face. "I'm glad we could come to an understanding.

"Yeah, can I be excused now, *fiancé*?" If I don't get away from this asshole, I think I may actually try to kill myself again. And that would be a waste of all those hours I spent in 'therapy'.

"Go ahead, I have business to attend to. I'll tell everyone that you were feeling ill, that should be believable, given your appearance." He just has to get another jab in, I suppose. "You'll find out what I want soon enough, *wife*."

With that, I spin and retreat as quickly as I can back to my room, trying to hold back tears the whole way.

Slamming the door behind me, I collapse against it, finally letting my emotions overtake me. Getting away from my father was still the goal I needed to focus on, but now that Leo was in the mix, it was a bit more complicated. I not only needed to get away, but also to find somewhere none of them could ever find me.

I wouldn't be heartbroken if Leo killed my father and took his businesses; he deserved it. But I'll be dammed if Leo thinks there's any chance in hell that I'll set foot in Briarwood ever again.

All I know is that I have one year to figure out my plan, so I'd better make the most of it.

4

Camilla

I've been at this school a couple weeks now, and I think I'm finally starting to find my footing. After the disaster that was meeting my intended husband, I gave myself the night to break down and feel sorry for myself before being whisked away to Hill Crest the next morning.

Michael was not a good travel companion, not that I was expecting him to be after our initial encounter. But thankfully, that meant that he was eager to drop me off with all my bags on the metaphorical front steps of the university and high-tail it out of there. Leaving me to my own devices.

Classes didn't start for a couple more days, the summer semester still wrapping up, so it left me with enough time to get acquainted with the campus, as well as my stuck-up, snobby classmates. I will admit, two of those days I spent most of my time here so far locked in my room, sulking about my arranged marriage and my father's parting instructions to keep up appearances.

I was not to tell anyone about my stay at Briarwood, I was to dress and act appropriately to represent him and his legacy. I was to maintain my required meetings with a therapist on campus that my father had selected.

So far, college was not my chance at freedom; it was simply trading one prison for another.

Those days in my room allowed me to look at my situation from all angles. I was trapped; I couldn't run, or I'd end up back in hell. But that didn't mean I couldn't find ways to make this year more fun. And if luck is on my side, then I'll find a way to escape my fate by the time this is all said and done.

With a whole weekend free of any plans and a newfound determination to do anything and everything I can think of with the small sliver of freedom that this college experience allowed me to imagine, I've decided to start a list of new things to try.

That starts today, first on the agenda is to do something that almost every young adult has done. Today, I want to get high.

Not the kind of high from prescription medication intended to put me in a comatose state, but the fun kind, like you see kids doing in movies. I just had to find it. I'm sure someone on this campus can lead me to what I'm looking for. I just had to find the right crowd.

Armed with a skimpy pair of cut-off shorts, courtesy of Maria, and a low-cut tank top that acted as a second skin and a large zip-up to hide my scars, I wander through campus. Observing groups of students hanging out along the pathway, filtering in and out of the cafe, and lounging in the grass.

No one immediately stands out as a drug dealer, but I suppose I didn't expect them to. It would take a little more work on my part.

Rounding the pathway, I'm coming up to the massive sports complex that the campus houses when I hear someone shouting my name.

"Camilla?" The voice sounds almost as confused as I am.

Turning around, I'm terrified for a moment of who I'll find. It's not like I have any friends I'm expecting to run into around here. Or anywhere.

Before me, in the flesh, stands a tall, tan, and handsome man. Perfectly taut muscles, emphasized by the dark t-shirt straining against his chest. Jet black hair that falls in perfectly messy curls, framing his face and leaving his bright blue eyes on display, striking against pale skin and chiseled features.

It takes a few moments of checking him out for the recognition to slap me square in the face.

"Gio?" I ask, stunned.

From elementary school until I was shipped off to Briarwood, Gio was my best friend. We had all the same classes, spent our summers together, and always watched each other's backs. For the longest time, I had a massive crush on him, until he finally filled me in that he was very much gay.

"I thought I was going crazy for a minute." He looks me over, shaking his head. "I can't believe it's actually you."

Holding my hands out to the side, I offer a shrug.

"It's me. Believe it."

"Where have you been? I haven't seen you in years." Of all the reasons I hated getting shipped off to Briarwood, Gio was one of the ones that made me most upset. After Dante, I felt so alone, so isolated. I needed a friend, someone to confide in. Instead of getting that, I got sent to my own personal hell. No one to talk to, and left to wonder if he would even notice my absence.

"Uh, studying." Wait, what was I supposed to tell people? Studying at home? Studying at my great aunt Ethal's? "Studying abroad!" I finally remember. "My father sent me to study abroad, thought I needed to expand my horizons, or something."

His eyes narrow into slits, clearly not believing a word I'm saying.

"Right, well, I'd love to catch up. What are you up to? Want to get lunch?" I'm thankful for his change of topic, giving me an out and taking my crappy excuses. Though I think that was always one of the things I loved about Gio, he knew when not to push.

I left my room today because I was determined to find something to get into. Maybe Gio could be my ticket to finding just that. He has to know someone on this campus who can get me what I need.

"Sure, where do you want to go?" I take a chance. Even if he can't get me what I'm looking for, I'll still get to catch up with an old friend. It's a win for today.

Falling into old habits, Gio takes control and leads me to what he says is one of his favorite spots near campus to eat. We find ourselves in a fifties-themed diner just on the outskirts of the massive campus. Neon lights, piano tiles, and a jukebox add to the atmosphere, giving the restaurant a nostalgic feel that instantly welcomes me.

A fleeting feeling of sadness hits me as I think back to the times Dante used to take me for shakes and fries at our favorite spot back home, but I push it away quickly, not wanting to be bombarded with the sadness that pairs with thoughts of my brother.

"So, studying abroad?" He asks after we've placed our orders, leveling a look across the table that says he's not going to let this go now that we have time to talk.

"Yep." Smiling widely at him, I offer no details.

He knows I'm full of shit. The question is, will he push me, or will he let it go?

Growing up together, he knew all the finer details of my father's actual business, and his family came from a darker past as well. His family is more involved in money laundering and street business, but he still understands how our world works.

"So, two seconds after your brother dies, your father decided you needed to go see the world?" His dry tone lets me know that he's not letting this go.

"Yep." Maybe if I stick to the same monosyllable answer, he'll give up.

Sitting back, he crosses his arms over his chest. A calculating look shrouding his face.

"So, where'd you go?"

I play with the sugar packets on the table so I don't have to look at him. Feigning not to hear him.

"Hm?"

He snatches one of the packets from my grasp, trying to draw my attention to him, but failing as I grab another.

"Where did you go, Cam? You were gone for years, so I imagine you got to see some really great places. Did you go sightseeing?"

Shit.

He's absolutely not letting this go. He wants details.

If I were smarter, then I would have at least googled some tourist information to fabricate some bullshit stories.

Unfortunately, my knowledge of foreign countries is minimal, which isn't going to help me out here.

"I went to Europe. Got to see a lot, but you know, I was very interested in my studies, so I probably didn't get to see as much as some other people. It was a great time, but I much prefer it here, definitely glad to be home."

Please don't ask, please don't ask, I silently beg, but as usual, luck is not on my side as Gio shoots out the question I already know is coming.

"Where in Europe did you go?"

Damn him. He knows I suck at geography, and to make it even more pathetic, I cannot tell you a single country in Europe. Not for sure, at least.

I abandon the sugar, shooting daggers at his smug expression instead.

"Fine. I didn't go to Europe." I begrudgingly admit.

His bark of laughter startles me, and he throws his head back, almost hitting the back of the booth.

"No shit, Cam. I'm not an idiot, and you've always been a terrible liar.

Well, I'm glad to see he's still honest and very blunt. It's good to know some things never change.

Sobering, he focuses on me again.

"Your brother died, and you disappeared. You never even called me or said goodbye. I know you didn't go studying abroad. Be straight with me, tell me what happened." Reaching across the table, he grabs my hand in his, offering silent comfort. "You were my best friend, you still are, I hope. I missed you like crazy, and I just want to understand."

I was warned not to say anything, but the thought of not telling Gio, my life-long best friend, who's been by my side through everything up until the last three years, makes me want to vomit.

Wouldn't I feel better having someone to confide in? It would mean I wouldn't have to feel suffocated with the burning secret of my impending marriage.

But what if he only ends up pitying me? I can't handle feeling like the weak and fragile little girl I've been made to believe I am for the past few years.

I should know Gio better than that, he's always been a strong support system. I don't think he'd judge me for what I've been through.

My only real hesitation comes from the thought of having to discuss Dante. His death still feels like a hot knife in my chest, and I'm not sure I can stomach reliving the day that I found out.

I've refused to think about him since the day I tried to take my own life. At this point, I'm almost terrified of how I'll react when I have to unpack all the emotions I've pushed down and locked away. I'm afraid the grief is going to consume me.

Aside from Dante, though, Gio is the only other person I've truly trusted in my life. I know if I don't tell him, then it's only going to continue to eat at me while my freedom hits its expiration date.

I weigh my options, studying Gio's sincere expression. I study the differences in him since I last saw him. He looks older, we both do. But he's grown harder over the years, more intimidating. But just under the surface, I can still see flickers of the laid-back, easy-going boy that I trusted with all my secrets when I was young.

I'm given a few extra moments with my internal debate as the waitress comes to drop off our food.

Gio digs in, clearly giving me the time I need to build up the courage to talk to him.

"I've been at Briarwood for the last 3 years." My voice is low, and I almost wonder if he can even hear me. I don't dare look up at him, opting to push my food around my plate instead.

Heavy silence lingers between us, making me question again if he heard me.

"Briarwood as in the mental institution from hell?" He explodes, outrage coating his words. "Why the hell were you at Briarwood, Camilla?"

Heaving a sigh, I drop a mask of aloofness into place, locking away any emotions I have to keep them from dragging me under.

"Because I slit my wrists when I heard about Dante. It was stupid, I don't want to talk about it." I swallow hard, clasping my hands under the table to hide their shaking.

"Father couldn't stand having me around, being *weak*, so he shipped me off immediately. I didn't have time to call you, and once I was there, I wasn't given any chances to reach you." Taking a breath, I make sure my emotions stay tucked away. I don't allow myself to feel as I give him the bare bones version of the story.

"I wasn't given a release date. I really didn't think I'd ever get out of there. But it seems my father has found some use for me, so he pulled me out and sent me here instead. Here I am."

Finally looking up, I see him staring back at me, slack-jawed, questions swirling in his eyes. He doesn't say anything. I can tell his brain is working, trying to process all the information I just dumped on him.

"What the fuck?" Sympathy flows from him, but I've completely iced myself out, ignoring anything remotely close to feelings. "I get you don't want to talk about it, I respect that, but fuck. I can't even imagine."

I don't respond. I already said I don't want to talk about it, and I don't need his sympathy. Whatever happened to me is done and over with.

We both eat our food, giving ourselves a few minutes to soak in the reality of my fucked up life.

"You said your dad decided to pull you out because he has some use for you." His suspicion peaks again. "What is it? What does he want to do with you?"

"Oh, he intends to marry me off." There's no beating around the bush with this topic, not with everything I've already dumped on him. "In fact, I met my miserable husband-to-be just before I came here."

He makes no move to respond, his slack-jawed expression firmly back in place.

"Yeah, that was pretty much my reaction as well."

"Are you shitting me right now?" He finally snaps. "Married? To who? Why? You didn't want to start with that?"

I wasn't expecting that strong a reaction from him. Sure, I figured he would think it was fucked up, but it's not like he's the one who's going to be marched down the aisle in a fluffy, white, monstrosity of a dress.

47

"Sorry?" I'm confused by his strong reaction. "I didn't think that was a good conversation starter after not having seen you in years. Figured it might be better to ease into things."

He continues to stare at me, reminding me that he asked a billion questions that he probably wants answered.

"As for who, that would be Leo Ivanni, and the why is because my father is using me as some bargaining chip to combine their businesses and become the all-powerful mafia don that he's always dreamed of."

Again, that doesn't seem to be the answer he wanted. He slams his fist down on the table, mumbling a string of profanities.

"The fucking Ivanni's?" He hisses, leaning further over the table now to keep his voice down. "Your father is trying to get into the skin trade?" *Wait, what?* "Running drugs and guns all over the country wasn't enough; now he has to sell people, too?"

I know I threw a lot of information out, but my mind is starting to spin with the added details that he just dropped into this shitty situation.

"Skin trade?" I ask, dumbly.

"Yes, Cam. Skin trade. The Ivanni's are notorious for running one of the largest trafficking rings in the country. All the families turn to them for directions, except for your father."

"Shit."

"Yeah, shit. If your father and the Ivanni's team up, they're going to have control over the entire country. What are you going to do?"

I wasn't aware that the Ivanni's had that much reach. I had learned that my father controlled practically the entire eastern seaboard into the Midwest, but it sounds like the Ivanni's make up the other half. If my father gets that much power, there's no telling what he'll try to do with it.

And what does this all mean for me? What is going to happen to me if I become the wife of the heir of this ridiculous empire?

Leo's threat still rings through my mind, reminding me why I have no choice in the matter, no matter how much I want to resist.

"I am going to live my college life to the fullest. That's what I'm going to do." I tell him, refusing to think about what my life might look like in a year.

Sitting back, he stares at me incredulously.

"Seriously? You're just going to go to college and live your life, knowing that you're engaged to a monster? You're not even going to try to find a way out of this?" He asks.

"What do you want me to say, Gio? I don't have a choice in the matter, and I've looked at this from every angle; there is no way out." Rubbing my hands down my face, I try to fight off the budding migraine blooming in my head. "Besides, Leo seemed nice enough. I'm sure it won't be that bad." The last part sounds unconvincing, even to myself, but I have nothing else to argue.

He hits the table again, harder this time.

"That's bullshit!" He's pissed now. "Leonardo Ivanni is one of the most sadistic bastards in the families. Did you know that he killed his last girlfriend? Strangled her in her sleep, all because he *thought* she talked to another man. And he killed his brother. His father told them he could have only one heir, and they had to fight for it. Before either of them could say a word, he slit his brother's throat and didn't spare a second thought."

I knew Leo couldn't be a good man, with what his family does and where he comes from. And the night we met, he didn't try hard to mask his insanity. But this was news to me.

I was truly trapped. I had no options. All I had was a few more months to try and come up with some plan to escape, to get out from under my father's thumb and off the Ivanni's radar. With them controlling practically the entire country, though, this seems impossible.

I'm tired of thinking about this. All I wanted to do today was get high. I wasn't prepared to talk about everything, and it's draining.

"I don't have a choice, Gio. Leo already made it clear that I either fall in line or my father will be dead, and I'll be right back in Briarwood." I say, "As much as I want to tell my father to go fuck himself and just run, the threat of going back is too much to even think about. This is what's happening, I'm not trying to dwell on it right now." I let my mask drop slightly, letting him see just how utterly exhausted I am with my life—begging him, without words, to just let it go.

"We'll think of something, I'll help you." He promises. He doesn't know how empty that promise is, just like he doesn't know that I only get a year to live out my college life, not four. Some things don't need to be said.

"Sure." I agree with no real promise.

Gio quickly covers the tab, and we head back out onto campus, walking through the footpaths with no destination in mind. He catches me up on his life for the last few years, the guys that he's dated and the ones that he'd rather forget about, and how much he enjoys living out of his parents' house.

It's crazy to hear how much he's gotten to do and experience since I've been gone. To think that while my world stopped, and it felt like there was nothing left for me, the world kept spinning. Life went on outside of my terrible little bubble.

Stepping off the path, we settle in a comfy spot in the grass, shaded by one of the large oak trees scattered about.

"So, you want to live out your college life, that's what you said." He starts, leaning back to look at the clouds overhead. "We can't solve everything right now, but that is something we can work on. What do you want to do?"

I lay back to join him in cloud watching.

"Well, I am so glad you asked." My excitement and determination from this morning bubble again, "First on my agenda, I want to get high."

Snorting, he rolls his head to look at me.

"Really? Three years in the crazy bin, and the only thing you can think of is getting high?"

"I have other things planned." I slap him on the arm, only mildly offended at his mocking.

"Oh, like what? You're going to get drunk too?" He asks.

I don't respond. He's mocking me, but also, getting drunk is one of the items on my makeshift bucket list.

"Oh my God! That's totally on your list!" He doesn't hold back his laughter now, getting all his amusement from my lack of life experience.

I sit up and stare down at him, unamused.

"Will you help me or not? I want to get high. I missed out on all these fun, stupid teenage rites of passage when I was gone." I explain, "I want to have fun and try all the things I missed out on."

Wiping the tears from his eyes, he sits up next to me.

"Fine, I will help you," He agrees, "It's not like it's exactly hard to find weed on a college campus." Waving his hands, he gestures at the space around us. "But we have got to work on this list of yours. If I'm going to help you, then I'm going to need something more exciting than a little Devil's lettuce."

He pulls me up from the grass to walk beside him.

"Fine, I'll work on adding more debauchery to my list." I agree as I follow along, off to my first of hopefully many new experiences.

5

Lev

I love the smell of fresh blood in the morning.

Muffled screams and whimpers greet me as I strut into our basement, fresh cup of coffee in hand.

I pass the cup off to Roman, leaning against the wall next to him to watch Dima at work.

Dima loved the violence and gore, more so than any of the rest of us. I enjoyed watching, getting a kick out of seeing grown men reduced down to sniveling puddles of piss, right to the very end. Roman loved to observe, taking his time to figure out what truly made a person squirm so he could jump in near the end to get answers. Abram, our fearless leader, only preferred the blood and torture when it was absolutely necessary; more often than not, he opted to stay away from it and keep an eye on the administrative side of things.

The poor excuse of a human we had tied to our torture table today was someone we'd been trying to find for a while. Franklin here had not only been double-dipping into the earnings for Lux, one of the many nightclubs we operated together, but he'd also been hiding some pretty questionable material on his office computer. Hidden away from the prying eyes of his wife, he'd been getting off to videos of little boys and girls while at work.

Usually, fucking with our money would mean the loss of a couple of fingers, maybe a hand if the amount was obscenely large. But the guys and I didn't take kindly to disgusting pedophiles and their fucked up interests.

There was also the matter of where he'd gotten the videos from; that's where Dima and Roman came in. They were going to get us names, or at least a name.

Abram has already sent the encrypted file to his father's tech contact to dig into and find any trail of where it came from, so we could hunt down every fucker responsible for the videos. But that could take time, so getting the names would expedite the process.

It was also a good idea to let Dima and Roman have their fun now and then. They tended to get restless when they went too long without bloodshed.

It just happened to be convenient that Franklin had fled to the States, not far off from our temporary relocation; it saved us the unnecessary round-trip. He probably thought he'd be safe, that we wouldn't come all this way over a bit of budget manipulation. Once we caught wind of what he was doing, we wasted no time taking a midnight drive over to our club in Chicago to bring back a new toy for the boys.

Our house back home was much nicer than the one we're in now, nestled on a large property with plenty of grounds to run, private, and we each had our own space to work or play.

The four of us have lived together since we were teenagers. Throughout high school, we all roomed together at Rosehill Academy, where our parents sent us to pursue higher education and hone our skills for each of the family businesses. We all connected and decided to attend college at the sister academy. We've been inseparable ever since.

Our conflicting personalities balanced each other well: my relaxed nature was the perfect counterpart to Roman's quiet, assessing nature, and Abram's controlling tendencies kept Dima in line.

Franklin let's out a blood-curdling scream behind the makeshift gag in his mouth, tears and snot running down his face to drip onto his already soiled t-shirt.

Dima laughs, holding up a hunk of meat that I quickly realize is one of Franklin's fingers. The garden shears in his other hand, as well as the finger, are both covered in blood, almost unrecognizable.

"One finger for every video we found on your computer. How does that sound?" He laughs.

Poor Franklin, the sick bastard, already wasn't walking out of here alive, but Dima hasn't been able to play in so long that it seems he's going to drag this out as long as possible.

Roman sips his coffee beside me, "He doesn't have enough fingers for that," He points out.

Dima tilts his head, angling a smirk at Roman over his shoulder.

Looking sinister, his long hair down today, an evil sparkle in his eye, soaked in sweat and blood, all his tattoos and scars visible since he'd discarded his shirt earlier in the morning.

The man loved blood, but hated getting it on his clothes. I'd once walked in on him torturing a man while fully naked, all because he said he was wearing his 'good pants' that day, and he didn't want to dirty them up.

"Well then, I guess we'll take his toes too."

Franklin whimpers, trying to talk as he shakes his head, but his pleas go unanswered as Dima tosses his finger at us. I narrowly miss getting hit with it before he starts to cut through the next.

I leave them in the basement as Roman steps in to help cauterize Franklin's wounds to keep him from bleeding out before we're done with him.

Stopping by the kitchen, I grab a fresh cup of coffee before letting myself into Abram's office.

He sits behind the desk, typing away on his computer. Looking fully put together in a full suit, despite working from home.

Taking a seat in front of the desk, I sit patiently, waiting for him to notice my arrival.

The clacking of the keys continues as the silence lingers between us.

"Did Dima and Roman get a name yet?" He asks, his focus not straying from the computer.

"Not yet, but they did get a few fingers." I watch the look of disgust wash over his face, taking amusement in the fact that he's much more squeamish than I am. "Did you get us what we need yet?"

He rakes a hand through his hair, grabbing a stack of papers off the corner of his desk.

"Class schedules for each of us," He hands me a sheet. "We each have a copy of her schedule, as well as at least one class with her. One of us will be with her all day."

I abhor the thought of having to sit through college classes, but it was the only way to accomplish what we came here for.

"Did you manage to get an updated picture?" I ask.

He taps his finger on the desk, lost in thought.

"The last photo we have is from just over three years ago. She's been a ghost since then."

My brows draw together. "Where do you think she's been?"

Camilla Russo was a hard woman to find. For years, we've had private investigators searching high and low for any trace of her, but until a couple of months ago, there had been nothing on her.

We planned to come and meet with her right after Dante's passing, but had sent some men ahead of us to check on her while we were tied up with work.

She was home one day and gone the next.

"I'm not sure," He admits, "But between her disappearance and the rising rumors about her father and the Ivanni's, I'm sure it can't be anywhere good."

"She's here now, though. Is the plan still the same? What if she doesn't need our help?"

"The plan remains," He says through gritted teeth. "We made a promise to Dante."

I shift in my chair, remembering the oath Dante made us all swear to him before he died.

"I know we promised him that we would make sure she wasn't left with her father if anything ever happened to him, but it's been years. She's not a little kid anymore. What if she's happy?"

His eyes narrow, "If she's happy here, then she can be happy back at home as well. Dante was convinced that nothing good would come from being left with Aurelio. Grown or not, she can still be used as a pawn in her father's stupid games."

He wasn't dropping this. One thing Abram stood by was honor: 'A Kozlov honors his word'. The promise we made to Dante may as well have been sealed in blood in his mind.

It was admirable, but sometimes became an obsession for him. I fear that's what's happening with Camilla.

He's flown us all across the world to check on a grown woman who most likely doesn't need saving. All because of a promise made one drunken night at school.

We all loved Dante; we clicked with him as soon as he'd arrived at the academy, bringing him right into our fold. It was apparent that he was protective of his little sister, always saying that she was his only true family.

She was important to him.

That meant she was important to us.

But I have to wonder if all of this is necessary after all this time.

Yes, she fell off the face of the Earth for a while, but that easily could have just been grief taking its course. She could have finished school at home before deciding to enroll in college. She could have travelled.

There were so many unknowns.

We've never even met her.

What if she's thriving now and meeting us, four of Dante's closest friends, throws her back into grief?

Could our showing up cause more harm than good?

And then there was Abram's plan to drag her back home with us, putting distance between her and her father.

It made sense when she was just a kid; we could offer her protection until she was old enough to make her own decisions. But now she was 19, an adult, we had no reason to take her from her home or school, to start a new life.

"So we find her, get to know her, and then what? Tell her she's coming home with us, and if she refuses, then we just kidnap her?" He flinches at the mention of kidnapping, but regains his composure quickly.

"If that's what it takes, then yes."

I drag a hand down my face, staring at him incredulously. Not believing how far he's willing to go for this promise.

"For now, just focus on blending in and getting close to her. We all need to see what information we can get from her. Find out where she's been, if she knows what her father's up to." He waves a hand, "The most important thing is building up her trust with us."

"So she doesn't try to stab us in her sleep when we kidnap her?"

Rolling his eyes, he continues.

"It will be easier to tell her why we came to find her if she already trusts us."

"Wait, you don't want us to tell her about Dante? About the promise?" My eyes are nearly bugging out of my head. It's one thing to keep the promise we made, but not telling Camilla about our connection to her brother seemed like a horrible idea.

"No, she's likely to be suspicious of our sudden arrival without adding in the emotional torment of having been close to him. We don't know how she'll react, so, for now, keep it to ourselves."

With that, he returns to his work, effectively dismissing me. I retreat to my room, my mind reeling with the thought of having to lie to Camilla to get close to her.

I might not know her yet, but if she's anything like her brother, she won't respond well to deception.

This wasn't going to end well for any of us.

I support Abram; I would do anything for him. But the voice in my head is screaming at me that we're making a mistake by lying about why we're here.

Maybe there was a way I could get her to realize who we were to Dante, without going directly against Abram's orders. I would just need to be friendly and become someone she could open up to. If I can get her talking about him, then it should be easy to direct her to the truth.

Then everyone could be happy.

I spend the rest of my day reading over the small file we have on Camilla, learning everything, which isn't much, and committing it to memory. I try to find any details that I can use as a common ground with her to strike up a conversation.

At dinner, Abram fills in the others on the plan, making sure we all give our word not to mention Dante's promise before we all retreat for the night.

Restless energy consumes me as I stare up at the ceiling from my bed, sleep not coming to me. Giving in, I head down to our gym out back, figuring a run should tire me out enough to get some sleep before tomorrow.

As I run, I recall all the stories Dante used to tell us about his sweet little sister. He used to talk about her like she hung the moon. He told us about the time she tried to save a dove that had flown into their window, only to be heartbroken when their father broke its neck. Or the time she'd nearly burned down the kitchen, trying to make him a birthday cake, all because she insisted she needed no help from their housekeeper. Then the following year, she had successfully managed to bake him a cake, but mistook the salt for sugar, resulting in the most disgusting thing he'd ever tasted.

I can recall the way his eyes shone when he told that story, saying he'd choked down an entire slice upon seeing the tears welling in her eyes, and how her smile lit up the room when he went for seconds.

After hearing about her for years, it felt as if I already knew her. I was eager to meet someone so close to Dante; it almost felt like meeting her would be like seeing him again.

Sufficiently worn out from my run and full of a new, optimistic outlook on meeting Camilla, I head back to bed.

I continue to recall all the stories we'd heard over the years as I drift off, dreaming of a sweet brunette who would threaten to bring me to my knees.

6

Camilla

Gio really should've warned me about hangovers.

Getting high was fun. We'd had a fun night on Saturday, scoring some weed from one of Gio's friends. We took that back to my dorm along with some trashy movies and a mountain of junk food.

Sunday had brought brunch and day drinking, leading to more drinking late into the night before we crashed.

I enjoyed both getting high and drunk. Something was calming about turning off your mind and just going with the flow.

But I was paying for it now.

Slumping into one of the seats in the back of my 8 am lecture, I attempt to use my hand to shield my eyes from the fluorescent lights beating down on me. I had barely been able to pull myself out of bed this morning, with the pounding in my head.

After I'd arrived on campus, I quickly found some girls who were willing to trade some of their casual clothes for the designer crap that had been bought and packed for me. But today, I took advantage of the bartered clothing, donning a baggy sweatshirt and black leggings.

Opting for comfort over giving a single fuck.

If I could've, I would have just skipped class. Unfortunately, one of the conditions of this fucked up arrangement with my father and Leo is that one, or both of them, would be notified if I wasn't following their rules on campus. One of those rules included my attendance.

It wasn't like I was going to be getting a complete education, so I'm not sure why it mattered.

If I'm able to stay awake for this hour of Music and Society Studies, it would truly be a miracle. I'm not sure who chose my schedule; with a class like this, I would assume Leo. He would want me to be refined enough to follow along with the stuffy conversations at his social gatherings.

I'm surprised he didn't find me a class on being a submissive wife, learning all the household duties, and how to care for his demon spawns. But the day is still young.

Someone slides into the seat directly to my right, sitting so close that I have to shift over so our arms don't touch.

I refuse to look up, not interested in conversation.

Whoever it is doesn't seem to understand personal space because every time I shift away from them, they move closer into my space.

Another shift and I whip my head up, ready to tell them to back off, but I'm frozen on the spot.

Holy hotness, Batman.

Piercing green eyes stare back at me, surrounded by warm olive skin. Complex features, paired with a dark buzz cut and a silver nose ring, gave this man an aura that screamed 'bad boy'.

This man was sex appeal in the flesh.

As if he can hear my thoughts, his mouth stretches into a blinding smile, softening his hardened features at once.

"Hey, I haven't seen you around before. I'm Lev," He holds a hand between us, waiting for me to accept it.

I have to shake myself mentally. Lev is hot, but I can't be interested, and I'm too hungover to make friends right now. I grab his hand with my fingers, pushing it back towards him.

"You're also in my space, Lev."

A surprised laugh rumbles through his chest as he shifts further back into his seat, giving me the space I need to think clearly.

"Sorry about that," He draws a notebook and pen from his bag, turning to me again. "I didn't catch your name."

"I didn't offer it." I doodle in the margins of my notebook to keep my focus anywhere but on his delectable body, accentuated by the grey t-shirt hugging his chest and jeans clinging to his thighs like a second skin.

"Ouch. If you don't tell me your name, then how am I going to know what initials to draw in hearts with mine when I start daydreaming about my future wife later?" He asks.

Rolling my eyes at him, I look over just in time to see him give me an exaggerated wink. I don't know if he thinks he's being funny, but he's coming off way too desperate for his looks.

There's supposed to be a fair balance between hot and crazy, and Lev was tipping the scales in the wrong direction at the moment.

"You might want just to leave that set of initials empty if this is how strong you always come on."

That draws another laugh from him.

"I like to be optimistic." He tells me.

I'm saved from having to respond as the professor walks in to start the lecture.

I do my best to focus on the never-ending lecture, but every time Lev shifts in his seat or laughs under his breath, it draws my attention. I'm hyperaware of his presence. He's setting my nerves alight without even trying.

It's a foreign feeling. My body is confused by the sensation, my skin feels too tight, and the scars on my wrists beg to be scratched.

I abandon my notes, listening to the professor as I rub my thumb over the jagged scar inside my wrist.

It helps, some.

I don't know why Lev's presence is putting me on edge. He seems overly eager to talk to me.

A jarring thought occurs that maybe he's connected to my father or Leo. What if he's here to catch me breaking the rules and report back to them?

That doesn't make much sense. If Leo sent someone, it would be Michael. The giant wouldn't fit in on campus, but I also wouldn't be stupid enough to do anything I'm not supposed to in front of him.

I have two options here. Either I can feign ignorance and ignore him, or I can woman up and face him head-on.

Both options make my stomach roll. But I did not lose 3 years of my life to act like a scared little girl.

I turn to face him abruptly, startling him from drawing hearts in the margins of his notebook. He recovers quickly, offering a flirtatious smile while he gives me a quick once-over.

I don't let his insane hotness distract me.

"Who sent you?" I hiss, not wanting to be overheard by the students in front of us.

His smile drops. Brows crinkling in confusion, he slowly shakes his head.

"Uh, my parents?"

"Your parents?" I ask, dumbly.

"Yeah…" He draws the word out slowly, "They wanted me to go to college, so that's what I'm doing?" He says it like a question, obviously not following.

Well, this isn't helpful.

He sounds sincere, but in my world, that doesn't mean anything. Playing along, I decide to get more information.

After all, it's better to know your potential enemies rather than be blind.

"Where are you from?"

He perks up at the question, eager to talk about himself.

Originally from Sicily. Moved to London for school and was there for quite some time before coming here."

Sicily. So he's Italian. I had guessed as much based on appearance, but I could have been wrong. That doesn't ease my suspicions any. He has the look of someone from my world. He looks strong and hardened, even through his flirty exterior.

"Why did you come all the way here for school? Don't they have schools in London?"

He chews his lip, contemplating before answering.

"I have some family here, plus they offer a great education. It just made sense."

Fuck.

If he had 'family' here, he could easily be connected to my father or Leo.

This was getting me nowhere.

Gio might know something. I could ask him after class, but I need more information from Lev first, something for Gio to look into.

"What's your last name?"

He shoots me a devilish smile, laughing to himself, he turns to face me fully.

"Why? You want to hear how your new name will sound once we tie the knot?" His hand covers his heart, "I'm flattered, baby."

I fear my eyes will get stuck in the back of my head from how hard I'm rolling them at his corniness. He doesn't answer the question, going back to his notebook.

This is going nowhere. It seems my best option is to ignore him until he gets bored and goes off to find another piece of ass.

We don't speak for the rest of the class. I finally mangage to take some notes on the lecture, and he continues to doodle.

Once class ends, I quickly try to gather my things, shoving my stuff into my bag and rushing down the stairs. As I cross the threshold to enter the hallway, I feel a hand wrap around my bicep.

Instantly, I go into fight-or-flight mode. My body, on high alert, chooses fight.

Thrashing and pulling, I try to dislodge my arm from the grasp. Memories assault me, the guards at Briarwood dragging me down the barren halls towards treatment rooms, pulling me from my bed. Unrelenting grips leave bruises, as I'm taken from one torture to the next.

My chest tightens, and my breathing intensifies.

I feel like I'm suffocating.

My world narrows down to the feeling of hands on me.

Nothing else matters but getting free.

I can't let them take me.

I can't suffer anymore.

"Camilla!" A loud voice breaks through the memories. It sounds familiar. "Camilla, open your eyes!" When did I close them? "Cam, you're fine. Just open your eyes, look at me."

Peeling my eyes open, I find Gio.

His brows are drawn together, and a look close to panic covers his face.

Blinking, I try to clear the images from my head.

Lev stands just behind Gio, his eyes trained on my trembling hands. I ball my hands into fists to hide the shaking, digging my nails into my palms to bring me back down.

"I'm fine," I reassure Gio.

"What the hell happened?" He cuts his eyes over to Lev, who stands next to him, rubbing the back of his neck sheepishly.

Lev clears his throat, but I cut him off before he can say anything. I don't want to draw any more attention to my moment of panic.

"Nothing, it's fine."

Gio's eyes narrow slightly, a protective instinct flickering behind his skepticism.

"It's my fault," Lev interjects. Shooting him a look, I try to convey to the handsome stranger to drop it silently, but he continues. "I had a note I wanted to give Camilla, when I was trying to get her attention, I grabbed her arm." Looking at me, he shifts uncomfortably, offering me the paper in his hands. "I'm sorry, I didn't mean any harm."

Gio snatches the note before I can grab it, shooting daggers at him.

"Yeah, well, impact matters more than intent. How about you keep your hands to yourself in the future?" He spits out, swiftly dismissing him as he steers me away from him and out the door.

At the last second, I turn to get a glance of Lev looking crestfallen in the empty hallway, now clear of any students. I feel an inkling of guilt for a moment before brushing it off. He couldn't have known how I was going to react, but that still didn't mean he should've touched me.

"What's his deal?" Gio asks as we walk outside, the sunlight instantly warming me and chasing away the lingering chill.

"I'm not sure," I say, "He sat next to me in class and was trying to be friendly." My voice trails off as I contemplate whether I should tell him my suspicions that he was sent here to watch me. Gio has always been protective, but I fear that with the intense protectiveness he just showed outside of class, my speculation might piss him off even more.

It may be better to try to figure it out on my own before dragging Gio into this. If Lev were sent here to watch me, then having him report back to my father or Leo how close we are wouldn't end well. He could easily be used against me. The last thing I want is to drag Gio down with me; I care too much about him to put him in jeopardy like that.

"Well, I don't like him putting his hands on you," He draws me back from my thoughts. "Let me know if he bothers you, yeah?"

"Why? Are you going to beat him up?" I laugh, but he doesn't join in, though.

Looking straight ahead, he smirks, "Something like that."

His words carry a sinister note, but his composure is calm, making me think I imagined it.

"Are you sure you're okay? I can skip my next class, and we can go get some greasy hangover food instead," looking over my attire, he grins. "It looks like you may have been struggling before that douchebag showed up."

I swat at his arm, trying not to smile.

"It's your fault! You didn't warn me about how shitty I would feel this morning."

Nudging my shoulder, he laughs. "Cam, you didn't drink that much. How was I supposed to know you're such a lightweight?"

"You still should've warned me, you're supposed to be my guide in all of this."

Amusement flickers in his eyes, "I'll be sure to give you the full list of potential consequences for all our future endeavors, no matter how obvious they may seem."

"Thank you, kindly."

"So are we skipping or not?" He asks.

I shake my head, not considering his offer. I have too many rules to follow and none I want to explain to him.

"Not today, I don't have much left today, and then I need to get my assignments done tonight."

"Aiming to be the perfect student?" he mocks playfully.

We come up to the building that houses my next class. Stopping before the steps leading inside, I turn to face him, squinting at the sunlight shining behind him.

"I just want to stay on top of all of it. I have a ton to catch up on."

His gaze softens with understanding. "I get it. Just text me when you want to hang out, and I'll be there." Pulling Lev's note from his pocket, he adds, "Or if he bothers you again, let me know. I'll take care of it."

He waits for my nod before handing me the slip of paper, both of us going our separate ways.

I'm early for my following lecture, settling in the back row of the empty classroom to enjoy the quiet for a few minutes.

Unfolding the piece of paper, I expect to see a page filled with the little doodles Lev was drawing throughout class, but I'm shocked at what I find instead.

The page is filled with an intricate sketch of me. Sitting in the classroom, Lev sketched me out in fine detail, down to the crease in my brows as I felt the scars on my wrist. It's both beautiful and tragic. I can see the anxiety written on my face that I was feeling in class, but the overall image is stunning.

Of course, he had to write 'The future Mrs. Marino' along the bottom, killing the vibe. Yet, I still find myself giggling at his antics.

I can't believe he drew this or had time to draw with this much detail.

It almost makes him seem too playful, too normal to be someone sent to watch me. Most of the men the families hired were tough, rugged assholes, like Michael. Lev didn't give off the same energy as them.

Even so, I still needed more evidence than a beautiful sketch to convince me that he could be a friendly face for me rather than a deceiving spy.

Time would tell, but in the meantime, my guard will stay firmly up.

7

Camilla

My next class goes much smoother than the first. After the incident in the hall, Lev and Gio went their separate ways, leaving me to my own thoughts.

I fully intended to throw away the picture Lev drew me, not wanting to entertain the fact that he could be an innocent new friend before I had proof. I'm not sure what possessed me to tuck the paper carefully into my bag instead.

Drained from the incident after last class, I opt to take a seat in the far back corner of the class, putting off as many fuck you vibes to everyone in the room to hopefully ward off any unwanted company.

The professor jumps right into the lecture, and I let out a sigh of relief when the seat next to me remains empty.

I try to stay focused and take better notes in this class to make my evenings easier by completing assignments and avoiding having to relearn the material later.

Halfway through the class, a door snicking shut behind me catches my attention. Not thinking much of it, I return to taking my notes, but stiffen as a presence looms beside me.

Out of the corner of my eye, I see a heavy body slip silently into the seat beside me.

The professor glances our way but dismisses the newcomer quickly.

Much like last class, I do my best to ignore whoever it is, but I'm unsuccessful as they lean over to whisper in my ear.

"What page are we on?"

The voice is deep, but smooth like velvet, wrapping around me like honey and silk.

Just like with Lev, this man's beauty slaps me upside the head. His sharp features and striking blue eyes that intensify closer to his pupils before fading to gray further out in his irises. Raven-black hair sits perfectly styled on top of his head, over the neatly shaved sides, a stark contrast to his smooth complexion, free of blemishes or imperfections.

Smacked silly with the unfathomable hotness in front of me, I can't think of a clever retort. He nods his head in thanks as I manage to mutter out the page that we're looking at, turning to open his book to read along with the class.

Thankfully, he doesn't crowd into my space as Lev did, but his presence is still impossible to ignore. Warmth radiates off him in waves, increasing the urge in me to fan myself.

Thick, corded muscles sit under his button-up shirt, causing the material to stretch almost to the point of bursting. Tattoos peak out from the edges of his sleeves, and I'm caught staring at his arms, wondering how far the artwork travels up.

A Cheshire grin stretches across his face as my eyes lift to meet his. I feel the heat rushing to my cheeks, caught in the act.

"I'm Abram," He offers his hand, "I'm a new transfer." His voice holds a twinge of an accent that I can't place.

I take his offered hand cautiously, quickly shaking it before releasing and pulling mine back to the safety of my desk.

"Camilla," I offer quietly, not having the same urge to be rude as I did with Lev earlier.

"A beautiful name." He smiles kindly, but I revert my attention to my notes.

I've never been one to receive many compliments; having only been around Dante or Gio for most of my life, it felt foreign to me. I don't know the appropriate way to respond. If I simply said thank you and didn't return the compliment, then I would seem like a stuck-up bitch. But if I returned the compliment too quickly, then it seems inauthentic.

There was no winning.

Avoidance has always been my favorite tactic.

If he's offended, he doesn't let it show, quickly jumping into another line of conversation.

"So, how do you like cultural studies so far? I was on the fence about joining for a few weeks, but finally decided to take a chance on it."

A few weeks? This lecture had been booked out for months, at least that's what the professor had told us on the first day. If he's a new transfer, then how did he manage to get a spot on the class roster?

Red flags start to wave in the back of my mind, the same fear from earlier coming alive, that he might be a plant here to spy on me. I'm never going to know unless I speak to him. Being stand-offish with Lev was a defense mechanism, one that I itched to use now, but it isn't the most innovative course of action if I want answers.

Keeping that in mind, I'm careful with my answers as I speak.

"It's alright. Nothing I envisioned myself taking, but it's interesting enough."

He nods, thoughtfully.

"What's your major?"

Fuck.

What is my major? Do I even have one listed in my file? I'm only here for a year, so I won't be receiving a degree, but what degree do I even look like I'd be studying for with the bullshit classes I've been enrolled in?

"I'm… undecided, and you?" I try to deflect, not missing the crinkle in his brow.

"Communications."

Great. What the fuck even is that? You can get a degree in communicating?

"Are you a first year? This class is usually for third years," He asks suddenly.

If by first year he means I haven't attended school since I was sixteen, then yes. I guess I would be a first-year. But my age would suggest I should be at least in my second year, which still doesn't explain how I'm in this class.

Fucking Leo. Could he have made this any more difficult to play along with?

The answer is yes, he probably could have if he had taken a second to use his brain.

"Second year," I decide to call it in the middle just to be safe. "I lucked out."

"Impressive," He says cryptically, "You must have done really well in high school to swing that. Where'd you go?"

Okay, what is this guy's deal? Where is the third degree coming from? What would where I went to high school matter to him?

"Crestwood, in Chicago." I name the school I should have attended all four years, trying not to let my mind drift to the place where I resided at the time instead.

He nods thoughtfully, as if he's taking mental notes of every response I give.

My skin crawls. I don't like being at a disadvantage because he knows more about me than I do him. He hasn't offered any information about himself during this inquisition, but he's been successful in getting me to tell him all he wants to know.

"Are you a third year then?" I jump to ask him, and he doesn't hesitate to nod.

I'd be more skeptical if he didn't confirm he was older. By the looks of him, I would have assumed he was a TA, or even just a fresh new professor.

"And what high school?" Since I've already answered, it's only fair that he answer his own questions—an even playing field for both of us.

"Hollow Hills," He says, "It's a boarding school in Europe, my father sent me when I was young because the education in Russia isn't what he wanted for me."

Russia. I guess that explains the accent I'd noted earlier.

Knowing he's Russian eases my concerns that my father or Leo sent him. Father absolutely hated Russians, a feud that dated back years before I was born, and meant that he still swore to this day never to work with them, but he extended that to not even interact with their kind. Most of the Italian families didn't take kindly to them. Tension has always run high between the Mafia and the Bratva.

Not that Abram was in the Bratva just because he's Russian, but I could never be too careful.

With my suspicion down, my curiosity is piqued. I want to know more about how he found himself at a college in the middle of Michigan, having attended school in Europe his whole life. Something about it wasn't making sense.

Before I can ask, the professor ends the lecture, students gather their things, and begin to filter out around us.

Mentally, I'm wrung out. I'd love to retreat to my dorm for a quick power nap before my next class, but my stomach has other plans. A deep growl sounds out, my stomach loudly announcing its displeasure in not having any food today.

Heat rushes to my cheeks as my eyes meet Abram's again, who seems to be fighting a smile.

"Well, I was trying to find a subtle way to ask you to join me for lunch, but I guess that's as good an opening as any."

My mouth gapes open and closed as I scramble for a good excuse to say no without coming off rude. I am starving after waking up hungover and skipping breakfast. Since leaving Briarwood, my body has started to get used to meals at regular intervals for the first time in years, as evidenced by another thundering growl from my midsection.

"Come on, we barely got to talk during the lecture, my treat." He coaxes, "I haven't braved the school cafe yet, you wouldn't leave me to suffer on my own, would you?"

I would, but my hunger and burning curiosity win out against my urge to deny him. He was nice enough and not nearly as forward as Lev. I'm interested in learning more about the Russian stranger who stands before me.

He gestures for me to lead and follows a step behind me out of the lecture hall, falling into step with me once we enter the sprawling courtyard.

I let the comfortable silence fall between us, soaking in the sun's rays as it warms me to my core. It feels nice, like a warm hug trying to breathe life back into me, but it still can't touch the cold void where my heart should be.

I much prefer the rain to the sunshine. I love the smell, the heavy feeling in the air just before a storm, and, most of all, the way gloomy skies make the colors of the outdoors seem more vibrant, more green, and just alive. I feel like the rain gets me, whereas the sun is trying to change me, shape me into a warm presence that I'm not, and will probably never be again.

"Did you live in Chicago all your life before moving here for school?" Abram's voice pulls me from my thoughts as we approach the cafe, reminding me of his presence beside me.

"Born and raised," I answer, distracted as I gaze over the offerings for today, debating if I want to down a whole pizza in front of him or if I want to settle for something smaller. "Russia and then Europe, and now Michigan. Anywhere else you've planted your roots?" I ask, saying fuck it and dropping the pizza onto my tray.

His lips tip up at the edges, a silent laugh shaking his chest as he grabs his own food.

"I've visited many places, but as far as long-term, just those three."

I still wonder what caused him to come to school here, of all places. It's a nice school, but it was by no means the most well-known university for one to fly across the world to attend.

We settle at a table in the corner of the cafe, and I make sure to snag the seat that has my back facing the corner, leaving my view of the rest of the room open. After years of being snatched up by guards or attacked from behind, I wasn't taking any risks. Abram takes it in stride, settling across from me with no questions asked.

"How does one end up moving from Europe, and what I assume are prestigious schools, to attend college here in Michigan?" I finally ask him the burning question, waiting to see if he'll answer or try to deflect.

Avoiding the topic would give me reason to be suspicious of his sudden enrollment. I wait with bated breath to see which way this will go.

He chews for a moment, lost in thought.

"One of my best friends, who I've known most of my life, wanted to move here to be closer to his family. His mother isn't doing well. After years of being away from them at Hollow Hills, he decided to move back here so he could be around in case things get worse." He avoids my eyes as he speaks, pushing his food around on his plate. "They live in Rockford; this was the closest school to attend, and I didn't want him to come here alone."

Sadness rocks through me, the deep seed of grief striking me right in the chest. Memories of Dante flash through my mind, the reminder of the pain of losing a loved one and the crushing pain that comes with it.

"I'm sorry about your friend's mom." I offer lamely, working hard to shut down the images of happier times that flash through my mind. Refusing to remember Dante, dead or alive, his memory burns too much to.

Looking up, he offers a genuine smile, "It will all work out, but thank you."

The rest of lunch passes in an endless game of twenty questions. He seems to have picked up on the fact that for every one question I answer, I'm going to ask one. He waits after each question, waiting for my turn to either throw the question back or ask something else that comes to mind.

All the questions remain very light-hearted and surface-level: pets, favorite colors, and favorite movies. I'm shocked to learn that Abram's favorite movie is Dirty Dancing. I even see a hint of a blush touch his cheeks as he admits that, just before he swears that he'll deny it if it's ever mentioned again.

Before I know it, my silent alarm is going off, reminding me that my next class is about to start. I feel a small sense of disappointment at having to end our lunch. I didn't expect to enjoy the time with him, but my cheeks are starting to hurt from how much I've smiled and laughed over the last hour.

"This was fun, but I have another class to get to," I tell him, gathering my things to be on my way. A silent part of my brain is hoping that he feels the same sadness about our time being up I quickly tell that part of me to shut up. I just met him, I don't know anything of substance about him, certainly not enough to be having those thoughts.

He stands to join me, walking me out of the cafe.

"It was fun," He agrees. "We should do it again, Thursday?"

I think about it for a moment, stopping on the footpath to squint up at him. His gaze remains leveled with mine, hope twinkling in his eyes as my burn from the sun beating behind him.

I promised myself that I wouldn't make friends when I got here. I lucked out by finding Gio again, but I didn't want to form an attachment with anyone else. Not when I know that I won't be sticking around, whether I manage to escape from the fucked up reality I live in, or if I get dragged back to suffer at Leo's hands. One way or another, this wasn't going to last.

But the short time spent with Abram has already weakened my resolve to keep that promise to myself.

For just an hour, it was nice not to feel so lonely, to have someone around who wanted to know more about me, and who didn't know about my life or my family.

Did I really want to turn that away so easily?

"Sure," I agree before I can talk myself out of it. I'll grant myself a friend, knowing this isn't going to last. I'll be sure to keep him at a distance, no personal details. I'll entertain his friendship with the heavy expiration date lingering over it, and when the time comes, I'll be sure to push him away, preferably before I make a run for it, if anything, to make the hurt sting a little less.

His smile is almost as blinding as the sun. "Perfect, I'll see you then."

With those parting words and plans in place, we both head our separate ways. I have to force the butterflies in my stomach to cease as I rush to make it to my next class. I spend the entire walk wondering if I just made a stupid mistake.

8

Dima

I watch the mindless students pass through the halls outside the lecture room. They all move aimlessly, their eyes buried in their phones, watching their stupid TikTok videos or snapping photos of themselves.

I don't understand how some people can move through life so carelessly, never worried about threats lingering over their shoulder. It's funny when I think about it. Here I am, an enforcer lying in wait right in front of them. They don't have the brains to fear the danger that lies just before them.

I look at the time again. Class is starting. But still, I remain in my spot against the wall, not willing to go in until I see *her* enter.

I tried to argue with Abram when he announced that we'd all be taking college classes. I'd never been one to appreciate education. I didn't see a need for it in my world. My job was to get answers, beat and torture, whatever it took. I didn't need a college degree for that; hell, I didn't need a high school diploma for that either. But I can see how it's the easiest way to get close to Camilla, since this is the first place we've managed to track her down in over four years.

My idea of just kidnapping her and bringing her back home with us was not received well by the guys. None of them can argue with me that it would be the most efficient way to do things; we could be home in days. They all wanted to take the gentle approach of befriending her. Who knows how long we'll be trapped here posing as students and making friends with a girl who's never been more than a ghost to us.

A dark flash of raven hair rushes past me, slipping into the lecture hall.

About time.

I wait another five minutes, making sure she has time to settle into a seat so that I can slip in and sit near her. If her bag is unpacked, then she'll be less likely to move anywhere else.

Part of me hopes she'll run; I do love to give a good chase. It's been too long since I've had a good, fun hunt. I'd love to see flashes of that raven hair catching the moonlight as she runs from me. Maybe in the woods, she can be the little deer running from the hungry lion. I'd let her pull ahead for a while, thinking she has a chance at escape, but really, she'll be tiring herself out for me. When she thinks she sees a sliver of hope, a light at the end of the tunnel, I'll catch her. Snuff out that hope like a dying flame, and devour her, body and soul.

Reality comes crashing back around me as a couple of giggling girls walk back, eyeing me and winking as they pass.

I again roll my eyes at the lack of self-preservation.

Slipping into the lecture hall, I immediately spot her. She's tucked herself in the back corner of the hall, seated alone at the end of the empty row.

Her hair forms a curtain around her as she leans over her books, doodling in the already full margins of her notebook.

She's completely oblivious to my presence, unaware of her surroundings.

I slip into the seat next to hers, noting how she stiffens with my arrival, suddenly aware and on edge.

Her eyes peek through her curtain of hair, widening as they take me in. I'm not surprised. I've been told that I can be intimidating, all rough edges, larger than most men, and the scars littered over my arms don't give off very welcoming vibes.

I stretch my lips into what I hope is a friendly smile, but the way her eyes widen even further before darting back to her notebook tells me that I've failed in some way.

The professor drones on about some ancient bullshit, and I fight not to lose my mind, thinking of how to start a conversation with the wide-eyed doe beside me.

The ground rules were that we find out what we can about Camilla and where she's been since Dante died. We're not to mention anything about knowing Dante or attending school with him, and we don't let Camilla in on the fact that we've all felt like we've known her for years. We've listened to countless stories about her in our time with Dante at school, always in the background of their weekly phone calls and video chats. I'd even travelled to the States with Dante on some of his visits home. I never met Camilla on those trips; I lingered in the shadows when Dante would take her out, acting as their secret security.

Dante never did share why he suddenly became interested in ramping up safety anytime he was around her, but I didn't think to question at the time.

She still sits stiffly and does her best to keep her eyes trained on her notebook. Every few moments, I catch her stealing glances at me when she thinks I'm not looking.

Pulling out my phone, I check the group text to see if the other guys made any progress with her.

LEV: I may have fucked up...

ABRAM: What the fuck did you do?

ROMAN: It's 8 in the morning...how could you have possibly screwed anything up already?

LEV: I didn't mean to. It was an accident, I swear!

ABRAM: What happened?

LEV: I talked to her during our class. She was very hesitant, but I thought we might be making some progress before class let out...

ROMAN: ...

ROMAN: And?

LEV: I was trying to give her a note after class, but she didn't hear me when I called out to her. I reached out for her, and she freaked out. Panic attack... I was trying to calm her down, and her friend showed up. He was pissed.

ABRAM: Jesus, Lev.

ROMAN: Take it Easy. He had no way to know it would freak her out.

LEV: I didn't mean to!

ABRAM: I'm going into class with her now. I'll check on her.

***

ABRAM: She seems alright, but she did get tripped up when I asked her about her major and what year she was in. Like she had to think about it...

ABRAM: She says she was at Crestview in Chicago.

ROMAN: We checked their files for years, never found any signs of her.

We never found any paperwork or a diploma for her.

ABRAM: I know...

ABRAM: She seems to like me. We're getting lunch.

ROMAN: She likes you? Are we sure there's nothing wrong with her?

LEV: Why do you get to take her to lunch? I'm coming to join!

ABRAM: No.

ABRAM: We're not bombarding her. I barely got her to agree. Do NOT show up and ruin any progress we could be making.

LEV: Fine.

LEV: I want in next time.

LEV: Hello?

ROMAN: I'll take that as a 'no'.

LEV: Asshole.

Interesting.

So she took better to Abram than she did to Lev. I wonder if that has anything to do with his Russian descent rather than Lev's Italian.

I've always told him we have a superior heritage.

Of the four of us, Abram was hardly ever anyone's favorite. He was usually the most hated, as he gave the orders that determined who lived and who died. I'm usually a close second for most hated, dishing out the slow and painful torture. I am shocked that she didn't take to Lev; he was like a golden retriever, making friends wherever he went.

The professor announces that we'll be working in pairs on a project for our semester grade. The perfect opening to speak to Camilla, I can't hide my smug satisfaction as he continues to say whoever is sitting to your right would be your partner.

I watch Camilla's wide eyes slowly drag away from her notebook to stare at my borderline feral grin.

A blush rushes to her cheeks as I shoot her a wink, quickly averting her gaze to her notebook once more.

She doesn't look up again as the professor discusses the project parameters, then dismisses us to plan with our partner for the rest of the hour.

Everyone breaks off into their pairs to start planning. I wait for Camilla to make her move.

Reluctance rolls off of her in waves, and she tries and fails to sit in silence. She lasts all of two minutes, listening to me drum my fingers on the desk before she sucks in a sharp breath, sitting up to turn and face me. Her wide eyes take me in, roam over all of my features, while she keeps her face carefully impassive.

She studies my long hair, pulled up into a bun, and the tattoos that cover my hands and arms, probably wondering if they extend farther under my shirt, onto my impressive chest and abs. She stops on my septum ring and the small barbell through my eyebrow, mesmerized by the small pieces of metal. If she likes those, then she'd be melting at the sight of my cock and its impressive collection of hardware.

She doesn't look like she's going to speak first, so I decide to break the ice and introduce myself, even though I'd love just to sit here and watch her check me out.

I clear my throat to grab her attention. "I'm Dima." My voice comes out gravelly, making her eyes widen even further. "Looks like we're going to be partners."

She swallows heavily, her eyes not leaving mine as she whispers.

"Camilla. Nice to meet you."

Oh, the irony. It's fantastic to meet her officially. After knowing her all these years, my heart feels like it's trying to jump out of my chest when she speaks to me for the first time. I've heard her speak so many times, but always to Dante. Her voice is the perfect mix of soft and sensual, a current of innocence lingering just beneath the surface.

I want to bottle her up and keep her with me forever like a sexy little Tamagotchi.

"So, any ideas what you want to do the project on?" She tears her eyes off me to flip to a clean sheet of paper, one without her doodles filling the margins.

I glance around the room, looking for a clue as to what this class is even centered around. The whiteboard outlines the project's parameters, and it seems Camilla is copying them down in her notebook while I ponder. Her textbook finally catches my eye: *Interpersonal Communication.*

What the fuck is that?

"Whatever you'd like to do," I offer, "I'll follow your lead." I've never taken a college course, and I have no clue what we're supposed to do for a written project on conflict management, support, and influence of romantic relationships. My favorite method of communication is torture, and I've never had a relationship beyond a one-night stand. I don't think I fit the requirements for this project, let alone this class.

"Okay…" She drags the word out, almost annoyed that I'm giving her full rein on the project. I can't bring myself to feel bad about it. I shouldn't even be enrolled in this class, let alone making any decisions for both of us. "I guess we have some

94

time to figure it out. The first outline isn't due for three weeks."

Here it is, my opening laid out right before me.

"We can meet outside of class to figure it out when you're free. Let's exchange numbers, and you can text me."

Her hand stops writing, freezing in place.

"Um, that's okay." She lets her hair fall back into a curtain between us, obstructing my view of her profile. "We can just plan it out when we're in class."

Was I just rejected?

This has never happened to me before. I don't like it.

"It really would be easier if we could meet outside of class. We're only in here once a week. There's not much time to plan this out if we can't meet up." I don't want to sound desperate, but my ego is already hurting. "I won't even take advantage of having your number by sending you pleasantries or funny jokes."

"You have jokes?" Her eyes peek around her hair, skepticism heavy in them.

"Of course," I scoff. "What, you think because I have a man bun and tattoos I can't have jokes?"

She blinks, processing. "It was more the whole being Russian thing, actually."

Now it's my turn to blink.

"What gave it away?" I ask, crossing my arms and leaning back in my chair, hoping that she faces me to give me a better look at all of her soft features. "My devastatingly good looks and superior Russian genes?"

Victory swells in my chest as she moves her hair out of the way to study me closely. Her gaze lingers on my tattoos; she traces the designs with her eyes.

I let her study me, giving her time to analyze me and all I have to offer.

"I think it was more so the accent, actually."

Interesting, my accent was not anywhere near as prominent as when I was younger, after the years I've spent in London at school. Most people had to really strain to hear it, unless they were used to it.

"Hm, I didn't think it was that noticeable."

"It's probably not," She concedes, twirling her pen around her fingers. "But you're actually the second Russian I've met today, so it makes it a little easier."

Damn, Abram, stealing my thunder. Now I'm just the second Russian in her eyes. He probably did it on purpose, knowing that it would grate on my nerves.

"What are the odds?"

She makes a sound in the back of her throat that I'm assuming is her agreement, and the silence falls between us once again.

"So, now that you know about my descent and that I have an extensive array of jokes, can we exchange numbers now?" Her pen stops, now clutched between her fingers; they turn white as she strangles it. "In the name of effective group work, of course."

"I can't." I'm worried for the state of her bottom lip as her teeth start to dig into it.

"Do you not have a phone?" I guess, though I'm not sure how anyone can go without one these days.

"I do, it's just… complicated. I really can't have you texting me."

She sounds defeated, only adding to my confusion. I can't think of a reason she wouldn't have my phone number. Her sullen demeanor is screaming at me that she's not just trying to brush me off; she seems genuinely disappointed to have to admit she can't text.

I don't like the feeling of putting this crestfallen expression on her face. For now, I'll drop it. But I make a mental note to look into this more later. She just met me; there's no reason that she should have to share all of her secrets with me now.

"Okay, we'll figure it out," I reassure her, quickly dismissing the topic.

We spend the last few minutes of class having a casual conversation, agree to start outlining our project next week, and then make plans to meet up on our own time. Her mood doesn't pick back up, sadness lying just below the surface and tinging her words as we talk.

Once the hour is up, she's packed and out of her seat before I can blink, rushing out of the room and leaving me no chance to catch up. I don't try to follow her; I decide to give her space. I have to remember that she's being bombarded by all of us today; it's probably overwhelming to have four new men crashing into your world out of nowhere.

I'll stand down for now, give myself some time to listen to what the others may have found out about her, and do my own digging as well.

No matter what I find, come next week, all bets are off, and I'll do whatever it takes to find the answers I'm looking for. She's been a ghost for years, but we've found her now.

Come hell or high water, we'll find out where she's been.

9

Camilla

I rush out of the lecture room like my ass is on fire, chancing a glance over my shoulder to make sure Dima doesn't follow.

A sigh of relief is dragged from my lungs, seeing that I'm alone. I don't know how many more surprise meetings I can take with hot Russians and transfer students before I completely lose my mind.

Dima was nice, much like Abram and Lev, as much as I hate to admit it. But something about their insistence on befriending me put me on edge.

And Leo, the jackass. Every second of the day, I figure out new ways that he's ensured he can control me. Once Dima asked for my number to meet outside of class, reality slapped me across the face, reminding me that Leo had access to my phone, all my calls and texts, anytime he wanted.

The only reason I hadn't thrown the damn thing in a lake was that I was expected to respond to all of his check-in messages.

All day, I haven't even been able to enjoy the prospect of talking to new people; instead, I've been weighed down with anxiety, wondering if they were planted by Leo or not.

My skin feels tight with all the anxious energy that's flowed through me today. My only saving grace is that I'm done with classes for the day, and tomorrow I have a break only for the pleasure of my first appointment with the school-appointed counselor.

I guess when you've already tried to slit your wrists once, you become a walking liability for this school. These appointments were "crucial to gauge my mental state".

In other words, I need to make sure that I have my best, mentally stable, well-adapted mask on tomorrow if I don't want Leo having any reason to pull me out and drag me back home early.

I just hope that Leo couldn't find anyone as sadistic as Dr. Watson. I know if my father had chosen the therapist, he'd probably have paid extra to fly the bastard out here just to fuck with me. But, I'd learned over the last few weeks, or so, that Leo practically made all the decisions regarding me, my father had washed his hands of me and was just on standby until I made it down the aisle and fulfilled his side of the deal for him.

It seems that after years, my father was the same thing he'd always been: a fucking coward.

I make it back to my dorm without any interruptions and move around, still buzzing with anxious energy.

I try to get some homework done, but my mind won't focus. Looking in the fridge, I try to find something to eat, but nothing sounds appealing. I flip on the TV, but the voices coming from the screen are like nails on a chalkboard. Flipping it back off, I lay back on the couch, staring up at the lines in the ceiling.

I could call Gio and see if he can find us something to take my mind off it, but he's probably going to try to ask about Lev and what happened this morning. I don't want to think about it right now, especially when I still don't know how I feel about him and if he's here as a plant or not.

An idea hits. Jumping from the couch, I rush to my room to throw on a pair of spandex shorts and a sports bra. I throw on a baggy shirt that comes down to mid-thigh and pile my hair up into another messy top knot, slipping on some flip-flops and grabbing my keys and phone as I rush out.

Years ago, well after Dante had left, I was missing him so much and going out of my mind. I'd forced Gio to sign up to take a dance class with me just for something to do. It was something my father didn't know about, which made it all the more fun for me. That, and Gio hated it. Even still, I continued to sneak out to go to any of the classes I could get into, right up to being shipped away.

It became a nice outlet whenever I was missing Dante too much or when I started imagining ways I could stab my father with a butter knife; I ran out to one of the classes.

Technically, you were supposed to enroll and pay for classes at the studio I snuck into, but the lady who ran it was kind and said she was happy to let me join. I always figured she thought I came from a rough home life, which wasn't entirely untrue, so I just went along with it.

I don't know what reminded me that the campus has a whole private studio attached to the gym. Rooms and rooms full of mirrors and stereos where I can get lost for hours.

Sounds like the perfect distraction for my head right now.

Moving quickly across campus, the hair on the back of my neck stands up. The sinking feeling of being watched chases me around every corner. The worst part is, I have no way to know if that's just a sick side effect of being at Briarwood or if someone is actively here, watching my every move.

I have no way to know. If Leo put someone here to watch me, then they'll be well camouflaged, giving me no chance of finding them. That would defeat the purpose, after all, if I knew exactly who to avoid.

Glancing around me, I can't see anyone who looks suspicious or as though they're following me, but still, I quicken my steps to close the distance to the gym quickly.

Music blasts through the crowded gym. Student athletes and fitness fanatics litter every open space and machine. The stale stench of sweat hangs heavy in the air.

I don't pay attention to any of the faces scattered around as I hug the perimeter of the room to the far side, where the entrance to the rec spaces is.

The door closing behind me is like taking earbuds out after blasting music; all at once, the gym noise stops. My ears ring from the sudden silence.

Lucky for me, the rec spaces don't seem to be a popular spot, if the lights are off and empty rooms are anything to go by.

All the rooms are relatively similar, with mirrors, ballet bars, and stereos. But the two on the end make my eyes widen with excitement.

The first room on the end is just like the others, but there are mats spread out across the floor, each strategically placed under sets of silks hanging from the high ceilings.

And the last room at the end, the holy grail. A typical dance studio, just like the others, but the back of the room holds small platforms spaced out, each with a pole situated right in the center.

There's no hesitation in my choice. I push through the door, claiming the room as my own.

I probably never should have been allowed to take a pole dancing class, given I was only sixteen, but it was one of my favorite classes to sneak into back at home. The girls in the class were always so lovely, and it was so fun to do something that felt so forbidden. I knew that my father would lose his shit if he ever caught me.

But he isn't here, and he had no say in what I did. Leo might think that he does, but he isn't here either, so I'm going to do what *I* want. And what I want is to spin around a pole and feel sexy, dance around the room, and let out all my emotions that are running like a live wire under my skin.

It doesn't take but a second to connect my phone to start playing music through the speakers in the room, quickly working to drown out the noise in my mind as I drop down onto the floor to work through some stretches I can remember from classes.

My muscles ache and protest the foreign movements, but I keep pushing, knowing that I'll hurt worse later if I don't get loosened up.

The music shifts, a new song blaring through the speakers, the bass rattles faintly through the floor. Standing, I close my eyes and focus on releasing the tension in my body, picturing it rolling off me in waves and down to the floor.

Without much thought, I let the music move me. I focus on the words of the song, allowing them to capture each of the emotions I shoved down today, letting them go, one by one.

I feel lighter as the song comes to an end, blending seamlessly into the next as I can't fight the draw to the pole across the room.

Exhaustion already hovers over me like a dark cloud; my body isn't used to this exertion after years of being sedentary, but I push through.

Feeling the grip of the pole between my hands is like a welcoming hug from an old friend. Everything feels right. All my worries cease to exist as my energy is pushed towards my grip and what I'm doing.

Song after song, I work on running through old moves I learned years ago. Savoring the stretch and pull in my muscles and not worrying about the aches I'll feel tomorrow.

I'm not sure how much time has passed by the time my body threatens to collapse, but I finally feel lighter once I'm done. Lying out on the floor, I savor the feeling of lightness and sweat drying on my skin, thoroughly soaking through the t-shirt I threw on before I left. I can already feel the blisters budding on my palms, but I can't be bothered to care.

I make a mental note to add this to my daily routine, a good way to let out all of my pent-up frustrations without having to vent to Gio at every turn. Dr. Watson always said that exercise was a good stress reliever, though it was laughable at the time since we weren't allowed to do anything even remotely close to exercise.

Once my breathing is leveled out and I don't fear that I'll collapse, I gather my phone and shoes to make my way back to my dorm.

I keep my head down as I walk through the crowded gym, not wanting to be distracted by the room full of jocks. The night air is stale as I step through the doors, the humidity still clinging to the day, with a small promise of reprieve from the slight breeze that occasionally sweeps through.

Walking back towards the dorm, I check my phone, seeing messages from both Leo and Gio waiting for me. Before I can open either thread, I slam into a wall. More specifically, I slam into a wall of pure muscle, sending me flat onto my ass to stare at the man towering over me.

Broad muscles against a black muscle tee, and cropped black hair frames a face full of harsh lines and sharp features. Black ink swirls over both of his sculpted arms as one reaches out for me, the other pocketing a phone in his loose gym shorts.

"I'm so sorry about that. I wasn't watching where I was going." His voice comes out rough, his words not matching his concerned tone as he waits for me to take his offered hand.

I stare at his offered hand like it's about to strike me, more curious than anything as to why he's easily taking the blame for me running into him.

He doesn't have the same reservations, bending over to lift me by the arms when I still hesitate to move. He steadies me on my feet before grabbing my phone to offer it to me as well.

His striking blue eyes lock on mine again, keeping me entranced, standing here like a fumbling idiot trying to find my way out.

"Sorry". I finally manage to blurt out, realizing how rude I may seem just standing here.

A crooked grin pulls at his lips, "All good, I just hope that fall didn't hurt too bad, this gravel looks harsh."

He's not wrong. My ass is throbbing. I know this, combined with the fatigue already settling in my muscles, is going to be a bitch come tomorrow.

"No," I laugh it off, "Mostly just a hit to my dignity."

He laughs with me, the sound warming me to my core as I watch his Adam's apple bob in his throat. The sound is rough, but smooth like honey at the same time.

"I'm Roman," He offers his hand once again. This time, I take it, noting how it dwarfs mine.

"Camilla," I try to smother the stab of disappointment as he pulls his hand from mine. "Nice to meet you."

His eyes roam over me before jumping over my shoulder to the gym.

"You just coming from a workout?" He asks. "Too bad, maybe I'll see you around then," He says at my nod.

With nothing else, he steps around me, walking into the gym without a backward glance, leaving me watching him, dazed and confused.

My phone buzzing in my head draws my attention. Looking down, I see Leo's contact on my screen. In my collision with Roman, I didn't get a chance to read his message, something I'm sure I'll pay the price for now.

Taking a breath to steady myself, I answer the phone, waiting in silence.

"Camilla, my useless excuse of a wife. Where have you been?" His voice is like venom, striking me through the phone as he wastes no time on pleasantries. Why pretend to be pleasant with someone whom you intend to own?

My teeth ground together at his high-handedness as if he doesn't already know where I've been.

"I had classes all day and then decided to go to the gym." I try to focus on the scenery passing by as I talk, hoping the pretty trees will bring back some of the calm I found in the studio.

"Ah, trying to look good for me, dear?" I fight the urge to vomit at the thought. He chuckles at my silence. "Well, I called to remind you that you have your first appointment with Dr. Pitts tomorrow morning. I advise you not to be late. I'll be informed immediately," He lets the words linger between us,

"And I'd hate to have to end your little college expedition so quickly after it started."

How could I forget the dreaded therapy session that I've avoided thinking about since I got here? He's using that against me as a way to keep me in line, which only makes me hate it more.

"Yeah, okay. I'll be there, I don't need a time keeper." I can't help the childish retort. It seems that when I've been stripped of everything else, I fall back into a less mature mindset.

What I'd like to do is tell him that he can shove his misogynistic class schedule and forced therapy where the sun doesn't shine. But somehow, I manage to refrain.

"You should be thankful for the short leash I've granted you; you never know when I'll decide to use it to choke you instead." He laughs cynically. "I'll be checking in on you soon; you'd better answer when I call." With the ominous threat, he disconnects before I can utter a single word.

Making it back to my dorm, I'm seething. All the work I put in at the gym is washed away with one phone call.

Exhaustion weighs heavily on me, but it's easily overshadowed by my rage and the need to wash away the sweat sticking to my skin.

Standing under the hot water in the shower, I try to figure out how I got here.

What have I done so wrong in my life to have ended up getting locked away, then freed, only to be handed to another monster who wants to keep me on a leash? Like a fucking *pet*.

The bigger question weighing me down is how I'm going to get out of this.

I haven't put much effort into finding a way to get away before my wedding day. A way to escape the pull that both my father and the Ivanni's have. Their power stretches over most of the country, leaving my options limited, practically nonexistent.

There's got to be someone who can help me get away undetected, but who?

My top priority is finding someone who can help and laying out a plan to leave before my time is up. Everything needs to be planned meticulously, every outcome considered.

If I end up pulling this off, I'll only have one shot. And no room for any mistakes.

10

Roman

The photos that Abram provided us did not do Camilla any justice.

Even standing before me, in an oversized T-shirt and sweaty from the gym, she was nothing less than stunning.

The way the afternoon sun shone behind her gave the illusion of a halo around her head, highlighting both the innocence in her eyes and the demons she had locked inside.

It's clear to me that she's been through some shit, not just the invisible demons I can see in her eyes, but also the scars on her wrists read a very telling story. She's no stranger to struggling, to torture... to pain.

All day, I'd watched the group chat with the others, waiting for updates from them. Until now, it was my turn to finally plant myself in her path and introduce myself.

I was much more on Lev's side, wondering why we couldn't just tell her who we are or who we were to Dante. It seemed like a lot less effort than the plan that Abram had come up.

But Abram was our unspoken leader; what he says goes. And if he thought this was the best idea, then this is what we'll do for now.

I was firmly against Dima's idea to kidnap her; I didn't think that would go over well, for her or for us.

While I may have been the last of us to get to meet her, I wasn't the last to see her. I'd been following her around for days, watching. Much like now, after waiting for her to head back to her dorm, I abandon the gym looming behind me as soon as she's out of sight. Following at a distance and watching her stiffen as she speaks on the phone, wondering who was on the other side.

Whoever it is, they don't make her happy.

She remains on the phone, mostly listening as she treks back to her dorm, disappearing inside and out of sight. I could follow her into the building, but that puts me in a more vulnerable position to get caught, and I don't want to be seen just yet.

Backtracking to the house, I find all the guys arguing over pasta preferences in the kitchen when I arrive.

"Gnocchi isn't even pasta! It's potatoes, we have potatoes every night. I told you I wanted pasta, that was my one request for my night to choose!" Lev yells.

"Gnocchi is a dumpling, this is pasta," Dima retorts, "Plus it tastes better than orzo. And doesn't look like maggots."

"Abe! Please tell him it's my choice today, we're having orzo." Lev sounds almost feral as he begs Abram to save the day.

Abram's bored tone doesn't surprise me.

"I told you two that I'm not getting involved in your petulant bickering."

"Oh my God! By not picking a side, you're taking his side, you know." Seeing me round the corner, he perks up instantly. "Oh, Roman, would you please tell Dima that Gnocchi does not qualify as pasta?"

Looking from his begging stare, desperate before me, to Dima's crooked grin, telling me that he's loving fucking with Lev, I decide to join in the fun.

"Gnocchi is my favorite. When's it going to be ready?" I ask, watching his face crumble at the betrayal.

Grumbling, he drops into the seat beside Abram,

"I don't know why I even hang out with you fuckers."

Rolling his eyes, Abram directs his attention to me. " I thought you were going to run into Camilla at the gym?"

Everyone perks up, instantly interested at the mention of her name.

"I did, she was already on her way out for the night. I'll have to go earlier next time. Dima didn't give me much warning." Dima had texted me after she left her dorm shortly after her last class of the day, having followed her back. By the time I got word from him and left the house, she was already leaving.

"Why does she want to work out anyway? She's too tiny." Dima shrugs.

"You are a mountain of muscle," Lev points out. "You of all people should know that some people enjoy working out."

Dima stops rolling the gnocchi on the counter to level his gaze on him.

"I work out because I need to, not because it's *fun*."

"So did you get a chance to talk to her at all?" Abram interjects, looking to me.

"Briefly, she ran into me, and I got to introduce myself. Then she got a phone call, and I followed her back until she was at her dorm."

"You think it was her father?" He asks thoughtfully. At the same time, Dima mumbles,

"So she does have a phone."

I look between the two of them, "No way to know, and why would you think she didn't have a phone?" I direct the question to Dima, wondering why he would think someone in this day and age wouldn't have a cellphone. They were practically necessary for survival these days.

He looks cagey, trying to avert his attention to the food prep instead. "I asked for her number so we could work on our project together, and she freaked out, saying she couldn't do that. She was panicking, so I just guessed she didn't have one."

Silence settles over us for a few moments as we contemplate. That reaction isn't exactly normal, and she definitely does have a phone. I handed it to her earlier. Why would she be so hesitant to exchange numbers?

"Aww," Lev breaks out into a goading smirk, effectively breaking the silence. "You finally got rejected! And I wasn't there to see it?"

Dima snarls, ready to launch himself over the counter. Abram reaches over to smack Lev upside the head, ignoring his complaints.

"Knock it off."

Lev can't help but laugh, even as he rubs the back of his head.

"Something to look into, we need to know why she's acting weird about it. It could be because of her father, but we still don't know why." Abram muses, "Stick to the plan, continue to get close to her, and see what we can find out."

He leaves to retreat to his office, saying he needs to finish up some business meetings. The three of us hang out while dinner cooks, watching TV and talking about mundane topics.

Abram rejoins us briefly for dinner, all of us noting how Lev shovels two plates of gnocchi down his throat like it's the best thing he's ever tasted, forgetting his earlier protest. Soon after, we all head our separate ways for the night.

The next morning, I head out early. Deciding to go for a run in hopes of catching a glimpse of Camilla. We know that she has a free schedule today, with all her classes scheduled in blocks on Monday, Wednesday, and Thursday instead. I'm curious to see what she'll get up to today.

Since I started following her, I've only seen her hang out with one friend, Giovanni Ruiz, a childhood friend she recently reconnected with.

From the little bit of research I've done, he doesn't seem to be a threat. I'd worry about a possible attraction towards her if I didn't already learn that he preferred men. Not that I care, but his protectiveness over her could be an unnecessary obstacle. I decided to leave him for now. I wouldn't step in to tell him to back off until he made himself a problem.

We'd only arrived on campus about a week after Camilla, leaving me little time to follow her and get a feel for her usual route. Granted, it's only been a few days since she started coming out of her dorm, but it's hard to say if she even has a routine at this point. I'm blindly fumbling around in the dark, trying to get a feel for what her next move will be.

Outside of yesterday for class, she leaves her dorm sporadically since we arrived. Once she did, the only thing she did was go with Giovanni to buy some weed off a wannabe dealer on campus.

I opted not to tell the others that she went to buy drugs. It was only weed; it was practically harmless. Abram would disagree, but all she did was go back to her room to smoke. Nothing to write home about. She deserved to have a little fun, let loose.

What he didn't know wouldn't hurt him.

Luck seems to be on my side today, as I round the bend approaching her dorm, I see her step out into the morning sun. The early morning light shines off her dark hair. She keeps her head down, quickly moving down the steps and setting off towards the administration building.

She's ditched her cut-offs for a tight pair of leggings that hug every curve of her ass, tucked into a pair of Chucks. She has a tight tank top on, highlighting her slim figure with the ugliest cardigan I've ever seen thrown over top. It has baggy sleeves that she's had to roll at the ends to keep her hands from being swallowed. The beige and brown checkerboard colors don't complement her at all. If anything, it makes her look washed out, in contrast to her pale skin and raven hair.

I keep a safe distance behind her, watching to see where she's going but not giving myself away.

I watch her slip into the admin building before disappearing into the office for the freshman counselor, the door shutting firmly behind her.

I shoot a quick text to Abram, waiting in the lobby to see if she'll come out. His reply comes a few minutes later.

Abram: Looks like the counselor has her blocked out for an hour and a half. No reason listed.

He isn't the most skilled with hacking, but he at least has enough skills to navigate the school's system. It's how he got each of us into her classes, and now we can see how long she's scheduled for each appointment.

With over an hour to kill, I decide waiting in the lobby isn't my best option. The receptionist at the desk is already looking at me like I'm a snack and she's starving.

I turn on my heel, leaving the office and finishing my run back to the house. I give myself plenty of time to jump in the shower before grabbing the keys to my bike and heading back to the campus.

Parking in a lot one building over, I leisurely make my way back over. Timing it perfectly so that I'm walking up the steps to the front doors just as she's coming out.

Luck being on my side again, she isn't paying attention. Her gaze focused on the ground as I wait for her to run into me.

Unlike last time, I catch her before she can fall this time.

"Whoa, careful now. I'm sure you don't want to hit the concrete again." I joke.

All the air gets sucked from my lungs as she looks up to meet my gaze. Her eyes were bloodshot, and her cheeks were blotchy from crying.

"Sorry, I was just distracted," She sniffles.

My brows pull together, wondering who I need to kill for making her cry. Her glassy eyes make me want to seek vengeance in the deadliest ways possible.

"Is everything okay?" I ask dumbly.

Of course, it's not okay. She's standing here in front of me, holding back more tears.

She laughs without humor, sucking in a shuddering breath before wiping any emotion from her face right before me.

One second, she's a broken, fragile soul trying to hold it together, the next an emotionless ice queen. The difference is startling.

117

"Yeah, it's fine." She shifts her weight, subtly pulling away from my hands. I tuck my hands into my pockets to refrain from pulling her into me.

I search for something to say, something to keep the conversation going. Nothing comes to mind.

"Do you want to get out of here?" She asks suddenly, shocking me into silence.

She must take my silence for reluctance, tucking her hair behind her ear and shaking her head.

"I mean, if you're not busy." Shaking her head, she blushes. "Sorry, you've probably got better things to do. Just forget I asked."

"Where do you want to go?" I finally pull my head out of my ass long enough to compose an answer.

She contemplates for a moment, staring off into the distance and chewing on her bottom lip.

"Know any good bars around here?" She asks. Her wide doe eyes stare up at me, sparkling with hope and a little bit of mischief.

Narrowing my own, a smirk pulls at my lips.

I don't know what she wants to run away from, but I'll happily be her knight in dark denim to whisk her away for a distraction if that's what she needs.

"Let's go."

11

Camilla

I'm fuming.

If I could drive all the way back to Chicago and shoot Leo square in the face, I would.

That fucking bastard. His bullshit "therapist", his rules, and our stupid impending marriage. He can shove it all up his ass.

I'd gone to the session, sat and tried to zone out, but Dr. Pitts wouldn't allow that. He required participation in the form of my having to describe what I remember from the day I tried to kill myself. When he wasn't happy with that, he dug out the autopsy report for Dante, reading it in great detail and describing every single second of suffering that he went through before he met his end.

All to evoke some emotion, he said. To find the root of my depression.

I've shut out thoughts and memories of Dante since I went into Briarwood; it was easier than facing the pain of knowing he's gone. Dr. Pitts managed to ruin that within an hour in his office. And I'm expected to show up every week to relive this shit and suffer anything else his convoluted mind can come up with.

Roman taps my thigh, letting me know to grab onto him as the bike approaches a winding curve up ahead.

I don't know why I decided to leave with him; I don't even know the guy. But overall, it seemed like the better option than going back to my dorm to stew in my memories and raging emotions.

Sitting on the back of his bike, my arms wrapped around his massive torso, barely able to interlock my fingers, feeling the wind whipping around us and the sun shining down, I know I made the right call.

He didn't have a spare helmet, obviously, so he fastened his over my head, and we were on our way.

I'm thankful for the cover it offers me, shielding my face from the passing world and allowing me time to recompose myself before we get where we're going.

Roman guns, the gas, sending us flying down the narrow, open road. My hands tighten around him, and my stomach flutters at the sensation of flying. I've never felt anything this freeing before; it's like we're untouchable, like we could run forever and never get caught.

Soon enough, he slows back down to a normal pace, matching the traffic flowing into the small town just outside of the campus. I find myself wishing for more time on the open road, to get lost in the illusion of freedom.

The town isn't overly busy; a lot of smaller mom-and-pop shops line the main street, no big-name companies or stores in sight. He pulls into a barren parking lot for a bar that probably would have been popular back in the day. Now, the outside is weathered, slats of wood hang by a single nail, and the color is stripped away. The sign, if you can even call it that anymore, has 'The Tipsy Lamb' barely just visible from where we park.

The bike cutting off beneath us instantly steals the quiet peace I'd found on the ride over. Thoughts start seeping in through the cracks and putting me back on edge.

Roman seems to know that I'm teetering on the edge, not offering any words of comfort, but simply offering me a hand off the bike and leading me into the bar.

The inside doesn't fare much better than the outside: dusty floors and chipped table tops. Dull neon signs and years of character scream from every corner. An old-school jukebox sits to the side, filling the bar with soft 80s classics.

A few customers litter the space, some in small groups making small talk over a beer, others spread out along the bar top, nursing their drink of choice in solitude.

Roman leads me over to one of the tables to the side, away from the rest of the customers, with an illusion of privacy.

I settle into one of the seats, but he doesn't join me.

"What'll it be?" He asks.

I've only ever tried beer, and that was just two days ago with Gio. I don't know any other drinks, so I let him take the lead as he's done thus far.

"Whatever you're having." My voice comes out rough, a lingering sign that I'd been crying earlier.

He raises a brow, staring down at me, assessingly. Then, without a word, he heads for the bar, leaving me to gather my thoughts.

I don't know what I hope to get out of coming here, but getting drunk and forgetting the last hour sounds like as good a plan as any.

The atmosphere in here is calming, despite its rugged appearance. The sounds filter together: the music playing from the corner, the conversations of friends, and the buzzing of the ancient air conditioner create a perfect symphony of static. Knowing that no one here gives a shit where we came from or what we're dealing with. They're only here to drink and have a good time, and I'm happy to do the same.

Roman strides back over with two glasses in hand, one a lowball glass with an amber liquid, the other with iced water. He gives me the lowball, settling in the seat across from me, sipping the water.

"Bourbon," He nods towards the glass as I eye it skeptically. "Best thing for a rough day."

Laughing cynically, I choke down a sip, "Any suggestions for a rough life?" The burn from the liquid threatens to choke me, warming me up straight from my core. The longer I sit with it, the more comforting it feels.

"Get a new life, leave this one behind, and make your own perfect world." He suggests it so easily, leaning forward on folded arms, looking stoic as if it were that simple.

"Right, because getting away is always so simple." I down another gulp.

He contemplates, studying me closely, looking for any cracks in the mask I put on to cover the truths of what's really going down in my life to lead me to this moment.

"I didn't say it would be easy," He corrects, "I said that the solution to a rough life is to go out and create a better one. It's not going to be easy, but anything beats staying in a shitty situation and suffering."

"What if the risks of getting away from the shitty life are high? Like paralyzing fear-type risks?" I try to stay vague, but the bourbon is already loosening me up, making it easier to voice my inner concerns.

He hesitates, "There's no reward without risk. The question is, would it be worth it in the end? Would you be willing to face the risks if it meant trying to better yourself? Or would you rather stay where you're at because of the fear of not making it?"

His words sit heavy on my chest; he obviously doesn't know the specifics of the situation I'm in. The risks of not being able to get away from Leo and my father would be the end of me. I can't face Briarwood again; it would destroy me from within. But on the other hand, I think a life being tied to Leo would end me much faster than the institute ever could.

"Guess we'll have to wait and see." I toss back the rest of the bourbon, savoring the burn as it goes down and not missing the impressed glint in Roman's eyes as he watches me.

I feel it go straight to my head, effectively taking me out of the serious conversation and into a more neutral mindset, where none of this matters anymore.

"Another round?" He asks, already standing to head back to the bar, at I nod.

My phone buzzing in my pocket draws my attention from swaying to the music flowing through the bar. Pulling it out to look at the screen is instantly like a bucket of ice water over my head, effectively killing my buzz. Leo's contact flashes on the screen with a string of texts.

LUCIFER: I was informed that you left your session crying today. Don't think that you can get out of attending with some waterworks; you're still expected to show up weekly.

LUCIFIER: And for the record, you cannot go to the bar after every session you have. I'll excuse it today, but grow up and face your problems without turning to alcohol.

LUCIFIER: I will not have a drunk for a wife.

Rage burns through my veins as I power the phone off, slamming it on the table for good measure.

Looking around the room once again, I try to find anyone who stands out, anyone who could be here to spy on me. All the other patrons look like normal people, not mafia henchmen.

Fuck him. Who is he to tell me that I can't drink after having to sit with Dr. Asshole berating me for my choices and reliving my brother's death for an hour?

Really, what can he do about it, from all the way in Chicago?

I've been locked away long enough, and I'm a fucking adult. If I want to come out and drink with a literal stranger, then that's what I'll do.

Leo can't tell me shit. We aren't married, and if I can help it, we never will be.

So, bottoms up bitches.

Roman comes back just in time for the end of my internal rant, placing two more glasses on the table with more of the dreaded bourbon. He slides one to me while keeping hold of the other, offering it up for a cheers.

"You going to join me this time?" I arch a brow towards him. He seemed reluctant five minutes ago, so what's changed his mind?

He arches a brow back, "I am. I already texted a friend who can pick us up whenever you're ready to leave, so I may as well drink alongside you."

The glasses clink together, and we both down a gulp; he doesn't even flinch at the burning liquid.

"A friend?" I ask.

"Yeah, you can't really ride back on my bike after drinking. He'll take us back to campus, and I'll come get my bike tomorrow."

I have no reason to trust him, but I find myself completely willing to go along with whatever he suggests. If he trusts this friend to take us home, then I guess that's what we'll do.

And if I end up getting kidnapped and found face down in a ditch somewhere, that's okay, too.

With that thought in mind, and the immense comfort of accepting that Roman is going to watch over me, I throw back the rest of my drink before dragging him by the hand to the middle of the empty floor to dance.

Others glance over at us with amusement in their gazes, but don't pay us much attention as I begin to move and weave around Roman's bulky frame, probably looking more like an annoying mosquito trying to attack him.

I watch him try to fight a smile, to remain stoic and serious, but he fails miserably as the song shifts to a faster pop hit. He swoops down to my level, grabbing me around the waist and swinging me up and around him, like I weigh no more than a rag doll. He spins me around, this way and that way.

My laughter spills out around us, startling me and sounding foreign to my own ears. It's been so long since I've laughed so freely and carelessly, not worrying about who was around or what guilt I may feel from feeling such happy emotions when horrible things were happening around me.

Feeling this lightness, I'm not sure if it's the liquor or the company bringing me this relief. But I do know one thing: I made the right call jumping on the back of Roman's bike today.

12

Roman

It sounds cliché, but I don't want this night to end.

I'd love nothing more than to stay here and lose myself in Camilla forever, but she's already had a bit more to drink than she can probably handle, and I promised myself that I would get her home safely, and preferably not with a raging hangover tomorrow.

She's been dancing for what feels like hours, moving around me like a snake, slithering up and down each side of me and driving me crazy. I would have expected her to start crashing by this point, but she's still going strong. Luckily, I've been giving her water in between glasses of bourbon all night, so she isn't completely hammered.

I also may have requested that the bartender start watering down her drinks as the night progressed, having guessed that she would be a lightweight.

I'm just glad I could offer her a distraction. I felt horrible earlier today, seeing her walk out of the counselor's office in tears. It had me ready to go back inside and destroy whoever hurt her, make them suffer in the slowest and most demented ways I could think of. But then she asked to leave with me, her eyes silently begging me to take her away and make her forget all of her problems. I was powerless to resist, so I brought her to a quiet local spot. Somewhere, I knew we wouldn't be bothered by anyone from school since it was a run-down bar, mostly kept open by local drunks from the town.

I'd already texted Lev, asking him to come and pick us up. Another choice I contemplated, given that she didn't have a good interaction with him yesterday, is that I can't be sure asking him to come is the best choice. But, I figured that it would be the easiest way possible to show her that he's really a good guy, and hopefully will build that trust with him that she seems to be forming easily with Abram and now, me.

Lev sends me a text to let me know he's headed this way, so I get Camilla to sit down and drink another water while we wait. Her eyes are heavy and glassed over, but she isn't stumbling around like I'd expect her to.

She makes no arguments about chugging another water, throwing it back like it's just another shot, while I go ahead and close out my tab.

She leans forward on her barstool, looping her arms around my neck. The height of the stool puts her high enough that she doesn't have to strain to reach me. I watch her calm expression, a complete one-eighty from when I ran into her earlier, savoring the feel of her fingers running through the hair at the nape of my neck.

Her teeth dig into her bottom lip, looking at me like she wants to eat me. My cock strains against the zipper of my jeans, and I have to remind myself that she's drunk; now's not the time to start anything.

128

I run my thumb along her lower lip, freeing it from the abuse she's putting it through, unable to keep my hands off of her.

"My friend will be here soon. Why don't we get some fresh air?" I suggest.

She slides off the stool easily, the change in height forcing her arms from around my neck.

"I have to pee." She tells me, abruptly spinning away to make her way across the bar towards a broken restroom sign hanging on the wall.

I follow closely behind her. I'm not a perv, but someone in her very well could be. And I'll be damned if I let her out of my sight, not with the way I see a few straggling eyes follow her across the floor.

I see her slip into the women's room just as I come to stand in the hallway outside the door, leaning up against the wall. I wait, daring anyone to come through here and try to walk in.

Only a couple of minutes pass when the door slowly creeps open, and Camilla's sultry smile meets me through the small gap. I haven't seen this playful side to her yet, but I'm eager to see what comes from it.

I meet her at the threshold, looking down to see the mischief sparkle in her eyes.

"You ready to go?" I ask, clearly she's not, but I'm willing to play along with her game.

Her lashes flutter, and her teeth bite into her bottom lip yet again. "I need something else before we go."

Arching a brow, I fight the smirk that tugs at my lips at her coy attitude.

"What's that?"

Her hand finds my chest, sliding up slowly over my muscles and curling into the collar. Before I can blink, she's pulling me into the bathroom with her, pushing me against the now closed door behind me. Her hands wrap behind my neck again, forcing her into my chest as she has to raise on her toes to reach. My hands instinctively grab her waist to steady her.

"You," She says it quietly, almost like she's nervous to admit it. Maybe afraid of rejection? That could be possible; another man would probably refuse, knowing that she's had enough to drink tonight to question if she really means what she's asking for. But I'm not another man, and I can't ignore the way her eyes have been devouring me all night, or the feel of her pussy rubbing up against my thigh, searching for any friction.

Spinning us around, I shove her back into the door, reaching down to grab her thighs and hoist her up to my height. Her legs wrap around me instantly as she catches her breath.

I rub my nose along her neck, savoring her sweet vanilla scent and watching her pulse race before pulling back to search her eyes for any hint of hesitation.

Her hips move aimlessly, rubbing against my waist as I watch her become more desperate by the moment.

"Did your little pussy get wet rubbing up all over me on the dance floor all night?" I ask, the whimper that escapes her is enough of an answer as her hips begin to move faster, more frantically.

My lips find her neck once more, latching onto her skin right at her pulse point, sucking hard enough to leave my mark for everyone to see and causing a moan to spill out of her.

Pulling back, I see a mark already forming on her porcelain skin, the sight making me feral, wanting to mark her everywhere I can.

My hands slide up to her hair, grabbing it at the roots and pulling tightly, forcing her head back against the door while her eyes roll back into her head. Her chest heaves with her panting breaths.

"Or maybe it was the ride over here? My bike vibrating underneath you, your thighs clenching around me?" I ask, diving forward to bite one of her breasts through her tank top, listening to her mewl in pleasure and pain. "Or is it just the fantasy of it all? Fucking a stranger in a filthy bar bathroom?" I don't give her time to answer, rushing to bite her other breast, driving her higher and higher.

Pulling back, I watch her chest heave, complete with wet spots over both breasts from my mouth. Her eyes are heavy as she watches me, a deep flush covering her cheeks from her arousal and probably a hint of embarrassment from my words.

Overshadowing it all is the warmth I can feel radiating from her pussy, threatening to soak me through her leggings and my own shirt. I can feel her desperation through the wetness soaking her, begging me to fill her up.

I use one hand to support her against the door, leaning back so I can slip the other into the waistband of her leggings. Diving into her silky underwear, I'm instantly met with what I already knew was there.

She's fucking soaked.

The zipper of my jeans is the only thing holding my aching cock back from diving right into her.

Slipping one finger into her, I'm met with tightness that makes me see stars, imagining the feeling around my dick, suffocating me in the best way possible.

Her wetness soaks my hand as I thrust my finger into her, pulling out only to add another before pushing roughly back in.

Her moans echo off the bathroom walls. I'd be surprised if no one in the bar could hear the sounds she's making. She doesn't seem to care at the moment.

Head thrown back in wild abandon, her pussy grips onto my fingers, strangling the life from them and trying to suck me in further.

"Maybe it was all of it, hmm?" I pull my fingers out, ignoring her desperate mewling as I drag my fingers through her folds, spreading her wetness around. "All of it made your needy cunt this wet for me, so you just had to drag me in here and beg me to fuck you?" I watch her eyes roll back the moment I thrust three fingers deep into her again, roughly fucking her once again.

She doesn't answer, more focused on moving her hips, riding my fingers, trying to chase her release.

I sink my teeth into her neck, halting my fingers and ripping her from the release she's craving.

I didn't break the skin, but I suck on her neck before soothing it with my tongue, pulling back to meet her frustrated gaze.

"I asked you a question, *Kukla*." I arch a brow, daring her to ignore me.

She licks her lips, staring back at me with hooded eyes.

"All of it," She barely manages to whisper.

My lips pull up into a savage smirk, leaning in, I reward her with a kiss, her tongue fighting with mine for dominance that she won't win.

If she wants me, she can have me. But she'll have to beg me for it.

I drop her back to her feet, ignoring her confused look, to reach around her and flip the lock on the door.

Her wide doe eyes stare back up at me, eagerly waiting, silently begging for more.

My hand wraps around her throat, not cutting off her air but gaining her full attention. I tip her head back to force her eyes on mine as she pants.

"You want me to fuck you? To shove my cock into your needy, weeping cunt until you're dripping my cum? Until you'll be able to feel me between your legs for days, a constant reminder of me?" With each question, my hand grips her tighter, forcing her back into the door.

As best she can with my hand around her throat, she nods.

Tsking at her, I shake my head.

"Not good enough, *Kukla*." I tighten my hand, "When I ask you a question, I expect an answer."

She whimpers again, arching into my hand.

"All you have to do is ask me to bend you over and fuck you. Just say the words."

She writhes against me, pushing herself onto me wherever she can touch, searching for friction, any pleasure, but only choking herself further on my hand.

"Please," She finally gasps out, latching onto my wrist with both hands, simultaneously trying to push me away and drag me closer.

She looks beautiful this way, begging and desperate. But the same way she's craving dominance, I crave obedience. A pretty please isn't going to cut it to get what she wants from me.

"Please, what, Kukla? Tell me." I push her closer to the edge, pushing my thigh roughly between her legs, giving her something to try and chase her own high. But, much to her utter disappointment, just as I feel her climbing higher and higher, I rip it away, loving the sounds of her cries that fill the space.

"Please -," she chokes out another broken plea, not able to finish the request.

"Please, Roman, bend me over and fuck my needy pussy?" I help her out, feeling almost bad at how feral she's become in the last five minutes of being teased. If I had to venture a guess, I'd say that she's never been left wanting, teetering on the edge again and again until her head was ready to explode. If she sticks around me long enough, I'll show her just how rewarding it can be to hand yourself over to that kind of torment.

Her cheeks become an even darker shade of crimson, her eyes leaving mine to study the floor. I think she's about to give up, not willing to repeat the words back to me, to beg for it.

But surprise rushes me as her small voice squeaks out, "P-please Roman, bend me over and -" She stops, licking her lips and taking a moment to steady herself before jumping straight into the deep end. "Fuck my needy pussy, please!" The last please is tacked on frantically, as if I'd change my mind. Absolutely not, especially when she asked so sweetly.

It's always the sweet ones that have the dirtiest thoughts and the most delectable pussies. Now that she's asked, I'm about to see if that theory rings true with our pretty little Camilla.

13

Camilla

I feel like all the air has been sucked out of my lungs. I'm left standing here breathless, waiting for Roman to do something now that I've asked him to fuck me. Not just that, I asked him to fuck my '*needy pussy*'.

It's possibly the most vulgar thing I've ever said, but it felt right because that's how I feel right now.

Heat floods my leggings between my legs, wetness pooling to the point that I left a wet spot on Roman's shirt, one that mocks me as I stare at it, waiting for him to reject me or laugh at me for thinking that he'd want to hook up in a bar bathroom, let alone anywhere with me.

His hands brace either side of my face, tipping my head all the way back to meet his eyes. Two pools of molten lava look back at me, simmering with desire and need to match what I'm feeling. His lips devour mine, conquering me and making my knees weak as his tongue fights with mine before claiming dominance over me. I'm just here for the ride, clinging on for dear life and hoping I make it out the other side.

Growling, he rips his lips from mine, staring down into my eyes once again, his cocky smirk back in place.

"Good fucking girl," He growls, making another rush of wetness flood into my already soaked panties.

Throwing my arms around his neck, I try to climb him like a tree, my core now throbbing, seeking some relief, something to get me off so I can tame this burning ball of fire inside me.

Roman seems to be done with giving me any illusion of control, though, roughly grabbing my hips and spinning me to face away from him before marching us over to the cracked and broken countertop to the side of the room opposite the stalls.

His palm on my back pushes me forward. I put my hands out to steady myself, not wanting to lie on the counter and enjoying the view of him in the mirror.

His hand stays on my back, but the other reaches up, fisting a handful of my hair, pulling on it painfully until tears prick the corners of my eyes. My eyes meet his in the mirror, awkwardly, as he has my head pulled back.

"Hands behind your back, *Kukla*." He whispers, biting on my ear.

I don't understand why he wants my hands behind me, but I'm too interested in what he plans to do to care. Without thought, I shove both hands behind me, resting them in the small of my back while he pushes me to lie flat on the counter.

I can't stop the whimper bubbling in my chest as my cheek meets the cool surface, taking away my view of him as he shifts around behind me.

His hand still holds me down, so I know he hasn't left. But I can't make sense of the sounds I'm hearing behind me.

He slides the cardigan off my shoulders down to my hands, wrapping it around one wrist, tightening until it feels like all blood flow to my hand has stopped. My noise of distress must be understood, though, because a moment later, he loosens it slightly, allowing a tingling sensation to flow through my hand as he moves on to repeat the process with the other.

Once he's done, I feel him step back. I test the ties, pulling at both my hands, but the cardigan remains strong in keeping my hands trapped behind me.

No time to dwell on it, my leggings and underwear are ripped down to my ankles, effectively keeping my legs in place as they become trapped by my shoes. Shivers rack through me as the rough denim of his jeans brushes against the backs of my bare legs.

His hand pulls my hair again, lifting my head roughly to face the reflection in the mirror. The sting from his grasp burns my scalp, but as much as it hurts, it also centers something within me. An oddly calm feeling washes over me as he takes control of me. I'm at his mercy here, but I couldn't be more excited at the thought of it.

"Is this what you want, *Kukla*?" He growls in my ear, "You want to be used like my own personal whore right here over the counter?" His words are harsh but hold no bite; the insult almost sounds affectionate coming from him. Being his whore sounds like a badge of honor that I'd proudly wear.

Why does the thought of being owned by Leo terrify me, but the thought of letting Roman have total control leaves me with nothing but the idea of bliss?

The question is forgotten as Roman spears two fingers into me, fucking me with them and dragging back out to spread my wetness around.

"You don't have to answer, your body tells me everything that you don't want to say." His teeth bite into my neck again, evening out the bite that he left on the other side earlier. The sharp pricks of pain on my neck drive me higher and higher as his fingers continue their devious torture, thrusting deep inside me, hitting a spot that makes me see stars. The hand in my hair snakes down my front, flicking roughly against my clit and sending me over the edge, crashing into a blissful explosion of sensations as I come.

He gives some words of praise from behind me, but my ears are too muffled to make them out, my vision hazy as I continue to come down from my high, savoring the cool touch from the counter on my flushed cheek.

Just as the spots in my vision begin to clear and I start to catch my breath, he grabs both my hips, thrusting into me without warning. His whole length splits me in half and settles deeply into my core. Fire rips through me, putting me on the verge of tears while another wave of heat pricks at my core, begging me to chase another high like the one I just rode.

The pain is intense, but even still, my hips strain against the rough edge of the counter, trying to force movement from him.

His hands grip me tighter, forcing me to stay still as he stays nestled deep inside me.

"*Kukla*," He all but growls the word, "Are you a virgin?"

My eyes slam shut, trying to ignore him in hopes that he'll keep moving.

I knew there was a possibility that he would realize I was a virgin, but a much larger part of me tried to cling to the hope that I could lose my virginity without him ever knowing. Stranger things have happened.

It's not like I planned to sleep with him tonight; that was an impulsive decision only partially brought on by the many glasses of bourbon. But the horrible session with my new therapist had brought on too many emotions that I didn't want to face. When Leo blew up my phone to gloat, I'd caught a glimpse of some texts he sent me days ago, telling me how much he can't wait for our wedding night so he could take what was '*his*' and completely own me. It didn't take a rocket scientist to figure out what he was referring to, not with the graphic images he was painting.

I didn't have much to rebel with, but my virginity seemed like a good start. Once it was gone, it could never be Leo's; it would forever be something that I freely gave away.

Giving it to Roman was a coincidence more than anything; he was in the right place at the right time. But now that I can feel him inside me, filling me so completely that I want to die with the feeling of him inside me, I know it was the right decision.

His hand wraps around my hair, wrenching my head back to meet his in the mirror.

"Please tell me you did not just let me steal your virginity in a dirty fucking bar bathroom like a cheap hooker."

A string of Russian expletives meets my silence. He starts to ease away from me, and my panic flares. I don't want to lose his touch. I can feel him, hot and throbbing inside me, and the ache in my core grows, not to be satiated until I feel him brutally pounding into me.

"Please," Tt comes out like a broken plea. I'm not above begging him to finish what he started. He stills, waiting for my following words. "You didn't steal it; I gave it to you, and I really want you to move right now. Please."

The last word is choked and desperate, but it doesn't make my words any less accurate. I'm teetering between immense pleasure and uncomfortable rejection, and I need him to take me to the land of orgasms. From the feel of his dick pulsing inside me, he is going to destroy me in a few thrusts, and I'm ready. I don't think anyone ever complained about death by orgasm.

His hands tighten on my hips, and he mutters another curse in Russian that I assume translates to "fuck it." Without any warning, he pulls his hips back and thrusts back in, slamming my hips into the counter hard enough to bruise, picking up his pace.

Every nerve ending in my body comes alight as his pace quickens, and pressure builds in my core once again. Without the use of my arms, I do my best to push my hips back into his and meet him thrust for thrust, chasing that high while he tears away my innocence.

"Such a good girl, taking my dick like a slut," he pulls my head back further, a pinching pain pricking the back of my neck. "I love that I'm the first to stick my dick in you, and you're sucking me in, begging for more."

His tongue slides up the side of my face, bringing to my attention the tears I didn't realize spilled over, slowly running down my face.

My moans and cries echo off the walls, even louder than before. I don't have time to care.

It hurts so good.

I'm so close to the edge again, but can't find the friction I need to send myself over.

My moans turn to desperate mewls and whimpers, trying to ask for what I need to get me there, but not knowing how.

The hand in my hair snakes around to grab my throat, not cutting off my air, but keeping my head facing the mirror to meet my tear-streaked face and Roman's intense stare watching my every move.

"You look so gorgeous with tears down your face and my cock deep inside you." Affection rings through his words, overshadowing his gruff and strained tone. "You wanted this, *Kukla*, and now you've got it. Now, I want you to come on my cock, show me what a good whore you can be."

As he growls the words, his hand tightens on my neck, cutting off my air.

Immediately, my fight or flight kicks in, and I begin to struggle, gasping for air. His body keeps me pinned to the counter with nowhere to go, and he picks up his pace, becoming punishing.

My ears start ringing, and my head pounds in time with his brutal thrusts, but the heat in my body ramps up, setting me on fire from the inside out.

"Be a good girl, come for me, *Kukla*," he bites my ear, his hand back in front of me, flicking my clit and sending me diving headfirst into the abyss. My vision blacks out, and my body convulses violently as I come harder than I ever have in my entire life.

His hand must release my throat. I don't have the strength to keep my head up, so I lie it back on the counter and swallow lungfuls of air.

His hands grip my hips, thrusting three more times into me before stilling, releasing a groan of his own to rival mine. I feel him pulse inside me as his warmth fills me in short bursts.

As he stills, the pain sets in. It's like a buzzing in the back of my head, still overshadowed by bliss as I continue to float around consciousness, but refusing to be ignored.

I stay over the counter as Roman pulls out of me, drawing a desperate whimper from me as the discomfort amplifies with the loss of him.

I can't find the strength to move, even as I can feel his cum dripping down onto my legs. He moves around behind me, the sound of his zipper deafening in the now quiet room. He grabs my panties, dragging them up my legs and ensuring they capture all of his cum, settling it against me, feeling wet and uncomfortable. He follows with my leggings before swiftly releasing my wrists to drag me off the counter to face him.

My legs shake and threaten to give out, I can feel the tears caked on my face, and I'm sure I look like a hot mess.

I should be feeling something, right? Some torrent of emotions, maybe regret, maybe gratitude? Instead, I feel a light, blissful emptiness and a freeing feeling of nothing.

I expect to see remorse in Roman's gaze, since he took my virginity without knowing at first. But his features are soft as he looks down at me, studying every detail he can and maybe trying to gauge how I'm feeling.

He won't be able to tell, now that I've had a moment, I've slipped my mask back into place, shielding my emotions behind it and leaving a blank stare for him to look at.

"You look beautiful, freshly fucked," He brushes a thumb over my bottom lip. Leaning over to whisper in my ear. "But knowing that you have my cum dripping out of you, keeping you wet is fucking hot."

Oh, hot damn. It should be illegal for words to make me feel this needy after just facing death by dick.

Would it be too soon to beg him to fuck me again? I'm sure it would hurt, but my vagina doesn't seem to give a fuck and instead is pulsing and yearning for him to fill me yet again.

"Come on, time to go." Offering me a hand, he leads me from the bathroom and towards the front of the bar. I make sure to keep my eyes averted, deeply intrigued by the patterns on the floor, to avoid eye contact with any of the other patrons.

Stepping out into the night air, I suck in lungfuls of the fresh air, trying to steady myself after what we just did.

Roman said that his friend was picking us up I assume he isn't here yet, by the way, he pulls me to wait against the side of the bar.

The silence that surrounds us was comforting earlier, but now it feels suffocating and awkward.

"Why did you tie my hands?" I stupidly ask, mentally slapping myself for filling the silence with such an obtuse question.

The corners of his lips tip as he hides a laugh at the abruptness.

"I like to have full control when I fuck," He answers, turning. He places both hands on either side of my head, boxing me in against the wall. "Plus, I know it turned you on. As soon as I restrained you, your cunt was dripping with need."

Heat flames my cheeks. I think I almost swallow my tongue at his bluntness. He isn't wrong, but I'm not sure I want to admit that to him and give him the upper hand again.

Going for my best nonchalant attitude, I shrug.

"It was okay."

"Okay?" His brows shoot up to his hairline.

"Yeah, I imagine that it could be better."

He grounds his teeth together, narrowing his eyes at me. "Kukla, I just pounded into your virgin cunt and ensured you came harder than you possibly ever have, not once, but twice. Pray, tell me how you think that could've been better? Considering your lack of experience to compare it to."

"Well, I would have liked to see you, maybe touch you the way you touched me." I tiptoe my fingers across his chest, avoiding his eyes, fearing that I'll fall into a fit of laughter at his offended stare. "And I may not have any real experiences to compare to, but I've read enough to imagine a great time."

His hand shoots up to stop mine in its tracks, waiting for me to meet his eyes.

"I can promise you that whatever you can imagine, I can top it. Just say the word, and I'll drag you home, tie you to my bed, and work your little body over until you're begging me for a release, for some reprieve. Then, when I finally give it to you, I'll make you do it over and over again, on my tongue, my fingers, until you're trembling and incoherent with pleasure. Only then, when I've said you had enough, will I make you beg for my cock. I'll pound into you so hard that you'll be left feeling me for days. I'll pump you so full of cum that it will leak from your needy cunt, soaking through every pair of lace panties that you own. Then I'll finish by pounding into your throat to clean the taste of you off my dick, only to do it all over again, so you can't forget the feeling of me. Don't test

146

me." He emphasizes his words by sucking my bottom lip into his mouth, biting hard enough for me to taste a metallic tang of blood when he finally lets me go.

He pulls back to give me space to breathe and study my expression, leaving me wondering yet again how his words can make me want to fall apart all over again, even with the soreness I feel left behind.

I don't get a chance to answer, a blacked-out SUV pulls up next to us, the tires squealing from the quick stop.

The passenger window rolls down, and a familiar face grins back at me.

"Wifey! I didn't know I was coming to your rescue, I would've sped the whole way here." Lev bounces in the driver's seat like a kid on Christmas waiting to open presents from Santa.

"That's your friend?" I spin to pin a glare on Roman, who ignores me, moving to open the passenger door for me.

"Unfortunately, get in." He nods towards the empty seat.

My mind races with confusion. Yesterday, I was suspicious that Lev was a plant from my father or Leo; now I'm supposed to believe he's nothing more than Roman's friend? I didn't have the same suspicion towards Roman, and even if he were a plant, then it would work in my favor, pissing off Leo when he reports back that he took my virginity.

None of this was making sense. I don't know who I can trust. I still want to believe Roman isn't working with Leo; his disgust for Russians makes that an unlikely possibility. And surely if he were working for them, then he wouldn't have fucked me, or let me go out and get drunk, for that matter.

I need answers, but I also need sleep. All this back-and-forth in my head is driving me crazy, and after the day I had, I'm thoroughly exhausted.

I avoid Roman's impatient stare, stomping towards the car, bypassing the door Roman holds open, letting myself into the back seat, needing space to myself.

He rolls his eyes before jumping in the front seat and slamming the door, shaking the car in the process.

None of us tries to fill the tense silence filling the car as Lev starts driving, heading back towards campus.

I watch the streetlights streaming through the window as we drive further away from the bar, trying to shut my mind off but failing miserably.

"So, did you two have fun?" Lev breaks the silence, eyeing me in the rear-view mirror.

Roman grunts in response, turning his head to wait for my response.

"It was *okay*." I can't help but poke the bear some more, knowing Roman can't corner me where I sit in the back. I get the satisfaction of seeing his jaw flex as he grounds his molars together.

Lev snorts, oblivious to the hidden meaning behind my words. "Well, that's what you get for going out with him. Next time, just hit me up, I'll take you out, and we'll have a blast."

"Actually, we already have plans for another night. It will be nothing short of extraordinary, isn't that right, Camilla?" Roman's clearly trying to goad me the way I did to him. He's probably expecting me to think about his words and melt into a puddle at the thought of it. But I'm ready for it this time.

"I don't know, it sounds to me like you talk a big game. Maybe I want to try a night out with your friend here, he seems like he could offer a great time."

Roman starts to turn in his seat, quickly cut off by Lev's bark of laughter.

"Your friend? How swiftly you dismiss our love connection, wifey." He palms his chest, "But, you are correct in that I could show you a much better time than Roman here."

"Oh, I don't doubt it."

Roman is practically foaming at the mouth now, holding back his irritation poorly as his chest heaves.

"How about we show her a good time together?" Roman suddenly throws out.

That motherfucker.

He knows where my head is at, now, filled with flashes of what we did tonight, but suddenly, instead of just the two of us, Lev is in the mix. An extra set of hands to drive me crazy, sending me over the edge, again and again.

He can't actually mean that, right?

"Three sounds like a crowd." I quip back.

Lev, thankfully, agrees. "Yeah, no fair. You got a night with my wifey all to yourself, I want to take her out."

"You always say, the more the merrier." Roman shrugs.

Any response is cut off as we pull up outside the dorms. I don't waste the opportunity to run, jumping from the backseat, barely managing to throw a quick thanks over my shoulder before scanning into the building, before either can follow me. I'm not sure if it's my imagination, but I swear I heard Roman's laugh echoing behind me from the car.

Once the door to my room is firmly shut and locked behind me, I fall against it, finally able to catch my breath. It's then that I can finally take stock of my body, feeling my thighs tremble and the cold and wet feeling of Roman's cum still lingering.

What the fuck did I just do?

14

Camilla

The next morning, I luckily don't wake up with another raging hangover.

My own impulsive decisions seemed to have wiped away any traces of the alcohol I consumed and, instead, left me with sore and aching muscles that scream and protest with every movement.

I'm not sure how much of the discomfort is due to Roman and how much is due to dancing the other night, aside from one central area.

Another stroke of luck is that I didn't wake up with any dooming feeling of regret. What Roman and I did last night was hot as fuck, and despite what I told him, it was terrific, and I can't deny how my body begs to do it again, and again…and again. The only regret comes in the sticky feeling of him still dripping out of me, which also reminds me that Roman didn't use a condom.

I'm not naive enough to believe that I can't get pregnant just because it was my first time, which leads me to my current predicament, needing a morning-after pill. Which also means I have to tell Gio about my adventure from yesterday, since I have no other way to get to a store on my own, as there are none on campus.

Armed and ready to go in another set of leggings and a baggy t-shirt, which seems to be becoming my go-to style, I set out to find him. I know he usually stops for coffee at the small cafe by the dorms before classes, so I start my search there.

Luck strikes again as I catch him walking from the cafe, a fresh cup of coffee in hand.

"Gio!" I shout, dragging his attention away from the hot guy he's eye fucking beside him. His confused gaze meets mine, watching me frantically approach and quickly excusing himself from the conversation.

"Um, good morning?" He offers me the coffee, but I wave it off, not needing the caffeine to add to my already jittery mood. "You never texted me. What have you been up to?"

"Just hanging out, nothing crazy." I'm stalling, not wanting to ask him to take me into town and having to explain what, or more specifically, who I've gotten into over the last two days.

He eyes me over the rim of his cup.

"Okay… so what's up? Why are you running around and yelling for me like someone is chasing you down?" He looks up wide-eyed, "No one is chasing you, right?"

"What? No, no one is chasing me."

He relaxes instantly, going back to sipping his coffee.

"Oh, good, I thought it might be that guy from outside your class the other day. It's too early to have to defend your honor; no offense."

Rubbing my hand down my face, I try to keep my thoughts on track and not get distracted by Gio's guessing game.

"No, Lev is fine; it was just a misunderstanding. That's not why I came to find you."

"Lev? So you're on a first-name basis with the guy now, how'd that happen?"

"Gio," I growl, urging him to stay focused and not worry about the random men popping up in my life.

He must sense my urgency, going from joking to serious as he takes in my expression.

"Okay, what's wrong?"

"I need a favor." Okay, despite my urgency, I'm clearly still stalling. I know this is going to open a whole can of worms, and Gio will want to know everything. The thought of unpacking it all sounds exhausting, though it could mean asking him for his opinion on the guys, and if I can't trust them at all.

He doesn't rush me, letting me take the time I need to collect myself and steady my nerves.

"Can you take me into town? I need to get something, and it's urgent."

He doesn't miss a beat, "Yeah, you want to go now?"

Chewing on my lip, I try to think it through. I need to get the pill as quickly as possible for it to be effective, but I can't have Leo finding out that I missed class.

"Yes, but…" This is ridiculous; I feel like a child having to ask permission to simply live my life. I'm nineteen fucking years old; I should be able to move freely through my days without fear of being punished.

"But your sadistic husband-to-be has rules about you attending all your classes, and you're afraid that he'll find out?" He finishes for me, understanding ringing through his words.

"Right," I answer lamely. This is why he's always been one of my best friends; he knows what I leave unsaid, and we have an unspoken way of communicating. He's always ready and willing to listen, but also to fill in the gaps when I desperately need him to.

His fingers tap idly against the paper cup as he stares off into the quad, lost in thought.

"Okay, you have Professor Jones this morning, right?" He asks.

I'm not sure why he knows my class schedule, but I nod anyway, ignoring that for now.

He pulls me towards one of the benches lining the walkway, urging me to sit next to him as he pulls his phone out and starts tapping away. He doesn't speak as he works away at whatever he's doing, my tense anticipation growing with each tap of his fingers.

Only about five minutes pass when he finally pockets the phone, standing to offer me a hand.

"Alright, let's go."

"Go? What did you do? What about my class?" I need more clarification before I'm willing to go along. My fear of Leo finding out outweighs everything else.

He takes my hand, pulling me up to follow him.

"You've officially been marked as present for class. We can go into town, and Leo will never know."

"How?"

"We all have our special skills," He responds cryptically.

My mind races as I try to piece together what just happened and how he can make it seem like I showed up today.

We make it to his car, but before I buckle myself in, I turn in the seat to face him fully.

"Did you hack into my professor's attendance log?" I try to guess, since I have no other theories.

He side-eyes me, drumming his fingers on the steering wheel.

"Maybe,"

I process that for a moment, that's so fucking cool if we're being honest.

"Where'd you learn to do that?"

"I had a lot of free time while you were gone." He puts the car in drive, effectively ending the conversation. "Buckle up."

I don't know why he's being evasive about his obvious hacking skills, but I won't press the issue with him. I have my secrets; he's allowed to have his. And it really doesn't matter, but it's clearly something he doesn't want to talk about.

Now that we're alone and pulling away from the campus, he doesn't waste time getting to the bottom of our impromptu adventure.

"What's so urgent that you have to skip class to go get? And where should I be heading?"

No time like the present, I suppose, since he's literally driving me to my destination, so he'll find out sooner or later.

"The pharmacy, I guess." I start picking lint off my pants to avoid his curious gaze, burning a hole in the side of my face. "I need a morning-after pill." I half mutter the words, but it's apparent that he heard me.

"Back the fuck up! When did you fuck? Oh, WHO did you fuck?" He frantically switches between looking at the road and swinging his wide eyes over to me, an array of emotions flashing over his face, from confusion to excitement, and back.

"Does it matter?" My emotions are much more reserved, not anywhere near his level right now.

"Um, considering you were a blushing virgin last time I saw you before you showed up at school, yes. It *does* matter! That's a huge milestone, were you even planning on telling me, like before the whole morning-after-pill thing?" He

156

doesn't even take a breath in between his words, spewing everything that comes to mind. "Do I know him? Who was it? Was he good?" He looks over quickly, catching the crimson blush I feel rush over me as flashes of last night appear in my mind. "Yeah, it was good," He decides, smirking as he focuses back on the road.

There's so much to unpack there, where do I even start?

"It's not a huge milestone; it was sex. Sex happens; we're adults. It's really not a big deal." He's acting like this is some life-changing event, like punching my v-card means that everything will change. It was fantastic, and I'm more than willing to experience the euphoria I felt last night all over again because I'm not sure many things can top that feeling. And he's missing the bigger point here, the biggest fuck up of the night. "And I forgot the cardinal rule of making sure he wraps it up before sticking it in. I think that's what needs to be focused on here."

He shoots me a dry look, arching a brow in that annoying way that tells me he knows I'm deflecting to avoid his tirade of questions.

"So what, we'll get you a pill, and it will be fine. Now, who was it?"

"No one. You don't know him." I quickly answer, chickening out of that conversation once again.

"How do you know I don't know him? I know a lot of people."

"His name was Roman, and trust me, you don't know him."

His expression turns puzzled, and he falls silent.

"Roman? What's his last name?"

I throw my head back against the seat, studying the roof of the car, exhausted with the morning's events thus far.

"I don't know. We hung out after my therapy session yesterday, and we ended up hooking up. I didn't think to ask for his last name and social security number while his dick was inside of me."

He laughs at that, "A random hook up for your first time, good for you, girl."

"Yeah, good for me so long as I don't end up with a child."

The rest of the drive into town to the pharmacy, he tries to pry and get details of the encounter, but I manage to stay tight-lipped the whole way.

Once he parks, I unbuckle, ready to get this over with, but he stops me before I can get out.

"Wait, do you have any cash?" He asks.

"No, I was just going to use my card."

Confused, I watch him dig his wallet from his pocket, gaping at the stack of bills he has stashed away while he pulls a few out to hand to me.

When I don't immediately take it, he explains.

"You don't want your father or Leo seeing a charge for the pharmacy on the card, it'll look suspicious, especially if it shows up when you're supposed to be in class. Cash is a safer option since we don't know how closely they're monitoring you."

My throat tightens at his thoughtfulness, and I mentally slap myself for not even considering the possibility that my card would be monitored.

Shooting him a thankful smile, I take the cash, stashing it in my pocket as I rush into the pharmacy.

I quickly find myself standing in the middle of the aisle staring down three different brands of morning-after pills locked behind a glass door. I thought I'd be able to walk in, discreetly grab the damn pill, and quickly retreat, but it seems my good luck from the morning is running out.

I don't even know which one I need to get, and with already having to ask the sales associate for help to get the damn thing, I don't want to have to ask about the specs of each of them on top of that.

My frustration builds the longer I stand here. Along with it, irritation as I feel the sting of tears pooling in my eyes at the absurd situation I landed myself in. I shouldn't be crying over a morning-after pill, and I'm not, not really. I'm on the verge of tears because my life is a mess, my future husband is controlling my life so much that I went and did something irrational that led to me needing the stupid pill that I don't know anything about. And to top it all off, I can't even use my own card to pay for it, in fear that he'll find out, and I can't just reach out and pick one because they trap them behind an anti-theft screen.

Everything is piling up into a shit storm, causing my emotions that I keep tightly bottled up to rise to the surface in the contraceptive aisle of a fucking pharmacy.

"Camilla?" A voice pulls me from my impending meltdown.

Quickly stuffing my feelings back down and urging the tears in my eyes to dry up, I look to the end of the aisle.

Great.

In the flesh, Lev stands before me, eyeing me curiously as he smiles as brightly as he did last night.

"I thought that was you. Twice in two days, if I didn't know any better, I'd think you were stalking me, wifey." He tries to stay lighthearted, but I can see the corners of his eyes pulling in curiosity as he studies my face.

I've managed to get my shit locked down, only putting out my emotionless mask.

"You picked me up yesterday. I didn't come to find you. And I can't help that we're in the same pharmacy in the middle of the day, it's simply a coincidence."

Palming his chest, he acts as if he's hurt.

"Wifey, you keep dismissing our love, and I'll start to think you don't like me."

I offer a blank stare in response, making him laugh before he finally notices the aisle we're in. His eyes fill with a mischievous glint.

"I suppose it's also just a coincidence that you're grabbing a morning-after pill the night after I picked you and Roman up from the bar?"

If he's offended at finding out that I hooked up with his friend, he doesn't let it show. He looks more ready to tease me about that rather than get upset. Plus, it's not like he has any claim over me simply because we met first.

Even still, without any baiting from him, I start to feel the overwhelming crush of emotions I stuffed down bubbling up again at the reminder of my frustrations. Wrapping my arms around my middle, I try my hardest to keep everything in, not willing to show any weakness in front of him and really just needing this fucking pill and to get out of here.

My mask must slip, showing some of my distress, because he goes from casual and teasing to serious and concerned in a moment.

"Here, let me get it for you. Which one do you want?" He asks gently, taking control of the situation.

But my earlier dilemma strikes again; I still don't know what fucking pill I need.

I feel my mouth open and close, but no words come out. I'm still just lost and frustrated.

"Okay, here." He offers me a crumpled list and his shopping basket, shoving them in my hands when I make no move to grab them. "Do me a favor and grab everything on the list, pay attention to the parentheses, some of the items are really specific. Then meet me at the checkout." Without another word, he gently pushes me to the end of the aisle, and my feet finally start moving on their own as he hits the button to summon a sales associate to the aisle.

I'm thankful for the distraction, even if it means doing his shopping for him. The list is filled with random crap, and he wasn't lying when he said it was specific, down to the brand name and ounces needed for the dish detergent.

I try to clear my mind as I shop, not dwelling on everything from this morning, or yesterday, or the last two weeks, really. I focus solely on the list in hand and pick out the required items.

Putting the last item into the basket, I round the corner and find Lev leaning casually against the checkout counter, chatting up the elderly cashier.

"Ah, there she is!" He grabs the basket, pulling items out to scan as he talks. "Thanks, babe. Looks like you got everything."

His items start being scanned, along with the tiny box holding the pill I need. I try to protest his paying for it, but his hand finds my shoulder, and he silently shoots me a look telling me that I won't win this fight.

The cashier picks up the pill last, shooting me a nasty look as she scans it. I wrap my arms around my middle again, trying to make myself smaller, hoping she'll move on.

"Do you have a problem?" Lev all but growls at the poor woman, causing both of us to jump. Red colors her face, and she averts her attention back to bagging the items, letting him pay in silence.

Grabbing the bags, he leads me from the store, stopping just out front.

"You didn't have to snap at her; people are going to have their opinions about things."

He stops rummaging in the back to arch a brow at me.

"Just because someone has an opinion doesn't mean they get to make you feel shitty about yourself."

He offers me the pill box, waving me off when I try to hand him the cash from Gio.

"Keep it. It's not your fault that Roman forgot to wrap it up." A smirk pulls at his lips as my face heats.

"True, but that doesn't mean it's your responsibility."

He eyes me over, contemplating.

"Roman is like a brother to me; we look out for one another. And by extension, that means you now." His severe facade drops, leaving me with his teasing grin once again. "Besides, I've claimed you as my wifey, so I'm happy to do it."

I can't help but roll my eyes, even as I fight the grin pulling at my lips. "You're insane, but thank you."

"I'll see you around. I'm sure you can make it up to me." With a wink, he retreats to his car, glancing back at me over his shoulder before disappearing.

Back at the car, Gio meets me with a raised brow, looking between me and where I just stood with Lev.

"Is that your mystery guy from last night? I thought we hated him."

"*You* decided you hated him after a misunderstanding one time. But no, he just ran into me in the store and helped me out."

His eyes narrow, "So Lev Marino just decided to help you out of the kindness of his heart? No other ulterior motives?"

"How do you know his name?" My own eyes narrow back at him. He's been acting like he didn't know him this whole time.

"I did my research after that little meeting in front of your class. Now, don't dodge my question."

Sometimes it was annoying how much Gio could see through me and my attempts at deflection. I could get away with it with many other people; most were too self-absorbed to care that I steered the conversation back to them. Not Gio, though.

Heaving a deep breath, I let it out.

"Lev decided to help because he and Roman are good friends. After he came to pick us up from the bar last night and now seeing me in the pharmacy this morning, he put two and two together and felt bad that his friend fucked me without a condom. Happy?"

Gio's eyes grow comically wide, his jaw going slack.

"Roman Vasiliev? Holy shit, Cam. You lost your virginity to Roman Vasiliev in a bar bathroom?"

"Yes," I draw the word out, daring him to say something negative to me right now when I'm already embarrassed.

Silence descends between us, filling the car with a suffocating awkwardness as I wait for him to process. He stares out the windshield before dropping his head back against the seat with a laugh.

"Oh my God. You are *so* bad ass!"

"What about this makes me bad ass?" I ask, confused.

He shakes his head, still silently laughing to himself.

"You don't even know, that's the best part."

"What? I don't know what? Tell me!" My irritation flares again.

He must sense my growing emotions, instantly sobering and turning to face me.

"Cam, you just hooked up with one of the Bravata's most promising informants. Also known as your Father and your fiancée's biggest enemies. Someone they would *murder* if they knew they were in their territory."

Every thought and emotion I had moments ago is washed away, leaving me with an empty, ringing feeling in my ear as I mull over his words.

The Bravata, my Father's self-proclaimed mortal enemies.

My father didn't send Roman.

If he were a part of the Bratva and not sent by Leo and Father, and he was good friends with Lev, then that would mean that neither of them was sent to watch me.

I'd spent the week worrying about four guys suddenly interested in me, and now, in a matter of seconds, all that worry is being tossed out the window.

And I can't do anything but laugh.

It starts with a slight giggle, one I try to stifle. But quickly it grows, refusing to be pushed down until I'm a hysterical mess in the front seat of Gio's car as he watches on with a slightly terrified expression as I try and fail to rein myself in. Tears start streaming down my face from how hard I'm laughing.

I was panicking this morning about needing a morning-after pill so I wouldn't have to worry about a slip-up, and I didn't even know that this little slip-up could cause an actual war. Once Leo or my Father killed me, that is.

That manages to sober me up some, finally allowing me to quiet my laughter and wipe my tears.

"Cam, you okay?" Gio hesitates, still looking fearfully over at me.

"I'm fine," I tell myself more than him.

He doesn't push me, sits silently as I finally work on cracking up the pill box and dry swallowing the tiny little pill. I'm thankful for the few moments of silence to pull myself back together and slip my mask firmly back into place.

"I spent the week wondering if Lev and Roman were being friendly as a front for being sent here to watch me by Leo or my Father." I tell him quietly, "It just took me by surprise that he's actually from the Bratva. And then the thought of getting knocked up by him - it's not funny, but my brain doesn't seem to get that." I have to smother another giggle from spilling out at the ridiculous thought.

He actually laughs with me this time, "They would be the last people that would get sent to watch over you. Your father would rather trail you himself day in and day out before sending either of them."

"While we're on the subject, there are two other guys that have talked to me this week that I've been wondering the same thing about." Since we've already opened up this can of worms, I might as well put my fears to rest or validate them so I can get back to my life.

He gives me a knowing look, "I have to assume you mean Abram Kozlov and Dima Sokolov, since where one appears, the others are never far behind. Definitely not sent to watch you."

Again, a wave of relief washes over me. I don't have to worry about them fishing for information or sharing the details of my lost virginity. Seems I get to live to see another day after all.

Another thought scratches at my brain, begging to be asked.

"If they're not here to watch me, then why do they all seem so interested in me? It's like everywhere I turn, one of them is there. It's unnerving, and the main reason I thought they were here."

"Maybe they like you," He shrugs.

"Like me? No, they most definitely do not *like* me." I sputter, shaking my head at the ridiculous suggestion.

His laughter is loud and sharp as he turns to start up the car, heading back towards campus.

"Oh, Camilla. Sweet, innocent, Camilla." Shaking his head, he continues to laugh. "Roman fucked you in a bar bathroom, and Lev bought you the morning-after pill. I don't know what the other two have done for you, but rumor has it that they all like to share. If even one of them is showing interest, then they all *like* you."

Grabbing my hair, I pull it at the roots, trying to center myself and make sense of this crazy situation. If it isn't arranged marriages and being locked away into mental facilities, then it's catching the interest of my Father's enemies.

I just need a fucking break.

"Hey, don't freak out." Gio gently tries to pry one of my hands out of my hair. "This could be fun."

"Fun? What about this sounds fun to you?"

"The way I see it, you have two to four sexy as sin men interested in you." When I look at him expectantly, he continues. "You said that you wanted to have all the fun college experiences, so have some fun hookups."

He makes it sound so easy. And if I didn't have so much shit to worry about in my life, maybe it could be easy. However, it was also perilous.

"You're forgetting the fact that I'm engaged," I tell him dryly. "Oh, and Leo and my father would actually murder me if they ever caught wind of this."

"They won't find out, and you don't have to tell the guys about the engagement if you don't want to. That's the beauty of a fling."

"A fling?"

"Yes, a fling. A basic right of passage for anyone, at any stage in life, really, but definitely in college." He tells me matter-of-factually. "You can hook up, hang out, have fun, but have no attachments, no expectations. You make the rules here, and you do what *you* want to do."

If I have to be honest, I feel like Gio's getting ahead of himself. I barely even know the guys, and even with the relief of knowing that they're not here to spy on me, I don't know if I want to do anything beyond what Roman and I did last night.

"It doesn't matter, I've already spent the last week stressed out about someone being here to watch me," I admit dejectedly, feeling a foreign stab of disappointment at dismissing the idea before ever really considering it. "Even if I wanted to, I don't think I could relax enough to have any fun."

"Don't let those assholes control every choice you make, Cam." His eyes flick between mine and the road, "If it's something you want to do, then do it. I'll help you out with making sure no one's watching over you."

"How?"

"I have my ways, just trust me."

He tiptoes around the topic, much like he did when he changed my attendance this morning. The more he avoids it, the more I want to ask, but I decide to trust him for now. He hasn't led me astray yet.

"Have I really been gone long enough for the mention of guys 'sharing' a girl to be normal?" I ask after watching the scenery pass by for a few minutes.

That minor detail almost slipped my mind with the way he glazed over it during our conversation.

He shakes with silent laughter, "I was wondering if you caught that. But no, it's not really normal, I happen to have a couple of friends who have a relationship like that, so I'm immune to the shock of it."

I want to ask more, but don't want to be intrusive. He must see right through my silence, though.

"Ask, I know you have questions."

"Who is it?" Immediately, I jump at the offer.

"Just some friends down in Florida, more like acquaintances, I guess. Eli and I met in a chat room when I was looking for information for my dad's business. He's super skilled at hacking and information gathering. His older brothers run their own company, and they all work together. We chat and catch up from time to time. The last time we talked, it came up that he and his brothers all fell for the Charlotte when they found her, and they made it work."

Again with the hacking, I file that information away for later, but continue to grill him.

"And you don't think it's weird at all? For a girl to be with multiple guys at one time?"

We've made it back to campus now. He parks the car but makes no move to get out, instead turning to face me.

"No, if everyone is on the same page, then I don't give a shit who they want to be with, or fuck, or do whatever with." He watches me closely, and I make sure to lock down my emotions to hide the relief I feel at his lack of judgment. "Plus, if it's just a fling, then I definitely don't see an issue with it. There are only the rules you make, fuck what everyone else has to say. Just be sure to tell them to wrap it up." He winks, and a grin splits his lips as he teases me.

Face flaming, I turn to get out of the car.

"I wasn't talking about *me*, I was just asking your general stance."

"Sure, we'll go with that." He follows right behind me, walking towards the main footpath.

After thanking him for driving me into town, we make plans to hang out over the weekend before parting to go to our respective classes. Just before I'm out of earshot, he calls out to me. The sun nearly blinds me as I turn to face him.

"In case you were wondering, if it were me with the chance to jump on those four sniffing around you… I wouldn't hesitate to take a *thorough* test drive."

And the blush is back, flaming my face.

"Good to know." I throw over my shoulder, rushing to class with the sound of his laughter echoing behind me.

15

Lev

I love being in the know.

Having information over others that you can choose when you want to play your hand, knowing you'll have the advantage.

After my little run-in with Camilla the other day at the pharmacy, I decided to swallow down my urge to run home and tattle on him to Abram and Dima - instead, I kept the information about their night out to myself.

I've been patient, allowing the others to fall into their routines with her, and so far, everything seems to be going well. Aside from having to talk Dima down from going out and kidnapping her when she refused to give him her phone number a second time, everything else was right on track.

We each had slipped into comfortable routines with Camilla, none of us pushing her too far, but just getting friendly with her. Thankfully, for me, she didn't seem as skiddish around me when we met up in class the second time around. She'd even cracked a few jokes with me in class and gone to get a coffee from the cart afterwards.

Her lunch dates with Abram had continued, but he still hadn't let me join them. He, like the rest of us, seemed to be very protective of the time he got to spend alone with her.

We all know the goal is to bring us all together and get her comfortable with the idea of us all being together, but it was a slow-moving process getting there. One that I wanted to play around with tonight.

I know that Roman plans to spend some time with Camilla tonight; he kept the details to himself because he wants to go alone, but I think I may have figured out a way to tag along.

See, I'm smarter than all the guys will give me credit for. I have a head full of wit and sharp senses, and I'm able to put two and two together.

After I ran into Camilla in the pharmacy, trying to buy an oopsie pill, I thought about it. She was skipping class, buying the pill the morning after I picked her and Roman up from the bar.

Coincidence? Not likely.

Add to that the conversation they had in the car that I've replayed in my head only about a hundred times over. She seemed to be poking at Roman, trying to get a rise out of him with something that I couldn't figure out. But then his comment smacked me in the head like a brick. He mentioned to her about having a good time with the three of us, and at the time, I was rightly annoyed. I selfishly wanted a date night of my own with Camilla, but figuring out his hidden meaning made me almost burst in my jeans like a prepubescent teen.

After putting the puzzle pieces together, I'm not mad at Roman's suggestion - I'm ecstatic. It sounds like a great bonding experience to me, to get us all closer together.

Dima and Abram couldn't even be mad as long as it worked, or at least I hoped so.

I can hear Roman heading out, telling the others not to wait up before walking out the front door.

I'm already dressed and ready to go, eager to follow right behind him, but not too worried about him leaving me behind.

As I said before, I'm smarter than they give me credit for.

Walking through the living room, I toss a brief farewell over my shoulder, not sticking around long enough for any questions.

I slow my stride as I step out onto the porch, whistling a tune and listening to the sounds of Roman's cursing as he kicks at his bike in the driveway.

"Having some trouble?" I ask innocently.

His narrowed eyes zero in on me instantly, furious, standing over his beloved bike.

"What the fuck did you do?"

"Me?" Holding a hand to my chest, I look at him with pure innocence. "Whatever do you think I could've done to your pride and joy, crotch rocket?"

"You know I'm going to see Camilla tonight. You think I believe it's a coincidence that my bike suddenly isn't starting?"

"Oh, that's right!" Snapping my fingers, I keep up with my ignorance, "Damn, that sucks. Hey, I'd be more than happy to give you a ride and tag along."

He moves to step around the bike to get to me, but I smartly step around, keeping the protection of the crotch rocket between us.

"I'm sure you would." He growls, "How about you give me your fucking keys and fix my bike back the way it was before I kick your ass?"

"I would, but I don't know anything about those death traps. Like I said, though, I'd be thrilled to play chauffeur. You said it yourself, the three of us could have a fun time together."

"That wasn't what I meant, dickwad!"

Oh shit, I've reduced him to preteen insults. He's more pissed than I thought he'd be.

"See, that's the thing I think I actually know what you meant when you said it." He's already mad; I may as well play my hand now. "Once I found little Camilla in the pharmacy after I picked you two up from the bar buying a certain morning-after pill, it all came together for me pretty clearly." I have the joy of seeing his face pale at the mention of the contraceptive measure that she had to take because he rushed into getting his dick wet and didn't think through the ramifications of their spontaneous fun. "I'll be dammed if I miss out on any more fun like you two clearly had, and I'm all for the three of us."

I can see his jaw working as he grinds his molars together.

"Fuck!" He spits out, dragging his hands through his hair to pull roughly at the roots.

Now time for my finisher, "Let me tag along, and I'll forget that you forgot to wrap it up. No harm done."

He continues to stare at me over the bike, stewing in his anger and probably thinking of fifty different ways to kill me.

"Seriously, I already bought her the pill. Think of it as an eye for an eye." I argue when he remains silent. "We're supposed to all spend time with her together at some point. Why not now?"

His stoic stare doesn't break, continuing to try to break me with just a look. Before I can try and throw another argument at him, he spins on his heel, stalking towards my SUV. I watch him dumbly as he turns and raises a brow at me.

"Are we going or what?" He barks, spurting me into action as I climb in beside him.

"Where to, my brooding brother?"

He spouts out directions to a club in the middle of downtown. We ride in relative silence, only the dull thrum of the radio filling the space between us.

"So, how do you forget to wrap it up? Hasn't that always been your golden rule that you drill into the rest of us?" I ask, looking for anything to talk about.

He rubs his forehead, looking much more tired now than angry, which bodes well for me being in such close proximity.

"I didn't exactly plan to fuck her in the bar bathroom. She pulled me in there, and it just happened. It didn't even cross my mind, I was just lost in her the second she looked up at me with those innocent doe eyes and begged for me."

The silence stretches again, and I can't help myself.

"Dude, that's hot."

"I know."

"But still, no rubber?"

"I know." He groans. "It was an honest mistake; it won't happen again. And thanks for getting her the pill." He adds the last part begrudgingly, but I'll accept the win.

"Do you think your bathroom escapades are what warmed her up to us all over the last week? Dima and Abram both said that she seemed more open, and I definitely noticed a difference with her anytime we've crossed paths."

"Could be," He shrugs, "She was having a really rough day before I took her to the bar, maybe having a chance to let loose showed her that we aren't a threat. We can be an escape for her, which is exactly what we want her to know."

"Hell yeah, we can, more than she knows." The logic is there as to why she would suddenly feel more comfortable around us after getting close and cozy with Roman while she was vulnerable. But something in my gut told me that there was more to her newfound acceptance of our friendships. Though I feel like the only one who could give me insight into that, other than Camilla herself, would be her little hacker friend.

We knew that her friend, Gio, had looked into us. He did a hell of a job on his own before he ever contacted Maverick and his team, who also happen to have a contract with Abram's father - well, technically, his girlfriend does. She gave us a heads-up right away when someone was asking questions about us, but we put it to rest quickly, figuring it couldn't be bad that he was doing what he could to look out for Camilla.

Perhaps he was the one who convinced her that we were actually awesome, and if that were the case, I suppose we would owe him a huge thank-you.

"So, what are we getting up to tonight?" I ask, realizing that I know where we're headed but nothing beyond that.

He shrugs, "Some party, I guess some rich kid rented out the club for his birthday. Camilla invited me when I ran into her at the gym."

I can't help but pout at the thought that Camilla only invited Roman, but I do my best to push past that, reminding myself that she's only just starting to get familiar with all of us. I'm also relieved that I went through with this on my own and didn't invite Abram or Dima; those two can be very overbearing and might not hold their temper well if they see

Camilla dressed for a club or dancing and letting loose. I wasn't fond of the idea of seeing her dancing around other guys, but I could at least keep a level head.

We make good time getting to the club and parked, Roman doesn't even hesitate to bypass the line of kids waiting to get inside. Stepping up to the bouncer, Roman slips him a few bills and instantly gains access to the crowded club.

The music is deafening the moment we step inside, with bass that rattles so loud I can feel it under my feet. Any remaining daylight from outside is cut off as we step through the entryway, leaving us in a dark, muted light that is only interrupted every few moments by various strobe lights.

I follow Roman as he easily clears a path towards the bar, wondering how we're going to even find Camilla in the mass of bodies filling the room from wall to wall.

I'm about to ask him, just as he settles at the end of the bar, turning to rest his back against the bar top with a shit eating grin on his face. Following his line of sight, my eyes almost bulge out of my head as my brain catches up with what I'm seeing.

Settled around the room are tall, shiny stripper poles, each with a beautiful woman spinning around to the music and capturing the attention of all the partygoers. The pole closest to the bar is currently occupied by Camilla, dressed in a long-sleeve top that stops just below her breasts, the tightest pair of spandex booty shorts I've seen in my 24 years of living, and a pair of cherry red stiletto heels. Her hair, which I've only ever seen down and around her face, is slicked back into a high ponytail that makes it hard for me to stop picturing it wrapped around my fist while my cock slides past her blood red lips and down her throat.

"What the fuck!" I look over to see the same shit eating grin plastered on Roman's face; he clearly knew about this. Yet another thing he didn't feel the need to clue the rest of us in on. "You knew she was going to be doing that?"

He shrugs, "Not technically. I know she pole dances at the gym a lot, she does other dancing while she's in there, and she's really good at it. I can tell she gets the most enjoyment out of pole dancing, though."

"What's wrong with normal dancing? Why the pole?" I mutter halfway under my breath, but he must still catch the words.

"I think she dances contemporary as a way to release her emotions, a way to speak without having actually to voice the words. But, to me at least, I think the pole dancing gives her confidence, makes her feel powerful. Plus, it's sexy as hell to watch."

"She's been letting you sit and watch her spin around the pole every time you run into her at the gym?"

That would explain the countless hours he's recently spent 'working out'. I can't even blame him. I could watch this shit for days, though, I'd prefer all these other perverts not be present.

"She doesn't know that I watch her." Well, that was borderline creepy, but Roman has always been keen on watching. He wasn't as downright stalkerish as Dina, but still watched

181

people more than most. It's what makes them both great at getting information out of the scum bags we torture; they can read the slightest shift in a person's demeanor to know whether they're still withholding information or if they've already given everything up.

"But she invited you here tonight? Knowing that she'd be dancing?" I clarify. He nods, a proud smirk screaming his satisfaction at that.

I might be lying if I said I wasn't jealous. I want Camilla to feel as comfortable with me as she does with Roman. Hell, she even goes to lunch with Abram twice a week while Dina and I are secluded to in-class only interactions with her.

"What's it like to be God's favorite?" I blurt out, my petulance slipping out.

That earns me a snort from Roman, but just as quickly, he composes himself again, never taking his eyes off Camilla. "Feels pretty good," He looks over to me, and must see my jealousy simmering under the surface. "Look, you just need to be casual with her, don't try to force a friendship. Just let her show you what she wants, when she wants. It's obvious she's felt controlled, at least for a part of her life, so our best shot is to let her take the reins and come to the conclusion that she wants to be around us."

"Why do you think she's been controlled?" I've thought the same thing, but I want to hear his take on it.

"We know who her father is," He rolls his eyes. "And we all see the way she acts like every new thing she tries here at school is a brand new life experience. I just put two and two together."

I didn't have much of the same insight into her reactions as Roman probably did, but I had noticed how much she threw herself into her school work, almost like it was a privilege to get to go to class. Abram always gushed over how excited she seemed to be about going to lunch with him, and Dima said she was weeks ahead on their joint project.

She seemed overly eager about her classes, and she'd even talked to me about wanting to see the team's football team play. She often had a childlike excitement as she started rambling about things she wanted to try in life, things from the bucket list she kept in her head.

All of that enthusiasm was nowhere to be found now, overshadowed by a sexy confidence that only amplified with each turn she took around the pole.

We sat in relative silence for about twenty minutes, only speaking to brush off countless attempts by rogue women who wanted attention. It'd be flattering, maybe, if our eyes hadn't been glued to Camilla since the moment we settled at the bar.

Finally, as the song comes to a close, she steps off the platform holding the pole, leaving space for another dancer to take her spot. Sauntering straight towards us, she offers polite smiles as she steps around many guys' advances.

Stopping in front of Roman, I can see the slight sheen of sweat covering her flushed face. A shy, cheeky smile graces her face as she stares up at him.

"Hi," I have to strain to hear her over the music, "I wasn't sure if you'd come."

"I wouldn't miss it, *Kukla.*" I have a front row seat to Roman's cocky, flirtatious attitude. Gone is any trace of his frustrations from earlier tonight, or any of the heaviness from our conversation. In its place is a crooked smirk as he looks her up from head to toe before leaning forward to place a kiss on her cheek. "I hope you don't mind, but I brought Lev."

He finally remembers my presence, gesturing over to me, and her eyes follow, offering me a much friendlier smile than I've received from her before.

She leans over to kiss me on the check as well. "Of course, the more the merrier."

God, I fucking hope so.

"Seems like a great party," I offer lamely.

She looks around, as if seeing it for the first time.

"Yeah, it seems cool. I haven't gotten to really enjoy much of it yet, but I'm free now and ready to see what's going on."

"Can I get you a drink?"

She nods, and I set about getting the bartender's attention while Roman suggests finding a booth to sit down for a bit to get her off her feet.

Armed with a tray full of beers and shots, I carefully make my way across the crowded space to find them huddled together in a corner booth.

The booths line the perimeter of the dance floor, offering ample opportunity for people-watching. They're built like coves into the wall, tucked back and offering a semblance of privacy as well as a slight reprieve from the booming noise from the DJ's set list.

The time it took to get all of our drinks gave me plenty of time to get my head back on straight and remember Roman's advice. Keep it cool and casual, that's all I had to do. We were just three friends hanging out, so there was no need to overthink this. I definitely didn't need to obsess over how every jackass in this club keeps throwing glances our way and devouring her with their eyes, definitely not that.

Camilla doesn't seem to pay any mind to the leering glances from around the room, offering me a sweet smile as I pass her a drink.

Up close, I can now see how heavily her makeup is applied tonight, a stark contrast to her usually bare, but still breathtaking appearance. Her eyes are cloaked in a smoky silver and gray hue with an exaggerated winged eyeliner, making her blue eyes all the more prominent against her pale skin and dark hair. The red lips I clocked earlier emphasize the plump shape of her lips, and do nothing for the rapidly hardening dick.

"So, how'd you end up dancing tonight?" I finally ask the question, luckily, without sounding like a possessive jackass.

Camilla downs the first drink I give her in three gulps, throwing back a shot before deciding to answer me.

"Oh, it's this guy Derek's birthday, and he's really good friends with Gio, who is my best friend. When Gio started throwing out ideas for his party, he asked me if I wanted to do it. He knows that I dance and thought I would have fun with it."

I have to stomp out the quick spark of jealousy within me, reminding myself that Gio is gay. It still lingers on the thought of this Derek guy getting to see Camilla dance at his birthday party.

Who even rents out a club for their birthday? He sounds like a pretentious asshole.

"Have you met Derek before?" Roman chimes in, I can see him battling with his own inner turmoil at the thought of someone wanting to make a move on Camilla.

Camilla doesn't seem to notice our building tension, focusing on plucking the stem off a cherry that was floating in her drink.

"No, Gio talks about him all the time, though. I think they might be dating and he just hasn't told me yet."

Just like that, both Roman and I visibly relax. Crisis averted.

But Camilla picks up our forgotten panic, eyes wide, she whips her head up, looking between the two of us.

"Shit! You weren't supposed to know that! Please, don't tell anyone. That's not my secret to share; Gio will be devastated if he knows that I told you. Please, forget you heard that!"

She's gone from relaxed to manic in a matter of seconds, her breathing picking up with every word until she's practically panting between us.

Grabbing her hand off the table, I squeeze it, trying to draw her attention back to me.

"Hey, it's alright. We won't say anything, breathe for a second."

Roman puts an arm around her shoulder from her other side, swearing his silence as well.

I don't see what the big deal is. Love who you love and all that, it's no skin off my back if Gio prefers men. But I can understand her panic, given that she doesn't know we're aware of Gio's preferences. In her mind, she had just betrayed her best friend and probably outed his biggest secret.

She looks up to me with wide, tear-filled eyes. "You promise?"

My heart fucking splits in two. She looks so fucking innocent yet hopeful at the childish affirmation.

Wanting nothing more than to promise her everything in the world, I settle for offering her my pinky, waiting until she links hers with mine.

"Pinky promise." I wink, cracking a laugh when she turns to Roman, offering her pinky expectantly until he caves, making the same promise.

What the fuck are we going to do with her?

This girl has us wrapped around her little finger already, and the fucked up thing is, I don't even think she realizes it.

16

Camilla

I lied the last time I told myself I was never drinking again, but to be fair, it's so much fun.

I invited Roman to Derek's party on a whim when I ran into him at the gym a couple of days ago, figuring that it'd be nice to have someone to hang out with if Gio ended up ditching me for who I assume is his new boyfriend - and I was correct in assuming that would happen. Not that I was mad at him, he deserves a night to let loose and party without having to babysit me. I just hope that if whatever he has with Derek is serious, then he'll eventually feel comfortable enough to tell me about it.

Inviting Roman had been a good idea, and it was even better now that he had brought Lev along. My face hurt from laughing so much with them all night, either because Lev was that funny or the drinks were hitting harder than I realized; I didn't care.

Currently, Lev was telling a story about how he and Roman got caught stealing candy from a corner store when they were kids, as part of their plan to start their own business at school.

"Roman tripped the store clerk just before he could grab me and call my parents, then he just jumped right over him, and we ran for our lives!" He has tears streaming down his face from laughing so hard.

"Always having to play the savior for this one, I swear it's like a full-time job," Roman grumbles out beside me, his lips twitching as he fights a smile.

"But did you two make it out with the candy?" I ask.

"Sure did, made fifty bucks off our haul."

"All of that for fifty bucks? You guys are insane!" My laughter sets off Lev, and then all three of us burst out laughing again.

Talking to them seems so easy; nothing is forced, and the conversation seems to flow freely from all of us. I was worried that things would be awkward with Roman after last week, but everything was normal. Gio and Lev had helped me with our slip-up, and life moved on. It was odd to think that the world didn't come to a screeching halt because I fucked up, but here we are.

"What about you?" Roman draws my attention back to the present.

"What about me?"

"What's the most rebellious thing you've ever done?" He asks. The question catches me off guard. Have I ever honestly acted rebelliously in my life? Outside of Briarwood, that is, because an easy answer would be any number of decisions I made to spite the guards after getting locked away.

Obviously, I couldn't discuss that without opening a whole new conversation I never wanted to have. Besides, anything I did while locked in that hellhole was for my own survival, not to act out and not for my own enjoyment.

"I can't think of anything, I'm not very exciting." I settle on the boring answer.

"Oh, come on, there has to be something." Lev pushes, leaning so close that I can feel his breath brush over my cheek. "One thing that you've done that you knew you weren't supposed to."

Memories flicker through my mind of my time at Briarwood, flashes of refusing pills, having them forced down my throat, and sitting in the lunch hall and staring at a room full of zombies eating lunch and fighting the hunger pains that stabbed through me while refusing the food being forced on me. Being strapped down, a tube forced into my stomach when they'd finally had enough.

Shaking my head, I scramble through the sad memories of my life, searching for something.

"I used to sneak out of my house, a long time ago." I offer the only thing that comes to mind.

"To do what? Meet up with boys?" Roman asks, looking irritated at the thought, making me laugh.

"No, nothing of the sort," I assure him, watching as his demeanor instantly melts back into his calm state. "I wanted to take dance classes; there was a studio not far from my house, so I used to sneak out to go."

"Well, that's not as exciting as it initially sounded." Lev actually pouts at the boring admission. "Why didn't you just sign up for the classes? Did your parents not want you to take dance?"

"My father was strict; extracurriculars weren't a big priority in our house." I need to steer this conversation away from my home life. If Briarwood hadn't been a safe topic, my home life would have been worse. "Plus, it was pole dancing, so I don't think that would fly with anyone's parents." I force a laugh to hide the hollowness I feel as the thought of my father carves away at me.

"Ah, so that's where you learned it from, I was wondering." Roman thankfully takes the shift in conversation in stride, leading us back to safer territory. And Lev follows right behind him, not missing a beat.

"You do look fantastic on the pole, I will admit." Slipping out of the booth, he extends a hand towards me. "I'd love to see if your moves on the floor are just as good. Would you like to dance?"

I don't hesitate to take his hand, thankful for the distraction. My skin feels too tight for my body, thoughts, and memories are trying to assault me now that the mention of my childhood has brought them to the forefront of my mind.

I need to lock it all down again, but they come up when my defenses are down. Unfortunately, as enjoyable as my conversations with the guys have been, they've led me to let my guard down, which is something I can't afford to do.

One day, the dam I've built in my mind to hide all my fucked up memories and sadness is going to break. I fear that day because I know it's going to crush me from the inside out, and I haven't figured out how I'll be able to put myself together once that happens.

So I let Lev lead me out onto the dance floor, using the time he has his back to me to rebuild some of those walls, stuffing everything back down as far as it can go for now.

I don't think, I just let the music and the mind-numbing bass drown out all my thoughts as my body moves freely with the beat.

Roman opted to stay back in the booth to watch us. My eyes collide with his as Lev settles at my back, moving and swaying effortlessly with the beat.

As the songs pass, Lev doesn't complain about how long we dance. His hands bravely shift from my hips up to my waist. Then another song, and one hand moves up to caress my collarbone, then up into my hair.

My body heats up with each roll of my hips, met with a thrust of his. I don't know if what we're doing even classifies as dancing anymore, but I can't find it in me to care when my body is buzzing the way it is, and with the heat I can see in Roman's gaze across the room.

Finally, the hand Lev has wrapped around my ponytail tugs my head to the side to meet his intense stare over my shoulder. His eyes stare into both of mine, looking down at my lips and back.

I'm not sure which one of us moves first, but in an instant, our lips collide, molding to one another. Sparks fly at the contact, his warmth washing over me as butterflies fight to escape my stomach.

Each breath is shared between us, a quick pull to my hair has me gasping, giving him the perfect opening to slip his tongue into my mouth to meet mine. I fight for control over the kiss, wanting to feel him under my power. Eventually, I give in, letting my mind clear of any thoughts except the feel of his lips on mine.

He starts to pull away, and I'm powerless to stop the whimper that escapes my throat. His teeth bite down on my bottom lip in response, before soothing the mark and pulling back to look at me.

His eyes are heavy with lust, his breathing quick, like mine.

Like a rubber band being snapped back into place, all the sounds of the club come rushing back in, assaulting my ears.

A brief flash of worry hits me, remembering Roman watching us from the corner. Swinging my gaze back to him, though, shows me the same heated stare locked right on me. Not an ounce of anger shows on his face, only reminding me of his comment in the car on the way back from the bar.

Could he really have been serious when he said that it could be fun to have Lev with us next time? Because if it sparks even half the amount of heat coiling inside me, then I fear that it might not be the worst idea I've ever heard.

Before I can fantasize more about that, Lev gently turns me around to continue dancing, seeing nothing but Roman's eyes on mine.

A few songs later, I'm parched and ready for a break. Lev must understand me when I gesture back to the booth, shooing me away and telling me he's going to grab more drinks.

Sauntering back to Roman, I feel a rush of confidence seeing the way his eyes rake over me, all the way down to my heels. I know he isn't seeing any of the scars that I strategically have hidden; instead, he's just seeing the sexy persona that I've painted on for the night. Cloaked in ruby red lips and tight little spandex, he can't see what really lies beneath it all.

Making it back to the booth, I bypass the bench seat; standing between Roman's thighs, looking down at him for once.

His hands settle on my hips, anchoring me in place with nowhere to run.

"You look like you had an *okay* time out there dancing, *Kukla*." His emphasis on the word makes me smile, reminding me of his irritation with my description of our hookup.

"It was pretty fun." I play along, seeing how far I have to push him before I see that spark in his eyes.

With no effort at all, that spark flashes in his eyes. A deep growl rumbles in his chest as he pulls me to him with a hand collared around my throat, clashing his lips against mine in a possessive air of control.

I don't have any time to react before I'm melting under his touch, savoring the flavor of whiskey that he leaves on my tongue.

Pushing me back, his hands clasp around both hips, as my back meets another warm body.

"You look parched." His head tilts as I feel another hand gently wrap around my throat, pulling my head back to rest on a shoulder.

Lev's face appears over mine, his mouth coming to meet mine.

I greedily accept his kiss and am frozen with shock as liquor spills into my mouth.

Not an ounce of revulsion is found in my body as I swallow every drop spilled from Lev's lips, claiming his lips again as soon as I'm finished.

Roman's hands tighten almost to the point of pain on my hips, and Lev's hand tightens in a subtle warning, pulling away to tilt his head at me.

"Don't be greedy, baby. Roman looks thirsty, too." Taking another sip from his glass, his lips meet mine once again.

Rather than swallow the liquor this time, I savor the burn in my mouth, turning my head back to Roman.

His eyes shine with a hunger like a starving man as he waits for me.

Lev loosens his grip enough to let me lean forward and meet Roman's lips, carefully spilling the liquid into his mouth.

I'm not as smooth as Lev, though, and a few drops slip down Roman's chin and onto his neck.

I don't hesitate to swoop down, using my tongue to lap up the spilled liquor, following the trail up the front of his throat and his chin, leaving him with one last chaste kiss.

My body blazes, a deep burning down in my core threatening to swallow me whole. If it weren't for both their hands on me, I'm sure I'd be a puddle on the floor by now.

Suddenly, the noise from the club is too loud, hitting me from every side, threatening to burst the bubble we've created for ourselves. I want to get out of here, but I keep my mouth shut, not wanting to end my time with them.

"Let's get out of here," Lev reads my mind, and I eagerly follow.

Once we're out into the fresh air, I suck in lungfuls of air, trying to tamp down the building inferno inside me, to no success.

I'm craving more of both of them. I want them all over me, inside me. I've never felt this deep-seated neediness, and I don't know how to smother the urge to beg them both to take me right here in the parking lot.

I make it to Lev's SUV parked in the corner of the lot, falling into the back less than gracefully. Lev slides in beside me, and Roman takes the driver's seat.

They don't ask where I want to go, and I don't bother asking where they're taking me, fully trusting them to get me somewhere safely.

As the streetlights pass by the tinted windows, the need inside me only grows until I'm practically riding Lev's thigh in the backseat.

"Fuck, baby. You need to stop doing that. I'm not going to be able to stop myself if you keep going." Lev groans, trying to keep me still and in my own seat.

"That's the point," I whine, fighting his hold on my hips, looking for the friction I crave. "Please," I beg when he doesn't let up.

Lev let's out a deep groan, throwing his head back against the seat and palming the growing erection in his jeans.

"Please what, Kukla?" Roman asks from the front, meeting my eyes in the rear view.

"Fuck me!" I practically shout, needing a release more than I need air right now.

Without missing a beat, his brow arches, his gaze never straying from mine. If I were in my right mind, I'd probably be concerned with his lack of attention to the road, but right now I couldn't give a single fuck if he crashes the car into a ditch if it meant I get to cum.

"Who?" He growls.

"Lev! Or you, both of you!"

"I'm not fucking you for the first time in the back of my car," Lev grumbles, but I can see his will crumbling before my eyes.

"He's right, we're not fucking you in the car." Roman agrees.

The sound that slips from me doesn't feel human; a raw, unguarded protest escapes me before I can swallow it back.

"But that doesn't mean that Lev can't help you out on the drive." Roman's voice sparks my hope once again, low and deliberate. His eyes move to Lev's, a silent exchange that hums like static in the air.

Lev lets out a string of curses under his breath, reaching over to drag me onto his lap, knocking the air from my lungs as my back settles against his chest, his legs spreading mine apart.

His presence fills every inch of the space around me until I can't tell where his tension ends and mine begins.

Without thought, my hips fight to find their own rhythm, chasing the friction that is my only anchor. Lev's hands are firm on my hips, but can do little to stop me from this position.

"*Kukla!*" Roman's bark stops me in my tracks, my eyes instantly finding his once again. "Reach back and lock your hands around his neck."

I follow his instructions blindly. Taking a handful of Lev's hair in one hand, while the other has a death grip around my wrist.

"Good girl, now, if you want to cum, then you better not let go. If you do, he'll stop."

"I will?" Lev questions from behind me.

Roman's sharp stare shifts to him.

"Yes, you will." He hisses. "Now, help her out. Give her what she needs."

Lev doesn't shy away from touching me. His hands instantly roam all over the front of my body, sliding over my thighs, up my stomach to my breasts, where he grabs a handful of each over my top. His hands find their way under the slip of a top I threw on tonight, pushing it up to reveal my sheer lace bra. Pulling the cups away, he bears my chest to Roman's burning gaze in the front.

Sharp pain shoots through both my nipples as he pinches both of them, sending my hips bucking wildly.

My moans and ragged breathing, along with Lev's labored breaths, are the only sounds filling the car.

Despite the awkward angle, Lev manages to fit his face against my neck through the hold I have on his, sending more shock waves of ecstasy straight to my core with each bite he inflicts onto my skin.

I'm no longer a person, I'm a melted pile of flesh and hormones dissolving right on his lap. I have no feeling other than where his hands are on me, and where the wetness is pooling between my thighs, calling to him and Roman, begging them for anything they're willing to give.

The combination of his lips on my skin and his fingers on my chest, inflicting bites of pain with every pass, has me chasing a high, rushing higher and higher towards the peak that will send me crashing into oblivion. But at the last moment, his hands release their torturous grip, dropping me back down to a disappointing place of wanting.

"Please!" I mewl his hands move back down to my hips.

A sharp bite on my neck has me crying out.

"You sound so pretty when you beg, baby." Lev murmurs - and I hate that the sound of it makes my pulse trip faster.

He continues to tease me, trailing his fingers along the waistband of my shorts before pulling them back, over and over again.

"Fuck you," I pant out the insult on his third pass of pulling back.

I more so feel his laugh against my back than actually hearing it; what I can listen to sounds more sinister than amused.

"Oh, baby, I intend to. But you need a bit more practice with patience, it seems."

"She was very demanding last time, if I recall correctly." Roman agrees as the torture continues.

"Hmm, that won't do, will it, baby?"

His question goes unanswered as I pull on his hair with all my strength, focusing my energy on inflicting pain on him without breaking Roman's rule to keep my hands where they are, not wanting to give them a reason to leave me wanting any longer than they already plan to.

"Aw, put your claws away. We haven't even gotten to the fun part yet."

Finally, his hand brushes past my waistband, sliding into the matching thong I'd worn under my spandex shorts, finally touching me where I need him most.

His hand is warm, but nowhere near as burning hot as I am. His touch almost feels like a cooling balm to the heat radiating off me in waves as he feels how wet they've both made me.

"Oh, fuck." A guttural groan spills from him as he slides his fingers through my folds, brushing my clit and sending me climbing once again.

When his pace doesn't quicken, my hips take control, thrusting forward and setting their own pace as he explores.

After an eternity of grinding, he takes pity on me, sliding one of his fingers deep inside me, meeting my hips thrust for thrust.

I'm close to the peak again, right there at the edge, and ready to nose-dive off the other side. It's so close, right there, but my body is holding on, needing something else to push me over. Tension coils in my chest, waiting like a tripwire ready to detonate, just waiting on the signal.

Lev adds another finger, a small bite of pain at the stretch, quickly overshadowed with pleasure.

As my hips become more reckless, he shifts his hand, allowing his palm to add the slightest bit of pressure to my clit.

That movement alone ignites the spark. My body shatters into an explosion of bliss, fireworks of pleasure expel from me in overwhelming waves, filling my vision with flashes of bright lights, blinding me until a cloak of darkness falls over my sight, leaving me in darkness but still thrumming with waves of pleasure.

Lev brings me down gently; I can feel the deep timber of his voice as he murmurs what I assume are words of praise behind me, kissing my head and running his hands softly over me to get the blood circulating again. It's then that I realize that he must have brought my arms down from behind his neck, wrapping them in front of me to hold me closer, giving him access to press his lips along my face from my jaw, up to my temples, and back again.

The hot tension in my chest settles into a glowing ember, muted for the moment but ready to be reignited with a single look from either of these men.

Sounds flicker around me, and my eyes fly open at the feeling of another set of hands on me.

I come face-to-face with Roman as he leans into the open door to our right, sliding my top back down to cover me before petting my hair like I'm something to be cherished.

"Come on," He tells me gently as he extracts me from Lev's lap, pulling me into his arms but never lowering me down to the ground.

Firmly in his arms, I watch Lev step out of the car and try to adjust himself as he follows. In front of us, a large white house sits at the top of the circular driveway. Floor-to-ceiling windows line the bottom of the house, shining light out onto the front lawn. The upper level isn't as open, but black shutters make a sharp contrast against the white paneling that covers the house. It's a house that screams money and reminds me all too much of the one I grew up in. But there's a warmth about it that feels foreign to me, even though I could stand out here and creep on those inside, it also beckons me, inviting me in to soak up its warmth.

"Where are we?" I ask, seconds before Roman pulls a set of keys from his pocket, answering my question.

"This is our house, we live with two more friends, but they're out for the night."

I noticed he didn't mention Abram and Dima's names, but I assume that's who it is, based on what Gio told me about the four of them. I don't know if it was intentional on his part, but I'm too busy gaping at the interior to question him.

Black marble floors sparkle beneath our feet, reflecting light in every direction. An iron chandelier hovers above my head, bringing warmth into the space despite its odd composition. The foyer features a small table with a lamp, seemingly intended for keys and mail, before leading to a wide staircase to the right. The short hall ahead of us opens into a spacious living room. Much like the front of the house, the back of the room is all glass, looking out into a moderately sized back yard. A pool glistens in the moonlight just off the patio, which is decorated with a dining table, daybeds, and a variety of cushioned loungers.

A U-shaped charcoal sectional is centered in the living room, facing a ship lap mantle with the focal point of the room, a 90-inch television, mounted in the perfect spot so that it can be seen from any place on the couch, as well as the open dining area and kitchen that sits just off to the right behind the sofa.

The kitchen is a chef's wet dream, stainless steel, top-of-the-line appliances, butcher block counters, and endless cabinet space. The large island separates the two rooms, and is sparkling under the lights, with how spotless it is.

I can't picture any of the guys cooking, so the thought of such a large and luxurious space in their house is almost comical.

"Your room or mine?" Roman's voice startles me out of my thoughts as he tosses the question to Lev as he pulls three bottles of water from the fridge across the room.

"Yours, you have all the toys." Lev winks, rushing ahead of us and up the stairs.

Roman follows, still carrying me as he climbs up the massive staircase.

"Do I get a say in this?" I ask jokingly, really, I'm looking for ways to tame down the nervous energy buzzing within me at the thought of going upstairs with both of them.

Being with Roman was hot, and being with Lev while Roman watched was hotter. Sleeping with both of them is going to be hot enough to incinerate me, but my insecurities are flaring, in fear that they'll see that I'm too broken, too tainted for them to waste their time on.

"You always have a say," Roman tells me, looking into my eyes. "You can say 'Yes' and 'Please', but you can also say no, or tell us to stop, and we will, no questions asked." His eyes soften for a moment, conveying his sincerity before flashing with heat once again. "But until you say no, we're going to show you a great time. Even better than anything you could come up with in that little head of yours, because I promise you that come tomorrow you won't be left saying that tonight was anything less than amazing."

We've made it into the bedroom now, and I don't have a moment to look around before I'm tossed onto a plush mattress.

"Now, any objections?" He asks, standing over me while I catch my breath. Lev hovers just behind me, propped up against the headboard.

My mind is racing, I could think of a hundred different objections and reasons not to do this, and I know that if I voiced any of them, then they would stop. But the biggest question is if I even want them to stop. I want to enjoy myself and say fuck the consequences, that was my big plan with coming to school. Despite the shitty expiration date on my fun, I deserve to enjoy myself.

A thought strikes me, my scars will be on display for them to see if we get undressed.

I haven't gone out of my way to hide them, but they're not something that I want to show off and have to answer questions about. My stomach and back have some more minor scars that they may have clocked by now, but those don't bring me shame as much as the angry, puckered ones that I inflicted on myself.

"Just don't take my top off," I tell him.

His brows pull together, curiosity in his eyes.

"You can move it around if it's in the way, but just don't take it off. That's my rule."

He nods, his expression sobering before asking me if there's anything else.

With my biggest insecurity out of the way, I shake my head.

A devious grin spreads across his face.

He lunges forward, pulling me off the bed by his hand on my throat.

It's at this moment that I know I'm utterly fucked.

17

Roman

Her neck fits perfectly in my hand as I drag her off the bed towards me.

I make sure I only squeeze hard enough to make her lightheaded, not actually choking her - we'll work up to that.

Crushing my lips to hers, I swallow her surprised gasp, savoring the lingering taste of liquor on her tongue and pouring every ounce of wanting and frustration that's been simmering inside me all night into the kiss.

Watching her dance with Lev was the highlight of my night. Getting to see her let loose and have fun was endearing. The only drawback was my aching dick fighting the confines of my jeans as I sat in the booth watching from across the room. Then Lev had to bring her over and pull that stunt with the shots, bringing me dangerously close to losing it right there in the middle of the club, like a fucking teenager. And then the car ride home; it's a miracle that we even got back here in one piece because I sure as shit was not paying any of my attention to the road, all of it was zeroed in on her and the sounds she made while he drove her crazy right there in the back seat.

Since the first day we found her, she's been driving me mad without even trying. I got to have her last week in that shitty dive bar, and now that I have her again, I'm not going to rush this time. I'm ready to savor every inch of her delectable body and make her absolutely sure that it can get no better than it will with us.

Whether she knows it or not, she's destined for us. She'll probably resist that notion at first, and softening her up with our dicks is maybe a shitty way to go about it, but we never said that we'd fight fair.

Lev steps up behind her, sandwiching her between us and reminding me that this is a party for three tonight.

He runs his hands over her shoulders and down to her hips, soothing her as she jumps from the unexpected contact.

She relaxes between the two of us, melting into our touches and moving in synchrony with us.

Reluctantly pulling away from her lips, I take in her dazed expression, turning her around to give Lev a turn. He wastes no time taking her lips with his while his hands continue to explore every inch of skin that's been left exposed by her outfit.

I step over to my dresser, looking through the bottom drawer, pulling out the items that I went out to find after our night in the bar.

Tossing some of it onto the bed, I hold on to the one that I know is going to drive her wild.

I grab both of her wrists from where she has her hands fisted in his hair, pulling them behind her back and swiftly clicking the handcuffs in place. The sound of the metal clicking stiffens her, and she pulls her hands, testing the cuffs. Lev must distract her enough with his tongue because she gives up the fight quickly, accepting the loss of control.

Thankfully, she wore her hair up tonight, giving me complete access to her throat as I lean in to kiss, bite, and suck up and down each side, making sure to leave my mark on her flawless skin.

I can feel the flush taking over her skin. Despite the car ride home, she's getting worked up again, ready and needy for us.

Lev and I pull away at the same time, leaving her to sway between the two of us.

"I think someone is overdressed." He says, his eyes meeting mine over her head, a silent communication ensues; he's following my lead.

"I'd have to agree with you." Grabbing her hair, I roughly twist her head to the side to meet my eyes—defiance flares for a split second before being engulfed by heat. "Don't you think so, *Kukla?*"

She doesn't answer, her eyes looking between my eyes and my lips as she pants and pretends to struggle in my hold. A whine slips through her lips as Lev pulls her shorts down to her feet, tapping each foot to guide her out of them before making quick work of her shoes.

Once the heels are gone, her head only comes up to our chests, making the angle of her head even more uncomfortable when I don't ease up on the hold I have on her hair.

I capture her bottom lip between my teeth, loving the groan she lets out when I bite down.

"Much better," I tell her.

Lev works his way up her body, trailing kisses up her legs, hips, and stomach, efficiently avoiding her pussy as she thrusts her hips towards him every time he leans close.

Standing back up, he continues the torture, moving over her collarbone and neck, her struggles becoming more prominent with each kiss.

"Almost, I think we're missing something."

Before I can say anything, he grabs the bottom hem of her shirt, pulling it up over her breasts to stretch across the top of her chest. Pulling the cups of her bra to either side like he did in the car, he leaves her bare to both of us.

Cupping both breasts, she pulls on my hold, leaning heavily towards Lev and arching her back to feel more of his touch.

He pinches her nipples, causing her to jump before he drops his head to pull one of them into his mouth.

The full body moan she releases has all of the blood in my body rushing to my dick. It's like a siren's call, screaming out to me.

I hold her steady while he teases her, switching from one side to the other while she writhes helplessly in our hands.

I drop one of my hands down her stomach, reaching between her legs and sliding a finger through her core.

"This greedy pussy is soaking wet," I growl, pulling her hair and pushing a finger into her, feeling the way she tightens around me before adding another. "You just can't help it, can you? You're a needy little slut just waiting for our cocks." I continue to goad her, feeling her clench around me with every comment. Even as she tries to shoot daggers at me and pretend to fight my hold and resist, the body doesn't lie - and hers craves more.

Her pussy tightens around my fingers, her body close to the release that we're working her up to. I pull my hand away, Lev follows suit, pulling back from her chest with a pop as she growls at us both.

I'm sure she means for it to sound aggressive, but she comes across as an angry kitten.

They both watch as I bring my hand to my mouth, sucking one of my fingers greedily, tasting her for the first time.

The sound of a starving man tasting food for the first time fills the room, and the sweet taste of Camilla floods all my senses. She tastes like sunshine and rain, the sweetest honey that I'll never forget the taste of.

"How does she taste?" Lev's raspy voice breaks my trance.

I don't think twice before offering my hand to him, watching Camilla's reaction when he greedily accepts, sucking my finger to clean her juices from me.

Her eyes widen, and she holds her breath. Watching his tongue as it trails over my skin, dipping between my fingers to collect every drop.

"Fan-fucking-tastic, wifey." He says with a wink towards her once he releases my hand.

She seems to be stuck in a trance, looking at him like he's from another planet while she rubs her thighs together restlessly.

With a hand still in her hair, I cup her chin with the other, drawing her attention back to me.

"Your turn, Kukla. Who do you want to taste?"

She doesn't answer, panting and writhing between us, she looks from me to Lev and back.

"Whoever you choose to taste, the other gets your pussy." I tell her, curious as to who she'll choose.

Her eyes roll back into her head, probably imagining the feeling of being filled from both ends.

"You," she gasps, "I want to taste you."

Lev looks to the ceiling, mouthing "Fuck yes" as she makes her choice. And I'll be honest, my chest puffs up at the fact that she chose my dick to choke on. I've already had her pussy, now I get to claim another part of her, and I get a front row seat to watching her fall apart for a second time tonight - but this time with no distractions. I pull her in to kiss her once again, silently rewarding her for choosing my dick, leaving her with a taste of herself.

Lev moves around us, stripping off his clothes and reaching for one of the foil packets I tossed on the bed earlier. While he does that, I drag Camilla to the head of the bed, keeping a hand on her so she doesn't lose her balance with her hands still secured behind her back. Sitting at the top of the bed with my back against the headboard, I guide her to straddle my knees, sitting back to admire her for a moment.

Her creamy skin glows in the soft light in the room. Chest heaving with every breath, her tits rise and fall with the motion, her puckered nipples glistening.

She hovers over my legs, looking nervous as her eyes refuse to meet mine. A pinch to her nipple draws her eyes back to mine.

"You want to taste, *Kukla*?" A shiver rocks through her, either from my words or from the feel of Lev brushing up behind her, anchoring her with his hands on her hips.

Her nod is timid, but determination sparkles in her eyes. Using one hand to free myself, the other cups her jaw, brushing over her bottom lip, plump from all the torment we've put it through.

I have the pleasure of watching her eyes widen as they take in the sight of my cock and the glistening Prince Albert piercing sitting proudly on the tip, glistening in pre-cum.

I take too much joy in the flash of fear I see, the sight of her throat bobbing. But then her tongue darts out to lick her lips, and the hunger from before is back with a vengeance.

Using her hair for leverage, I lower her head down, leading her to my lap to come face to face with my aching dick. I give her a moment to decide what she's going to do. I'd love to force myself down her throat, feel the way her throat squeezes me as she chokes on me, but I have no way of knowing if she's ever sucked dick before. For the sake of not having teeth marks in my most prized appendage, I let her get acclimated.

Her tongue pokes out, tentatively tasting the shiny drop of pre-cum, her eyes meeting mine when she hears my sharp intake of breath. She must see my desperate attempt to hold back. Diving forward, she takes me into her mouth, enveloping me in a delicious warmth and sending shock waves through me as her moan vibrates around my length.

I do try to keep my hands on the mattress, not to force her. But that restraint lasts only a few moments, and then her tongue is swirling around the tip, flicking the barbell in my cock, and I lose it, grabbing her hair and taking control over the pace.

I brutally fuck her face, setting a punishing pace while she gags and chokes around me, fighting and thrashing on my lap as saliva pours from the corners of her mouth, covering my lap.

Lev runs a hand over her back, soothing her as she gags, murmuring soft words of encouragement. Her breath stutters as one of his hands disappears between her thighs, and I let up on her to allow her to catch her breath.

Even as I let up, she suctions onto me with more gusto than before, her tongue matching the pace that Lev is setting with his fingers as he preps her to take him.

A quick flash of his eyes has me dragging her off my dick by her hair, loving the way her hooded eyes stare back at me, glazed over and unseeing. Her mouth gapes open, and she fights to pull air into her lungs, leaving Lev the perfect opportunity to shove his fingers into her mouth.

"Clean them off for me, baby. Taste yourself mixed with Roman." He growls, and she follows his command without hesitation.

He moves to position himself behind her, waiting a beat before thrusting in to the hilt and tearing a scream from her throat.

Diving forward, I capture her lips with mine, swallowing her screams and tasting our salty essences on her tongue as it wars with mine.

He starts to move, pulling back to slam into her again in short, hard thrusts, grabbing her bound hands for leverage.

Pulling back, I shove her face back down onto my dick, moving in tandem with his thrusts, listening to her muffled moans and cries of pleasure.

"Such a good slut, taking both our cocks at once," I tell her through a moan as she hits a particularly sensitive spot, swallowing me down further.

"I think I've died and gone to heaven." Lev agrees, "If there's a God, then he's looking down on me today, and my dick thanks him for it."

I have to agree with him, it doesn't top the night at the bar with her, but I could live with my dick in her mouth forever and die a happy man.

Pushing her head down, I force her to swallow my whole length, pushing her past her gag reflex as she fights against me. She struggles hard before finally going limp, figuring out that she's at a disadvantage here.

216

"Oh fuck, do that again!" Lev shouts, his hips stuttering.

I oblige.

"Fuuuuck, she strangles my dick when you do that. I'm not going to last."

I match my pace to his, her body rocking with us on each blow.

"Such a greedy slut, begging for our cocks and taking them so well." She tries to pull back, but I force her down further. "Now you're going to swallow our cum, every last drop. You'd better not waste it, or we'll have to start again."

"Come on, baby. Take it for me, take it." Lev chants, reaching around her to rub her clit, bringing her higher and higher with us. His muscles strain from keeping his pace and holding her bound hands behind her, but he doesn't let up. Neither of us does.

Her whole body tenses, becoming completely still moments before she convulses wildly, like she's being electrocuted as she cums.

I feel the brush of her teeth on my dick, giving me just enough to set me off, my cum shooting down the back of her throat.

I can hear her garbled protest as I push her head down further, forcing her to swallow, which sets Lev off to follow behind us with a shout, stilling her with his hands on her hips as he delivers his last two thrusts.

The room stills, all of us frozen in the throes of our pleasure as our panting breaths fill the space.

Lev pulls out of her, causing a sound of displeasure before collapsing onto the bed. She follows suit, melting into a puddle on my lap while I tuck myself back into my jeans.

Rolling onto his side, he brushes the hair that escaped her ponytail off her sweaty face.

"Baby girl, that was fantastic."

Humming her agreement, she doesn't offer much more than that. She seems to be in a haze, clinging to the edge of consciousness.

I pull her to sit curled up against my chest, releasing the cuffs from her wrists and rubbing the blood flow back into her arms.

Grabbing one of the waters, Lev unscrews the cap and offers her small sips as she practically purrs between us, the feisty little kitten tamed for the moment.

He runs to the attached bathroom, grabbing a washcloth so we can clean her up before sliding a pair of pajama pants on her, quietly laughing at the way we have to roll them over four times before her feet finally poke out the bottom. We leave her in her club shirt, even though it looks uncomfortable to sleep in. She told us that was her rule for the night, and we'll respect that.

Soon enough, once we're all as comfortable as we can get with Camilla not having opened her eyes once, we settle into the bed, Camilla lies between the two of us, and silence envelops the room once again.

She continues to perplex me at every turn. First, she was standoffish with each of us, and then, seemingly overnight, she became more comfortable being around us. Now, even though she stays firmly guarded with any personal information about herself, and with wanting to keep parts of her hidden from us, she's ready and willing to jump into bed for a good time. I feel like I'm getting whiplash from her when all I really want is answers. None of us has been able to get any intel from her on where she's been for the past couple of years and why she ended up enrolled at Hill Crest out of the blue. It all remains a mystery; she's a mystery.

But with her aloofness and carefree attitude that she tries to project around her, there's the sadness and shadows that we've all caught glimpses of just beneath the surface. There's evidence of pain in her that we've all seen at one moment or another.

She's a sexy little jigsaw puzzle. It's fun getting to see a new layer to her every time we meet up, but not being able to see the whole picture is starting to frustrate me.

This could all be so simple if we weren't all harboring secrets.

"I'm going to lock you away and keep you forever, wifey. I could live inside your pussy if you'd let me." Lev pulls me from my quiet thoughts, whispering sweet nothings to Camilla as she shifts around restlessly, blinking her eyes open to look around before dropping her head back down onto the pillow to burrow back into a comfortable position.

"You can't keep me." Her voice is muffled by the pillow but still audible.

"Sure, I can, you're tiny, I could take you anywhere with me. Plus, we just proved that we have amazing chemistry," He quickly assures her.

She's silent long enough for me to assume that she's slipped back into unconsciousness, but then her slurred words pique my interest.

"You can't. It's not allowed."

Jumping at the opportunity, I'm quick to ask, "Why is it not allowed?"

Lev and I both wait, holding our breaths to see if she's finally going to reveal something. When she falls silent again, I nudge her lightly, asking again.

I've almost given up all hope when she says nothing else, but just as I close my eyes, ready to drift off to sleep, I hear her whisper.

"My fiancé would be mad. Everyone would get hurt because of me."

My eyes dart to Lev, who looks back at me with the same shock-stricken expression, having heard her too.

What the fuck?

18

Camilla

I wake up feeling content — and hot.

The two bodies on either side of me are like personal space heaters, radiating an obscene amount of warmth from all sides. They each have a hand thrown over me, like they were afraid that I would slip away in the middle of the night.

Taking stock of my body, I look around the room we ended up in for the first time. The walls are barren, with only the dark gray paint to fill them. The king-sized bed that we're lying on with matching nightstands, a dark wood dresser, and a small armchair in the corner are the only pieces of furniture in the space.

The room is empty, but it has an almost relaxing feeling, a clean slate. Much like the last time waking up from a hook-up, I feel lighter than I did the day before. No remorse for the things I did, only a blissful feeling of nothing.

I'd even be happy to lie here and sleep all day, but my bladder protests that idea. Extracting myself from the guys isn't easy. Still, I somehow manage to escape their holds without waking either of them, making myself right at home as I stroll into the attached en suite, snooping around harmlessly as I take care of business.

Stepping out of the bathroom, the guys are still asleep, now cuddling against one another like long-time lovers, making me laugh.

I decide to sneak out and either call Gio to pick me up or walk back to my dorm to keep this lightness I have around me and avoid any awkward morning-after conversations.

My top is still in place from last night, but my bottoms are discarded and replaced with a pair of men's boxers; as comfortable as they are, I don't want to walk back looking the whole part of the walk of shame. It only takes me a minute to find the discarded shorts, then another minute to shimmy back into them, along with my shoes, as I do.

With one last glance at the guys, I slip out the door, taking extra care to close it silently behind me.

I'm pretty proud of my stealthy exit, and it gives me time to take in more of the house as I head back down towards the front door. The home exudes wealth and luxury; everything is clean and in its proper place. It looks nothing like what I'd expect from a house occupied by four men. It all makes sense when I loop my observations back to what Gio told me about the four of them. Of course, they would have money, and they'd be used to a certain standard, coming from the higher ranks of the Bratva.

The question remains as to what the hell they're doing here, of all places.

Coming down the stairs, the front door is finally in sight, my escape right at my fingertips. Just before I make it to the door, a tall and imposing body steps in front of me, blocking my path and making me jump out of my skin.

I feel my fight-or-flight instinct kick in instantly, adrenaline rushing through me, causing my ears to pound. Taking a few steps back, I look around frantically for an escape route as I try to make sense of the situation.

"Well, well. Fancy meeting you here." The rich voices cuts through the sound of my blood rushing in my ears, drawing my attention back to the figure before me.

Dima peers down at me, looking like the cat that got the cream, his eyes raking over me from head to toe.

"You weren't trying to sneak out before breakfast, were you?" He asks, a hint of teasing in his tone.

He can clearly see this for what it is: a walk of shame. Though I don't feel much shame, since last night was pretty awesome, sneaking out of their house at seven in the morning in yesterday's clothes paints a pretty vivid picture. I have to wonder how he feels about me sleeping with two of his best friends.

"I didn't mean to sleep over. I should head back to my dorm." I try to step around him, but he matches my steps, blocking my path to the door.

"Nonsense, it's Sunday morning, we always make a big breakfast on the weekends." Putting an arm around my shoulder, he ushers me into the massive kitchen. "You can keep me company while I cook."

Before I can even protest, he hoists me up by the waist onto one of the barstools on the far side of the island, checking me out once again.

"Nice outfit, by the way." With a wink, he's spinning around to pull random ingredients from the pantry and fridge to line the countertops.

Silence lingers between us as he moves effortlessly around the kitchen, adding ingredients to random bowls, stirring different pots on the stove, and taking things in and out of the oven. He seems to be at ease in the kitchen, like it's second nature to him.

I feel awkward just watching him cook; we haven't spoken much outside our shared class. Plus, I still think I hurt his feelings when I wouldn't give up my phone number, not that I think he'd ever admit it.

"Where did you learn to cook?" I finally ask, curious about his upbringing and who might have taught him to move so efficiently in the kitchen.

He looks surprised at the question, like he didn't expect me to strike up a conversation. In class, he's always the one to get us talking, since at first I was skeptical of him and then, after that, I was just intimidated by his striking good looks and towering form.

"My father had a housekeeper who acted as a nanny when I was younger and still living at home. She used to insist that I help her cook every day so that I could learn valuable life skills." His face fills with a sheepish smile at the memory,

"Really, I just think that she was trying to keep me out of trouble and away from attracting my Father's short temper."

The similarities to my own upbringing are striking. Memories flood my mind of spending time in the kitchen with Maria, especially once Dante went off to school. It was one of the few times that I didn't have to worry about my Father hovering over me.

"Do you cook?" He asks, snapping me out of my thoughts.

A laugh comes out before I can stop it, thinking about all the times that Maria did her best to teach me to cook the simplest of recipes, and I horribly failed every time.

"No, my housekeeper tried her best to teach me, but I guess I just lack the necessary skills to create anything even remotely edible."

His eyes sparkle with amusement, glancing up at me as he rolls out some pastry dough between us.

"So housekeeper nanny for you too, then?"

"Yeah, mom left when I was born, and my father was always busy." My hands start to sweat, worried about the impending questions that I'm sure will follow. The last thing I want to discuss is my father; it will only sour my good mood from yesterday.

He surprises me, though, moving swiftly past the topic without thought.

"Parents are overrated. Louis taught me everything I need to know to keep myself fed, and I suppose she sprinkled in a couple of lessons about how to be a decent person in there somewhere."

I don't know enough about him to know if that's entirely true, but I guess I'm about to learn firsthand how well he picked up on the cooking skills.

"So do you enjoy cooking? Or are you just the only one here that knows how to navigate the kitchen?" I ask the next question, ensuring that the topic stays on the lighter side and avoids any further details about our families and upbringings.

He laughs, head thrown back and showing off his bobbing Adam's apple, making my mouth water.

"I do enjoy it, it's fairly peaceful, and I like being able to provide." He moves to put the tray of perfectly rolled croissants into the oven, "But of the four of us, I'm the only one trusted in the kitchen alone."

Admittedly, I am surprised that of the four of them, he's the most trusted in the kitchen, but I can recognize that that's only because of my own bias I've made based on his appearance, and I should know that looks can be very deceiving.

"It's just you, Lev, Roman, and Abram, right?" I already know, but I want to try to dig for more information. "How long have you all lived together?"

"You figured that one out fairly quickly." He chuckles to himself, "We've lived together for years, we were in boarding school together and all shared rooms, so once we came here it was just natural to share a place."

"What brought you guys to Hill Crest?"

He's distracted now, stirring something on the stove and adding seasonings.

"Good business opportunities, we have a lot of connections over here that we don't have at home."

Well, that's interesting. Abram told me he was here because his friend's mom was sick, and Lev told me his parents wanted him to have a better education. Now Dima's story is that they're here for business opportunities. I just got over my skepticism of them, but now their stories weren't adding up.

I clock that information for later as Abram steps into the kitchen, looking much too put together for a Sunday morning, freshly shaven and wearing dress slacks and a perfectly pressed button-up with the sleeves rolled to show off the corded muscles in his arms.

His eyebrows jump up his forehead when his eyes meet mine, stopping him short on his way to the coffee maker.

"Camilla, hello." His eyes rake over me as he steps to the side of the island, leaving two stools between us. "I didn't know you were here. What are you wearing?"

Dima intercepts the question before I can ask Abram where he gets off commenting on my outfit.

"Kitten here had a little sleepover last night. I caught her trying to sneak out this morning, and before breakfast!" His back is turned as he finishes plating up the last of the food, so he misses the look that crosses Abram's face at the mention of sleeping over. A cross of intrigue with a hint of jealousy flashes in his eyes before being wiped away back into an impassive state.

It's such a quick flicker that I question if it was ever even there. Gio told me that they like to share, so he wouldn't be jealous, would he? Plus, it's not like any of us are together, so he has no claim over me, just like Lev and Roman don't either.

Abram continues to eye up my outfit, a hint of disapproval in his lingering gaze.

"We went to a club for a party." For some reason, I offer him an explanation for my skimpy outfit, feeling my skin start to stretch uncomfortably, and the scars on my wrists tingle the longer he stares at me.

"We?" He moves to take a seat at the head of the table, where Dima has now laid out his breakfast spread.

"Wifey?"

"Kukla!"

Frantic voices ring out from upstairs, followed by thundering footsteps as Lev and Roman come barreling down the stairs, sliding into the kitchen to come to an abrupt stop when they find me sitting at the island.

"Well, that answers that." Abram nods, filling his plate.

"We woke up, and you were gone; we thought you bolted." Lev moves to stand beside me, looking disheveled from sleep and missing a shirt. Instantly, all my focus is on the sprawling tattoos covering his chest and snaking down his arms.

I was a bit too distracted last night to notice them, but now I have the chance to admire them, up close and personally.

"You should have woken one of us up. Were you planning to walk back to the dorms?" Roman asks from my other side, drawing my attention to his also bare chest inches away from me.

My eyes are too busy tracing all the lines carved into his body, outlining the definition of the muscles lying just beneath his glowing skin.

"She's not even listening to me, is she?" I hear Roman ask.

Dima rounds the island, spatula in hand.

"Nope, go put some shirts on so she can enjoy the delicious breakfast I made her without swallowing her tongue." He delivers a sharp smack to both of them with the spatula, ushering me off the stool and over to the table.

"I don't know, I think she likes the view." Lev strokes his abs, taking the seat across from mine, earning a slap to the back of his head from Abram, who didn't stop scrolling through his phone to do so.

The spread on the table is mouthwatering, featuring everything from waffles and bacon to pastries, eggs, home fries, and a fresh fruit salad. I can only sit and watch as Dima piles enough food to feed me for a week onto my plate, nodding for me to start eating.

Roman strolls back into the room, unfortunately with a fresh shirt and another in his hand that he tosses at Lev.

Once both of them are covered up and I have nothing left to drool over, I try the food. It's a cacophony of flavors exploding in my mouth. Every single bite is better than the last.

Someone clearing their throat stops me in the middle of shoveling mouthfuls of food down my throat. Looking around the table, four surprised and slightly impressed expressions look back. I must look like I haven't eaten in days, but it's so damn good.

"Sorry," I mumble a half ass apology through a mouth full of food. It breaks them out of their trances enough to laugh at my expense and dive into their own food.

There's a comfortable silence as we all eat; no one tries to fill it with useless conversations, opting instead to enjoy the food in peace.

Once we're finished, I don't waste any time jumping out of my seat to clear the dishes, wanting to help out in some way since I sat on my ass and watched while Dima did everything already.

"You don't have to clean, you're a guest." Abram chides disapprovingly, though none of the others try to stop me.

"I want to help," I grab his plate before he can stop me, "And it's the least I can do to thank Dima for such a good breakfast."

"I can think of another way you can thank me," Dima slides his chair back from the table, mischief coloring his face. When I think he's going to make some innuendo, he surprises me again. "A kiss."

My brow arches disbelievingly, "A kiss? That's it?"

"That's it." He nods.

I contemplate for all of two seconds. A kiss is harmless enough, and I have fucked two of his best friends.

Decision made, I shuffle over to him, straddling his lap and enjoying the way his eyes widen in surprise.

I don't give him any time to think, diving forward and snaking my arms around his neck while drawing him in for a kiss.

I intend to give him just a quick peck, more of a tease than anything, but he reacts quickly, crushing my chest to his and conquering my lips with his, fighting for an opening to slide his tongue into my mouth to war with mine.

Everything else ceases to exist. This house could burst into flames and threaten to burn us to ash with it, and I don't think that could even drag me away from him.

"Oh, yeah. That's still fucking hot." Lev's voice startles me enough to pull away, looking shyly at Dima's cocky smirk staring back at me.

"Agreed." Dima winks, sending heat rushing to my cheeks. I clumsily stumble back to my feet to continue clearing dishes as the guy's soft laughter follows me.

Lev and Abram join me in clearing the dishes and cleaning everything up while Roman and Dima watch from the table.

"We should do something fun today. What's everyone up for?" Lev speaks up as he dries the dishes being passed to him.

They start tossing out ideas; even Abram, who looks dressed and ready for a day in the office, offers one to the group, and I feel a flicker of disappointment in my chest. Spending time with them sounds like a lot of fun. I've enjoyed my time with each of them individually, but hanging out as a group seems like it will draw a lot of attention, which is the last thing I need in my life.

I have to raise my voice to be heard over their brainstorming.

"I should really head back to my dorm,"

A chorus of protests and borderline childish whines answers.

"I have a lot of homework to get done before classes tomorrow."

"There's no way, you're always a week ahead on all your classwork," Lev argues, having teased me about it in class just the other day.

"I like to *stay* ahead."

Roman narrows his eyes at me, and I pretend like I can't see him from across the room, focusing on scrubbing an already spotless plate.

They need to stay just a fling, as Gio suggested. That means no sleepovers, no breakfast with them, and nothing personal—just quick and casual hook-ups, preferably like the first night with Roman in a shitty dive bar.

Gio told me they can look after themselves, and they probably would feel threatened by Leo or my father. Whether or not that's true, I can't put myself in a position to get close to them

232

only for them to be ripped away like Dante was. I don't want anyone's blood on my hands other than my own.

"So, Roman and Lev get to spend time with you, but Dima and I don't?" Abram's deep voice startles me from behind as he tucks away a stack of dishes.

So much for no jealousy, damn him.

Releasing a heavy sigh, I shut off the sink, turning to face him.

"It's complicated."

He doesn't waver, matching my stance; he crosses his arms across his chest, standing his ground.

"Uncomplicate it, spend the day with us." He shrugs.

Of the four of them, Abram was the one I would least suspect of fighting me on this. I've spent the most time with him on our lunch dates, and we've gotten to be friends, but I wouldn't think he would argue for me to hang out with the four of them.

"I can't." I shrug back, not offering anymore.

"Can't or won't?" Roman asks from the table, not giving me a chance to answer before adding, "Afraid your fiancé will be mad?"

I feel the blood drain from my face as Abram stiffens, his eyes flicking over my shoulder before trapping me in his burning stare.

Lev sighs deeply beside me. "Nice, way to approach it subtly there, man."

That draws Abram's attention as I hear Dima.

"Fiancé? What fucking fiancé? Is that why you wouldn't give me your number?"

"Oh my God! Give it up with the phone number already!" Lev gripes.

The three of them burst into pointless arguing over my rejection of Dima, the first day we met, but the distraction doesn't sway Abram; his attention is still laser-focused on me.

"So you can't hang around with us because your fiancé will get mad?" He asks, his voice eerily calm for the bomb that was just dropped.

Feeling backed into a corner, I try to offer up the smallest amount of information to get them to drop the subject, though I'm questioning in the back of my mind how they even found out about my impending marriage.

"No, I know he won't get mad. The whole marriage is a joke in my eyes, and he couldn't care less who I hang out with, not that he would ever know anyway." It's only half of a lie; it is a joke to me, but Leo absolutely would care that I was hanging around them.

His brows pull together, and the three behind me go quiet at hearing my explanation.

"If it's such a joke, then why are you getting married?"

Irritation flares in me. Where does he get off thinking that he can question anything about me? They don't even know me, yet somehow they know about Leo, and now they believe they have a right to ask me about it?

"Given your background, I'm sure you can put the pieces together." I fire back, using my knowledge of them the same way they are against me.

"Our background? What's that supposed to mean?" His brows furrow, forming an angry puckered line in the middle of his forehead.

"What does our background have to do with you being engaged?" Roman asks from behind me, his voice sounding tense, but I refuse to break eye contact with Abram to see his expression.

"It means that I'm sure, coming from the Bratva, that you've heard about an arranged marriage before. And with that, you should know that not everyone falls in love or even likes their intended spouse since it's all typically done for convenience or power."

Given the immediate silence that descends on the room and the frozen, shocked expression cloaking his face, I'd say they weren't expecting me to know that about them.

Lev is the one to break the silence,

"How do you know that we're in the Bratva?"

I turn just in time to see Dima deliver a smack to the back of his head.

"You're supposed to deny first, idiot. Not blindly admit to the accusation." He shakes his head with an eye roll, clearly disappointed.

"I didn't admit to anything; I was asking where she heard that."

"You did." Roman agrees, he and Dima share a look that I can't decipher, and I tuck that away to figure out later.

"How do you know that?" Abram finds his voice again, spinning back around; I see a stoic expression, one that gives nothing away.

"How do you know about my engagement?" I raise a brow, challenging him—a question for a question - just like our lunch dates.

I hope he will be just as stubborn as I am, dropping the subject for the sake of not wanting to answer the question, but rather, he shrugs, leaning casually back against the counter without a care in the world.

"I didn't," He tips his chin over my shoulder, "Roman brought it up, I'm just curious now. Your turn." He leaves the ball in my court, following the usual pattern from our lunchtime game.

My frustration is at a peak again, making my skin feel tight and my body thrum with anxious energy. I don't want to get into this with them; it's all my mess, and I can't have them anywhere near it.

The only thing I want from the four of them is a good time and some distractions, nothing more and nothing less. My personal life shouldn't be a topic of discussion.

Dragging my hands through my hair - which I thankfully freed from the slick back ponytail earlier this morning- I grab onto the roots and tug, relishing in the sharp sting it sends through my scalp, grounding me until the urge to scream is somewhat muted.

"It doesn't even matter; you all don't know me, we're just hanging out and having fun. The fact that I'm engaged doesn't mean shit to me, so it shouldn't mean shit to you, and if it does, then we can all go our separate ways and forget about it." My tone is harsh, but the facts are there; my engagement doesn't matter, and we should all forget about it.

They all fall quiet yet again, contemplating my words.

"So, what? You just want to hang out and sleep around through college before going back home to get married?" Lev asks, sounding confused.

I'm borderline offended by the way he threw out the term sleeping around, making it sound like I'm sleeping with every guy on campus. I'm not sleeping my way through school, but I ignore it to address the bigger topic here.

"I'm here to have fun before I'm shackled to someone I can't stand for the rest of my life. I've enjoyed my time spent with the four of you up to this point and would enjoy hanging out with you more, but if you can't accept what I'm here to do, then tell me now so I can go find someone who can, and who won't ask questions."

"I'm in!" Dima is quick to agree, "If it means I get to have a piece of you, then I'm all for it. Plus, I know once you have a taste of me, you'll never want to give me up." Tossing a wink my way, he adds, "Your little fiancé, whoever he is, won't stand a chance of getting you back."

Roman and Lev are both quiet, exchanging silent words like they did in the car last night before nodding in agreement.

"We're cool with that, last night was great, and we'd love a repeat." Roman finally speaks for the two of them, leaving me to face Abram.

He remains silent and stoic, clearly lost in his thoughts as we all wait.

I find myself holding my breath in anticipation of what he's going to say. Five minutes ago, I was ready to tell them to fuck off and walk out the front door, but now, after hearing three of them agree to a casual fling so I can enjoy my college life, no matter how short, I feel sad thinking about Abram wanting no part of it.

He rolls his head from side to side, trying to release tension from his shoulders as we wait.

"I still have questions," He starts, but I cut him off.

"And I won't be answering them. It doesn't matter, and this is all just fun, that's all I can offer." I shrug, leaving it at that.

The seconds feel like hours as he stews in silence.

No one tries to fill the silence; all of us wait for his decision.

Finally, his eyes find mine, holding me hostage as he tries to see into my soul.

"Fine, we'll have some fun."

Lev lets out a whoop behind us, running back and forth through the kitchen in celebration like a hyperactive golden retriever, being stopped short when Abram speaks again.

"But exclusively with us, outside of the four of us, we don't share with others." He says it in a way that implies that I would try to argue, and I savor his surprise as I quickly agree. Having no other experience aside from Lev and Roman, I'm not opposed; it was never my intention to sleep through every guy I meet while I'm here.

With that conversation out of the way, they all fall back into comfortable conversation, trying to think of something fun to do with our day. I don't even try to argue that I should go back to my dorm this time, as I don't have the energy if they start arguing again. Plus, there might be a part of me that's excited at the thought of them wanting me to say, of feeling wanted.

I listen to them banter back and forth while pushing down all my anxiety and fear that getting closer to them could be a horrible idea. As terrifying as it is, I want to try to enjoy myself and to do something for once to make myself happy. Even if this all comes crashing down, which I fully expect it will, I can at least come out of this with some fun memories to look back on to get me through the tough times ahead. That has to be better than nothing.

It's not until later in the day, as we're all having fun and enjoying our day, that I realize Abram never answered my question about knowing I was engaged. He deflected, giving me nothing and leaving me with more questions to add to the list of things I need to figure out about the four of them.

19

Abram

If someone asked me a month ago if I thought I'd be blowing off work calls with my father and abandoning my responsibilities to spend the afternoon sunbathing on a rented yacht in the middle of one of Wisconsin's self-proclaimed best lakes, I would have laughed in their face. But it seems Camilla has a way of bending us all around her little finger, drawing us out of our shells and igniting a childlike enthusiasm for the simpler things in life.

We've only known her for a short time, but the pull that we all feel for her is undeniable. Maybe that stems from the years we spent hearing stories of her and catching snippets of her voice through phone conversations with Dante.

They had an unbreakable bond, one that was evident anytime her name was brought up in conversation; his eyes would shine with adoration every single time. That could very well be the reason that she's throwing me off center as much as she is. In the time that we've been around her, she hasn't mentioned Dante once. She has a very meticulous way of steering any conversation away from the topic of family, acting as though her father and Dante don't exist.

One thing I've learned about Camilla for sure is that she has secrets, and she isn't going to give them up easily. She's guarded, always wearing a mask of faux confidence and aloofness, but every so often, if I watch her closely, I can catch a glimpse of the mask slipping to show her genuine emotions.

Right now, for example, she looks carefree and relaxed, lounging in the sun on one of the loungers positioned around the hot tub on the top deck of the boat. Her shoulders, though, are tense, and I can see a tic in her jaw from clenching and unclenching her teeth, revealing her discomfort.

Roman, Lev, and Dima took up residence in the hot tub, trying their best to invite her in with them, but she brushed them off, saying she just wanted to tan. And that's where my suspicion peaks, because she's lying out to tan... in a hoodie and bike shorts in the September heat.

Roman mentioned to all of us in the group chat about scars he's noticed on her wrists, and her request that she had last night about staying covered while fucking around with him and Lev. Our group chat has been buzzing behind her back all day with speculation about what she's hiding under the hoodie. Once it was brought up, I immediately thought back to every lunch date we've had so far; every time I've seen her, she's been in a jacket or a long-sleeved article of clothing.

One step forward, two steps back. Two more questions immediately follow every piece of information we learn about her.

My own teeth clench as her phone buzzes for the fifth time in the last twenty minutes. Her jaw clenches even harder as she glances at it before shoving it back under the chair cushion, trying to block it out. I have to tamp down the urge to grab her phone and find out who's putting her on edge, but I think I have a pretty good guess.

Lev's gaze flicks between the two of us, seemingly picking up on the silent tension simmering in us for two different reasons.

Doing what he does best, he tries to lighten the mood for everyone: "Let's play a game!"

Dima snorts, "A game? Are we back in grade school?" He slices his hand through the water, sending a wave crashing into Lev's face, which he shakes off like a dog drying off.

"Well, no one wants to do flips off the bow with me." He pouts as Roman shakes his head. Camilla watches the interaction from her lounger, biting her lip to hide her smile at their antics, her phone forgotten for the time being. "And we have a whole afternoon and this kick ass boat, may as well do something fun. Wifey is going to think we're boring if we don't do something soon!"

"I told you to stop calling me that," She tries to act annoyed, but her twitching lips give her away. "Besides, I'm having a great time."

"You're baking in the sun, probably sweating your ass off in a hoodie. How is that a good time?" Voicing what we're all thinking I expect the comment to dampen her mood, but she lifts her face to the sky, basking in the blinding rays.

"I'm comfortable, and I've never been out on the water. It's peaceful."

"You've never been on a boat?" Dima asks.

She shakes her head, prompting Roman to chime in, "Not even like a small one, or a kayak? Anything?"

Again, she shakes her head.

"Can you even swim?" I ask, doing my best not to let the memories of Dante's final night surface in my mind.

She keeps her face tilted up as the conversation carries on, either disinterested or as a way to mask what she's truly feeling. There's no way to know if she was ever told about the night Dante died.

"I can swim to save myself; outside of that, I've never liked it much."

I curse myself for asking as a silent somberness settles over the guys and me, our thoughts no doubt in the same place.

"Truth or dare! That's the game, who wants to go first." Lev makes the ridiculous suggestion with a hint of mischief in his eyes. It only takes a few seconds of contemplation before the rest of us catch on, seeing where he's heading with the game.

All too willing to go along with this, I volunteer myself. "I'll go." Setting my sights on Camilla, I think about my options. Either she'll play along, and we can finally get some answers to the burning questions we all have about her, or she'll take the dares, which, with the four of us, is only going to lead to some nefarious fun. "Camilla, truth or dare?"

"Dare," She says with zero hesitation. Taking what she assumes will be the easy route out, it seems.

A wicked thrill of excitement buzzes through me. Sharing a look with the others, I see the same reaction reflected at me. She doesn't understand what she's just unleashed.

We'll start light, ease our way into the more depraved options if she wants to dodge telling any truths. "Lose the shirt," I issue the dare, knowing that she threw on a swimsuit underneath, one that we picked up at a small shop on the way here.

She laughs lightly, like she guessed the dare before I even said anything. She moves quickly, whipping it off and over her head, making a show of dropping it to the deck beside her. The only tell that she's uncomfortable is the tick in her jaw and the way she lays her hands over her stomach once the cover of the shirt is gone, trying to tuck in on herself to hide.

The swimsuit she picked out at the store can barely be called a covering; the two triangle pieces held together only by a string leave little to the imagination, stealing my attention and making it hard to focus on the game. She's too thin, not sickly, but just lacking any curves, not that it takes away from how breathtaking she is. She's so small that it makes her look breakable, like one strong gust of wind could blow her away. The swimsuit accentuates her breasts, barely a handful but lifted and perky under the bright orange fabric. I can already feel my cock stiffening, begging to come out and play, and we're just getting started.

"Lev, truth or dare?" She shifts her gaze to him, catching him in the act of checking out her chest.

He doesn't even look chastised, simply offering her a smirk instead. "Truth."

"Where did you learn to draw?"

Interesting, I didn't know that he shared that secret talent of his with her. He's been drawing for as long as I've known him, but it's something that he tends to keep private. Hell, he barely even lets any of us see any of the sketches he does.

"We didn't have a lot of money growing up, but the nursing home my mom worked at held classes for the residents. I had to go to work with her a lot and spent most of my time in the art room while I was there." We all listen intently, having not heard this story before. "It ended up being something that I really enjoyed, and that allowed me to express myself and get my brain to slow down, even if just for a little while."

He swiftly moves on, continuing the game by firing right back at her. She chooses dare, unsurprisingly, and ends up losing her pants before aiming for Dima. He also chooses truth, giving her a chance to ask something she actually wants to know, but she keeps it light, opting to ask him if he has any hobbies. He lies, of course, telling her he likes to play video games, but in his defense, it seems a better alternative than telling her his favorite hobby is torturing others for information.

With his dare, Dima gets her to join them in the hot tub. They give her a wide berth, shifting to one side to leave her the other, a false sense of security for a while longer.

Moving on to Roman, she asks another easy question, as he too chooses truth. She asks how long he's been riding bikes - yet another hobby that they must've shared with her on their own time. He's been riding since he got his permit and found a cheap bike to buy off an upperclassman. I'm curious if he let her ride on his motorcycle, which has always been something that he's dead set against, but I have a feeling that little Camilla would have a way of bending him to his will pretty easily with that one.

She surprises us all when she chooses truth this turn. She either trusts Roman more than the rest of us, or she's trying to test the waters and see if we'll stick to surface-level shit as she did.

I'm silently begging him to go straight for a complicated question and get some answers, but to my disappointment, he keeps it relatively light.

"What do your parents do for work?"

Pussy move, we already damn well know what her father does for work, and that her mother has been MIA her entire life. He could have at least tried to ask about Dante and see if she'd deny it, to give us something to figure her out here.

"No mom in the picture, and my father works in shipping." Her answer is swift and short, as if it were practiced.

She's facing away from me now in the hot tub, so I can't see the tick in her jaw, but I catch the slight tension of her shoulders as the lie rolls off her tongue. I can't see her face, but I'm sure it's covered in a perfectly emotionless mask as it usually is when the topic of conversation gets anything remotely close to personal.

"Any siblings?" Lev blurts out, making her stiffen before forcing herself to relax in a split second.

"That's two questions; I already answered my truth." Shrugging, she looks over her shoulder, drawing my gaze from where it was studying a smattering of tiny silver scars etched into her back. "What'll it be?"

I'm not sure if I'll regret it, but I say, "Truth." Hoping that by doing so, I can provide her with some information and hopefully make her more inclined to open up, like all those games of twenty questions at lunch, where she only likes to play if it's an even match in information.

She looks stunned for a moment, studying me closely, looking for something to say. I'm against this like she is, but she won't find it, because I'm not. I want to share myself with her, and I'd love to know more about her, or read her like a book if she'd let us.

As much as this started about honoring the promise we made to Dante to look out for her, the more we get to be around her and talk to her, the more I want to chain her to us forever. She fits seamlessly between the four of us, bringing out different parts of us that we each thought we'd suppressed: my inquisitiveness, Lev's art, Roman's socialization, and Dima's less primal side.

It's as if when she's with us, the best parts of us come forward, the parts that make us seem more human and less like robots - which is precisely what we were becoming back at home, just blindly following orders day in and day out, wondering who was coming for us next.

For the first time, I see Camilla look shy, like she's afraid to ask the question she wants. That or she's scared of the answer she'll get.

"Do the four of you really run the Bratva?" Her voice dips with the question, making it hard to hear, but I manage to catch it.

The guys all stiffen a bit at the mention of what we do for work, but she was going to find out sooner or later; her knowing now means she won't freak out as much later when we take her back home with us.

"Not exactly," I continue to explain, not following her lead with the easy outs. "My father is head of the Bratva currently, so I am the next in line unless challenged. But while my father is still in charge, that's mostly just for appearances; he's taught me well and more so oversees now. Lev has been my best friend since I was a child, so I keep him around as my second hand. Dima is our enforcer, he gets information from those who are a bit.... Unwilling. And Roman is the one we send to negotiate our business contracts and also to collect information, though he's more public-facing than Dima is when it comes to that aspect."

Her lack of reaction suggests she already knew most of this. While I'm slightly irritated that she tried to set me up to catch me in a lie with that question, I have to respect the thought process behind it.

Hopefully, that will get her to see that she can trust us, even if just a little for now.

Turning her back to me, she silently indicates to keep the game going. I'm not sure that we've convinced her that she can open up to us just yet, but I have an idea on how we can help her get there.

"I want you to go sit on Roman's lap while we play the rest of our game," I tell her when she inevitably picks dare again.

Roman is settled on the far side of the tub from her, Lev and Dima bordering his sides, making him the best choice for what I have in mind.

She glides through the tub, standing before Roman, and without an ounce of hesitation, she spins to settle her ass right against his crotch, adding a few hip circles as she gets settled. He wastes no time wrapping his arms around her waist to keep her anchored to him and to not float away.

She takes her turn, starting her rotation with Lev again. He makes up some bullshit answer to whatever she asks, and once it's his turn, he might know where I'm heading with the game because he dares me to join them in the hot tub. Now closer to Camilla, I direct the next turn to Dima, who wisely chooses dare.

"I dare you to pull one of Camilla's legs over yours and keep it there." Before I can finish speaking, he has her leg locked in his grasp, tucking it over his lap. From the gasp and blush on her face, paired with his devilish smirk, I'd wager that he is rubbing his dick with her foot to show her how hard he is.

I don't think he understands that not everyone has a foot fetish.

I'm sure he'll figure it out eventually.

But I have bigger things to worry about right now.

Dina picks up immediately, though, directing his question to Lev, who also chooses dare, which is how Camilla ends up spread eagle over Roman's lap, each leg held hostage on either side.

We could pass it back to her to see what she would do with the opportunity, but rather than it becoming a game of keep-away, all of us volleying back and forth with our dares. Before I know it, Camilla has lost her swim top, showing off her pert little nipples standing at attention with her hands wrapped back around Roman's neck.

Lev's dared to tease her nipples with his mouth while Dina is dared to use his fingers to get her as close to an orgasm as possible without letting her finish.

With Dima's turn, I take truth.

"How badly do you want to take her for yourself right now?" He asks distractedly, not taking his eyes off her face as he watches her expression change as the rhythm of his fingers shifts.

Looking over her flushed cheeks and hooded eyes, her chest heaving as Lev tortures one breast with his mouth, leaving the other free to be pinched and plucked by Roman's free hand. Her eyes are completely glazed over; she's lost to the throes of pleasure, chasing that high. She may be looking right at me, but she's not seeing my starving gaze watching over her.

And in this moment, I wish she were seeing me, and seeing how hungry all of us are for her. We could tell her all day long that we want her, but she won't truly understand it until she sees it for herself.

"I'd throw all of you overboard right now to have her all to myself," I admit, flashes of her beneath me while I devour her mind, body, and soul, filling my mind.

We're past the point of trying to get information out of her. While that was the initial goal of the game, we've now moved on to a much more exciting end goal.

Camilla must sense this as well, because when I ask her once again, she chooses truth, giving me the perfect opening.

"How far do you want us to go with this today?" I catch her eyes with mine, making sure to catch her attention and that she's focused on the answer.

Everyone's hands still, causing her to arch and whimper while she comprehends my words. Her breathing picks up as her eyes clear, finally seeing me in front of her for the first time since we started.

"I want all of you," She begs through her heaving breaths, and who are we to deny her?

Before any of us can even move, she stops us in our tracks with another question of her own.

With an arched brow and her defiant attitude peaking back through, she asks, "Are you going to kiss me now?"

Just like a match lighting a flame, we all move at once. Diving forward, I take her lips with mine, leaving space for the others to torture her body, teasing her and bringing her right to the edge without letting her fall.

She just sealed her fate by asking for the four of us, whether she knows it or not. For as long as we can remember, we've been looking for the one that could fit with us, bring us together, and handle all we have to offer. Offering herself up to us for the taking is the green light we need, and we're not letting her go.

20

Camilla

Kissing all the guys is an entirely different experience. Kissing Abram, I feel an explosion of sensations barreling into me and threatening to crush me. He threatens to steal the air from my lungs as his lips move with mine, and I'd die happily if this is the way that I could go out.

Lev's mouth tortures my nipples, switching between biting and soothing. In contrast, Roman's hand on my other breast only delivers sharp bites of pain as he pinches and pulls, perfectly matching the rhythm of Dima's fingers as he thrusts them into me at an unpredictable pace, lingering at my entrance to tease me and stretch me before shoving them deep to hit that hidden spot that makes me see stars.

It's overstimulating, all the sensations crashing together, trying to swallow me whole. But the sun beating down on us, the water crashing against the boat, the jets from the hot tub all become muted, lost under the feeling of the four of us melding together.

The game of truth or dare is long forgotten, and all control has been surrendered to them.

Roman's hand snakes up the front of my body, collaring my throat and pushing me further into Abram, his tongue coaxing my lips to open and allow him in.

He pulls back abruptly, chest heaving, and his wild eyes studying every inch of exposed skin.

Moving back, he takes a seat across the tub from us, spreading his arms out along the sides to bask in the sun, golden skin fully on display, highlighted by the water droplets pebbled on his skin. He sits like a king on a throne, ready to rule over his disciples.

"Dima, switch with Roman and take her on your lap." His voice comes out deep and gravelly, making me jump with the sudden instructions. "Roman, sit on the edge of the tub."

The guys move quickly, shuffling around and splashing water in their wake to get into their new spots.

He doesn't give us any time to get settled. Once Roman is out on the edge with his feet in the water, he's directing us again.

"Camilla, turn and straddle Dima."

Much too happy to oblige, I spin around, making myself dizzy as I drop down on his lap, freezing at the feeling of his stiffening cock poking me at my core. My hips move on their own accord, grinding into him and savoring the blissful friction. My eyes almost bulge out of my skull when I notice the rugged ridges in his shaft, which can only be piercings.

Catching my expression, he winks.

Oh, God. They're going to ruin me.

"Here's what's going to happen, Camilla: you're going to ride Dima and give him what he needs while taking care of Roman with your mouth. Lev is going to continue to tease you with his mouth until you finish at least three times, and then he'll give you a break while you make sure Dina and Roman are satisfied." Abram's tone is commanding and almost businesslike, as if he were sitting in a meeting discussing trade routes and contracts.

"What about you? You're just going to sit and watch like a creep?" I'm not one to kink shame, and maybe watching is fun for him. But I feel irritated that he set this whole game up to get me right where he has me, and now he's not even going to join in? Part of me is a little embarrassed that I turn into such a mess, begging for all of them so easily, and now he gets to sit back, cocky as ever, knowing that I just begged for this, and he's playing the role of director instead of joining in.

Water sloshes up the sides of the tub as he stands. In an instant, he's towering over me, grabbing a fistful of my hair, wrenching my head back to look up at him.

"Careful, love." His cheek brushes against mine as he hisses in my ear, his stubble scratching roughly against my skin. "You almost sound disappointed."

"Disappointed that you want to sit and watch rather than get some for yourself? Not at all, it's your loss." I fall right into his goading. I'm not sure where this confidence in myself came from, but it's fun to watch the vein in his forehead throb as I challenge him. I don't think many people try to push his buttons.

"Oh, love, I'll get my fair share." Petting my hair, he looks at Roman and Dima's hungry stares. "I just need to let them have their turn first. They get antsy when they have to wait, and I'd hate for them to be too rough because they were impatient." Turning his face back to mine, his eyes darken even further, making them look almost entirely black. "Once they're done, then you're mine. And I'll be sure to make you feel it. Wouldn't want you to miss out on what you begged us for."

His lips crash with mine for another brutal kiss. A quick sting followed by the metallic taste of blood fills my mouth as he bites my lip in punishment before taking his spot across the tub once again. Roman's hand replaces his in my hair, pulling roughly and stinging my scalp, dragging my face down to his crotch, where he's freed himself from his shorts.

My mouth waters at the sight of his glistening cock, a combination of pre cum pooling on the tip and the water making it shine in the sunlight. I take him into my mouth, taking my time to swirl my tongue around the tip, the salty taste giving way quickly to the taste of him. Smooth like velvet, my lips glide around his shaft as I sink further and further down with each pass. A loan grows in him as I take a deep pass, feeling him in the back of my throat, swallowing so I can take him even further. As I sink down, I can feel his hand tighten even further in my hair, causing tears to pool in the corner of my eyes from the pain.

My hands are ripped from where they rest on his thighs to be pulled behind my back. I'm almost grateful for the tight grip on my arms, as it saves me from falling over with the way I have to lean over to get to Roman's dick from where I sit in

Dima's lap. Lev must have a hold of my hands because I feel Dima grab both my hips, lifting me and thrusting into me without warning. My scream is muffled by the cock in my mouth, not that I think any of them would care anyway. Out in the middle of the water, no one can hear me or see what we're getting up to. Dima gives me no time to adjust to the size of him, setting a brutal pace with his hips, lifting me with his hands to bring me down and meet him thrust for thrust.

Lev shifts both my hands into one of his, sliding a hand around to my front to alternate palming my breasts. My nipples stiffen instantly, begging for more of the delicious torture. "What a good little whore, look at you choking on Roman's cock while you take Dima." I barely hear Abram's mocking voice over the sound of my choked whimpers and muffled pleas. "One dick just isn't enough for you. You really need all of us to satisfy your greedy cunt?" His words send flutters through my stomach, making me clench around Dima, trying to keep him from pulling away with each thrust.

"So good, kitten." Dima praises, "She squeezes me so hard when you talk to her." He says to Abram.

He laughs, a deep velvety sound bordering on sinister. "Of course she does, she's our needy little whore. She loves this, she begged for this."

I feel my body ramping up, climbing towards that peak that I can't stop chasing since that first night with Roman.

I need to move, to find the friction I need to get myself there before I go insane with wanting. Between their words, their hands, and their dicks, I'm on the verge of self-combusting.

Lev must sense my desperation building, moving a hand down my stomach, brushing my clit with his fingers, ripping an animal-like sound from my chest, cut off by Roman pushing me down even further on his dick, cutting off my air supply.

I try not to panic, telling myself that he'll let me breathe again any second now. My lungs start to protest, causing me to thrash in their hold, fighting to free myself and get some air.

Their hands don't let up, keeping me firmly locked in place. Lev's hand picks up the pace, rubbing in tight circles and just the right amount of pressure, sending me crashing over the edge immediately.

At the exact moment that I cum, Roman lets me pull back and suck in lungfuls of air. My head is clouded, and all the sensations from before are heightened, every touch lifting me higher and higher, right back up to the edge again.

My ears are ringing from the pressure in my head and lack of oxygen to my brain, but I still hear Abram command from his perch.

"That's one, two more."

Fuck, I didn't think he was serious about that. Surely they're both getting close. My jaw is starting to ache from the stretch around Roman and Dima's pace hasn't faltered once, a constant pounding that is bound to leave me aching for days to come.

No sign of stopping in sight, they pick up the pace again. Lev doesn't let up on my clit, his mouth finding the back of my neck, biting and sucking, no doubt leaving marks as he curls over my back, pushing me further into Roman's lap and putting a strain on my neck between the awkward angle and the grip on my hair.

Dima takes over the torture on my nipples, freeing one of his hands as my body becomes more lax, and it takes them less effort to keep me in place. The extra pricks of pain shooting through me from all angles send me spiraling all over again. My vision darkens at the edges as I see stars, becoming halfway comatose as I feel Roman's thighs start to tense.

A string of curses flies from his mouth, and I'm pushed further down onto his dick, once again stealing the air from my lungs and choking me. I've not even come down from the last orgasm, and my body throws me into another. My body thrashes violently, fighting the sensations sending shock waves through every nerve ending, fighting for air, and now fighting to swallow the bursts of cum shooting down my throat.

Tears stream down my face, further obscuring my vision, and I can feel snot dripping from my nose as I fight for my life.

Roman pulls free of my mouth, tilting my chin up with a gentle grip to look at him.

"Good job, *Kukla*." He praises, swiping some spit off my jaw with his thumb, collecting it and pushing it into my mouth, prompting me to suck. His eyes roll back into his head as my lips close around the digit, making him growl in approval.

Lev keeps his fingers on my clit, bringing me back down to Earth and sending tiny jolts through me with his tender touches. Dima's thrusts start to become erratic, jerking my entire body as he chases towards his own finish. Three more

thrusts and he stills, clutching me to his chest so hard that he cracks my back as he spills inside me.

Our labored breathing mingles together as he holds me close to him, giving us both a moment to collect ourselves.

I'm lost in a sea of blissfulness, savoring the feeling of being held between them all with Roman's gentle caresses, Lev's reassuring and soft-spoken words behind me, and Dima's warm embrace.

The ache in my core and the now-overwhelmingly hot water in the tub are the only discomforts sneaking through the crevices of my mind, trying to disrupt my peace.

A new set of hands wraps around my arms from behind, dragging me through the water and into Abram's chest. The blood rushes back into my hands as they're finally released from behind my back, making them tingle with a pins-and-needles sensation.

His stubble scratching my cheek is overstimulating at this point, but I'm too weak to break out of his hold and succumb to him, sitting limply.

"Don't go all soft on me now, Love." He murmurs in my ear, biting my earlobe and awakening my body once more. "Did they wear you out?"

I know it's a carefully laid out trap, but I nod anyway, knowing that he'll have his way with me no matter what my answer is.

"Aw, but you begged for all of us, and you've only had two so far." He feigns sympathy while his hands roam, caressing my breasts and igniting those flutters in my stomach. "The fun's only just begun." His hands band around my waist, lifting me with his effortless strength as he drags himself out of the water to sit perched on the edge of the tub, like Roman was positioned on the other side, but with me on his lap.

The other three watch as he lifts me by the hips, sheathing himself inside me to the hilt and holding me in place.

My mouth falls open at the intense stretch. If it weren't for his hands holding me up, I'd fall face-first back into the water. He hitches his feet around my ankles, spreading his legs apart, and in turn spreading me open to display to the others.

Their eyes bore into me, seeing every inch of my body and settling on where we're joined together. My natural instinct is to close my legs, but Abram's hold on me is quick, not allowing me to hide.

"Lev, what do you think?" He asks over my shoulder.

Lev's eyes snap up from where they'd been staring between my legs, a look of pure hunger dominating his features.

His eyes rake slowly over me, from my face, down to my core, and back up to meet Abram's.

Licking his lips and palming his cock beneath the water, he groans, "She looks like a fucking snack."

"So why don't you have a taste?" Abram's offer shocks me, and he's quick to catch both of my hands, pulling them to the side to keep them from covering myself as Lev starts to slither through the water like a shark on the hunt for its prey.

Sliding up in front of me, his hands grip both of my thighs, burning my skin with his touch.

Shaking my head, I attempt to protest, but Abram quickly shushes me.

"Just relax, he's not afraid of tasting Dima if it means he gets to taste you, right, Lev?"

Lev's answer is to drag his tongue from my opening to my clit in one slow pass, his eyes locked on mine as he does.

His eyes fall shut, and his head falls back as he savors the taste.

"Absolutely," Bringing his eyes back to mine, he looks deranged now, a smirk pulling his lips, "Fucking delectable, Wifey."

With no other prompting, he dives back in, assaulting me with his tongue as he swirls it up and through my core, eating like a starving man and not holding back his moans of approval.

Abram holds me steady, running his hands all over my body and building the heat bubbling up inside. Pulling my head to the side, his lips lock onto my neck, biting my pulse point and making me scream. I feel the soft trickle of blood sliding down my collarbone and onto my chest from where his teeth broke my skin, his tongue coming out to soothe the mark but leaving the blood to run down.

Abram's hips start to move, a slow and lazy rhythm as Lev doubles down on his efforts, biting and sucking my clit.

His teeth scrape lightly on my clit before he bites down, sending me into another crippling orgasm.

I can't even scream this time; my body seizes up, and nothing but air comes out of my mouth.

Abram starts to move faster, using the seat of the hot tub for leverage as he begins to pound into me.

Lev releases my clit, sliding up my body with his tongue, exploring every crook and crevice as he makes his way up. Moving to both of my breasts, he swirls his tongue around each nipple, bringing them to painfully hard points before he stops to meet my eyes.

I try to focus my vision on him, but it's all becoming a blurred mess of colors and light.

His eyes drop down before he leans forward again. I feel his tongue where the blood dripped down onto my chest. He traces the path, following it up to Abram's mark, soothing it once again, and finally bringing his mouth to mine.

His lips maneuver mine, moving them with his to allow his tongue to brush against mine, bringing with it the mingled taste of myself and Dima as he matches his tongue to Abram's thrusts.

I think I black out, my body simply a puppet as they continue to move and shift around me.

I'm not sure how much time has passed when Abram shifts his angle, hitting that spot deep inside my core, making my toes curl with the pressure each pass brings.

I rip my lips from Lev's, a mumbled chorus of protests as I beg with Abram, trying to tell him that I can't take any more.

My body is wrung out, ready to give out if he keeps it up much longer.

"You're not done yet." He growls in my ear, "You begged for this, and you got it. Now, you're going to cum one more time."

My hair hits my face as I shake my head from side to side, refusing to give him another one.

His hand finds that familiar spot in my hair, pulling at the roots and making me hiss.

"One. More." He demands, finding my clit he continues the chant in my ear. His fingers rub tight circles on the bundle of nerves, almost uncomfortably so with the force he puts behind it.

As much as I try to fight it, I can't stop the rush of pleasure as the combination of his fingers and his cock causes an explosion within me once more.

A kaleidoscope of colors flashes in my eyes, blinding me as the waves roll through me. Just as I think I'm coming back down, it rises and peaks again, keeping me in limbo as my body runs through wave after wave.

Even as he stills, twitching deep in my core, it won't stop.

I can feel my limbs shaking with exhaustion, sore from the constant tensing of every muscle. I fight to breathe, but my lungs start to constrict, confused from the overload of adrenaline rushing through my veins.

This time, I actually do black out. My vision was completely cut off as the waves finally stopped.

My body is a live wire, though, every little touch sending sparks through me.

I can hear my tortured whimpers and the murmured words of reassurance, but my eyes are sealed shut.

Vaguely, I can feel myself being moved, feeling weightless as I'm lifted, and the sensation of floating follows.

I'm jolted as someone lays me down on something soft and warm, and I must make another sound because I can feel gentle caresses trying to soothe me as warmth envelops me from all sides.

The words being spoken around me are muffled to the point I can't make them out, and I'm too far gone to try.

The warmth is so welcoming, and the darkness is calm and peaceful, giving my mind a chance to catch up to everything that just happened.

I don't try to fight it, letting myself slip further into the darkness and away from trying to make out anything happening around me.

I know I'll come to at some point, but for now, I'm content to enjoy the peace.

21

Camilla

After the day on the yacht, things seem to fall into place. The last few weeks have been filled with more outings like the one that day, with the guys and me trying new things. It's always at least two of them with me anytime we go out to do something, but the majority of the time, all five of us go out together.

We all have our own little routines that we follow, like lunch dates with Abram, and study dates with Dima, but no matter what we end up doing, I feel light and free for the first time in my life. Leo ceases to exist in this little world that I've created for myself, and I spend more time drunk off sex than I do anything else.

If I'm not with any of the guys, I'm with Gio, and we've been steadily working through my bucket list of life. I got to see the water when the guys took me out on the yacht, but with Gio, I've tried nearly all the foods on my list that I've never had. From fast food to sushi, Korean barbecue, and Greek cuisine, I've found a lot of new things that I've clearly been missing out on.

Gio took me to the mall to walk around and shop, roller-skate, and bowl. He even took me to a bar that doubles as an arcade, making fun of me the entire day as I progressively got more wasted and became obsessed with the ski ball game.

It slipped out to the guys at some point that I had a bucket list of sorts, and they badgered me until I finally told them about some of the things I never got to do.

That led to Roman and Lev taking me out to an aquarium one town over, walking through patiently with me as I fawned over every single exhibit they had to offer. Abram and Dima took me to a zoo, which turned out to be a shorter trip than planned. It just made me sad to see all the animals caged the way they were; it hit a little too close to home for me to really enjoy.

I've had so much fun, getting to live my life freely and do all the childish things that I could think of. One thing about hanging around the guys, though, I was becoming a bit insatiable. No matter where we ended up, or what we were doing, I always seemed to end up right back at their house, naked in one of their beds.

The four of us have all only hooked up together one other time outside of the yacht, but I always have at least two of them. The things they do should probably concern me, like their obsession with choking me every time we fuck, or the way that my body reacts to it and craves it. But being with multiple men at once already isn't exactly a normal thing, so I haven't concerned myself too much with the details of it all.

I've been keeping up with my classes really well, even with my extracurricular activities. I worked out a good schedule for myself, giving myself plenty of time to make it back to the dance studio, keep up my practice, and get some well-needed stress relief. However, Roman usually joins me, watching quietly from the corner of the room as I push myself to my limits.

Leo's therapy sessions still suck, and I'd give anything to blow them off every week. However, I still go and suffer through, not giving Leo any opportunity to ruin my college experience.

Speaking of Leo, his name flashes up on my phone screen again, for the fifth time in the last twenty minutes, alerting me to another text that I quickly skim before swiping to delete it. He stopped trying to call me after about a week of the calls going unanswered. He never had anything important to say, only ever calling to verbally attack me, calling me a whore, or worthless, or any of the other uncreative insults he could muster up.

Initially, I wasn't ignoring his calls on purpose, per se. I was spending so much time with the guys that I just missed their calls, not wanting to answer in front of them and risk them hearing anything that might raise questions. But when there were no repercussions for unanswered calls, I decided to keep ignoring them.

His texts are more persistent, only becoming increasingly angry in tone the longer I go without responding. But I figure that he has too much going on in his perfect little world to do anything about it, so what's the worst that can happen? I won't let him bait me into an argument over whether or not I'm a useless excuse of a human and if I *deserve* to be his wife. I would gladly give the opportunity to anyone else and live happily on the streets by myself, far away from the so-called empire that he's building with my father.

Pushing away any thoughts of Leo, along with the lingering feelings from my therapy session for the day, I pick up my pace, eager to get back to my dorm and change before Abram picks me up to take me over to their house for the night. We're all supposed to have a movie marathon tonight, watching some dystopian franchise that was released when I was at Briarwood. It's more of a tween romance, but they all agreed to watch because there's some action, with the divergents creating their own rebellion.

I'm excited to watch the movies, but I'm even more excited to spend a chill night at the house with all four of the guys. And I'll admit, I am hoping to have a repeat of our day on the yacht... everyone wins.

Checking the time before I pocket my phone, I see I have about half an hour before Abram's supposed to pick me up. Rushing up to my dorm, I barely make it through the threshold before I'm slammed from the side, knocked into the wall hard enough to steal the air from my lungs while a hand locks around my throat.

I claw at the hand around my neck, trying to pry the fingers from my skin and get some air, but they only tighten further as the demented voice fills my ears.

"Well, well. Hello there, *wife*." Leo's evil sneer stares back at me, inches in front of my face. His hand tightens even further, pinching my skin and making my eyes bulge with the lack of oxygen. "Nothing to say to your husband? After I came all this way to surprise you?"

I try my hardest to tell him to go to Hell, but it just comes out as incoherent gasps.

"Just as rude as before, I see." He yanks his hand away, not caring as my legs give out beneath me, leaving me to slide down the wall into a heap on the floor.

"What are you doing here?" I ask when I can catch my breath, shooting daggers at him from where I sit.

Fixing his cuff links, he seems completely unbothered. "I can't stop by to see how my wife is adjusting to her little college experience? It's not like you could tell me how it's going, seeing as you refuse to answer any of my calls." His face shifts from impassive to stone, glaring down at me while he tucks his hands into his pockets. "Which I believe I specifically told you to answer, did I not?"

I refuse to answer, not giving him the satisfaction of thinking that I'm going to follow any of his bullshit rules.

"I allow you to have a phone. I allow you to come to school. I allow you to spend time with your little friend, and I don't say a thing about it." He emphasizes each point with a step towards me, until finally, he's towering over me, making me feel an inch tall, like a child being scolded. "I allow you to do all of these things, and you repay me by ignoring me?"

Head tilted, he waits for an answer. Of course, there's no correct answer in this scenario.

"I've been busy with classes and therapy." My voice is cracked and raspy from the assault to my throat, but I push through the discomfort to get the words out.

"Yes, therapy." He laughs without humor, "Therapy where you sit and refuse to participate most of the time, right?"

Faster than I can react, he has a hand fisted in my hair, dragging me up off the floor and making me cry out when I feel a couple of strands get ripped from my scalp.

"I know you might think you can get away with this crap since you used to sneak around behind your father's back, but that won't fly with me." He speaks through clenched teeth, spit flying through his lips and landing on my cheeks with my head locked in his steel grasp. "Keep this up, and instead of a wedding band on your finger, I'll lock a collar around your neck and walk you down the aisle on a leash."

My temper flares. Fighting against his hold, I push forward to slam my hands into his chest.

"Seems pretty fitting since all you want me for is to be your *bitch*. Why don't you save yourself the trouble and just cut me loose, go find yourself someone willing to lie down and spread their legs for you and answer your every beck and call."

Laughing, his hand captures my throat again, pulling me so close that our noses touch.

"Oh, but I hear that you've gotten fairly good at spreading your legs since you've been gone."

I feel my blood run cold, freezing me from deep inside my veins, and the shock registers in my mind.

He knows.

"Thought I wouldn't find out about that, huh?" He slams my back into the wall, causing my head to bounce roughly against the drywall. "I was mad at first, I'll admit. But then I found out who you were whoring yourself out to, and the irony was just too much for me. I think the best part about it is, you don't even know."

"They run the Bratva, I'm well aware." I don't even try to deny the fact that I'm fucking them. If he brought it up, then he already knows or has his suspicions, so my answer doesn't matter either way. "What's that say about how I feel about you that I would rather be their *whore* than your wife?"

The twitch in his hand is the only indication that my words struck a nerve; his face remains emotionless, studying me closely.

"It feels almost as good as knowing that you're enjoying whoring yourself out to the men responsible for your brother's death, and you don't have a clue."

My heart stops beating, it's gone from my chest, ripped out, and on the floor, I don't know, but there's a gaping hole left where it should be.

I heard the words he just spoke to me, but my mind can't comprehend them. There's no way that it can be true. This has to be another one of his tricks to fuck with my head. He wants me to feel bad about what I've been doing with them, so I won't be as upset about marrying him, as if that's the safer option. That's laughable. The only thing this would prove, if it's even true, is that there's absolutely nowhere for me to be safe in this world, no one I can trust.

Stepping back, he takes pleasure in watching me as my world crumbles down around me. Thoughts and memories bombarding my brain, questions of what if he's right, and the small voice in my head saying that the guys wouldn't do that to me, war with each other until my ears ring from the blinding pressure building in my skull.

The pure pleasure on his face at watching me fall apart makes me sick to my stomach. He truly is a sick son of a bitch to be getting joy out of any of this. And once again, I'm one step behind everyone.

Dante died, and I was the last to know; that too was turned into a sick joke, something for my Father to take joy in my pain. Then, I was locked up for years, while everyone's world continued to spin, relationships, experiences, time to grieve, and simple comforts all stripped away from me. Now, I get my first taste of freedom, a chance to make my own decisions and choose my own friends, and my own hookups, and again it's all just a big joke to everyone around me.

I don't want to fall for Leo's tricks if he is lying about the guys. But what reason does he have not to be telling the truth right now?

"I am so glad that I came all this way to tell you this in person. This is priceless." He beams, looking every part the villain that he is. He moves towards the door, stopping abruptly to turn around again. "Oh, I almost forgot." Digging in his jacket pocket, he pulls out a piece of cardstock, offering it to me and letting it flutter to the floor when I make no move to accept it. "I figured I'd deliver our wedding invitation while I was out here so you could see it. A Christmas wedding, it'll be perfect, well, for me."

Snapping out of my trance-like state, I process his words.

"Christmas? That's only halfway through the school year, you said-"

"I said you could have a year away. That deal became null and void when you decided to sleep with scum behind my back." He doesn't mask his disgust, not feigning amusement any longer.

I don't try to mask my rage, anger replacing the ice in my veins as the severity of the situation starts to sink in.

"That's bullshit! You have no right to go back on your word and drag me away from here six months earlier than you said!"

"I have every right, because in case you've forgotten, I *own* you." His chest begins to heave as he gets worked up, his face becoming red. His hand strikes out, I hear the sound of the backhand being delivered a split second before I feel it, pain blooming across my cheek and a sting in my bottom lip.

"Your little college experiment is done, and you'll walk down that aisle, willing, and say 'I do' to seal your fate for good. You have three weeks before I send Michael to collect you, so whatever soul searching you need to do, I suggest you do it fast." He's made his way back to the door now, dismissing the conversation, but not before he delivers his final blow. "Don't do anything stupid. If you run, or try to kill yourself again, I'll be sure to take it out on your little friend, what was his name again? Gio? From what I've heard, he could be a suitable replacement if you can't fulfill your duties."

The door slams shut behind him, leaving me in silence, with disgust filling me and bile creeping up my throat.

I stand frozen against the wall, unable to move and comprehend everything that just happened. I don't even realize that I'm crying until I taste the salty flavor on my lips as the tears track down my face.

Starting down at the cardstock lying on the floor, I'm paralyzed with fear. I don't want to look and see the date, real and in print. That seems to make it too real, but I know putting it off won't make any difference.

Picking it up, I'm faced with a beautiful design.

Red rose petals form the backdrop, overlaid with a gold emblem of overlapping lines and vines resembling a crest. A swirling font fills the open space of the crest, with both our names and the date that signifies the end of my life as I know it.

December 24th, 2025

Crimson red droplets fall onto the edge of the invitation, drawing my attention back to my face, realizing that Leo must have split my lip when he struck me.

The blood blends into the rose petals, easily missed unless you're looking for it. It makes me wonder if it'll be as easy to hide all the wounds he plans to inflict on me once he has me tied to him forever.

This isn't just a wedding invitation, it's a ticking time bomb, counting down until my life is officially over.

I'm at a loss for what to do. I don't know who I can trust, and even if the guys didn't have anything to do with Dante, they can't help me out of this like I once had hoped. Even if there was something they could do, I can't put Gio in a position to be hurt. Gio's always been there for me, a shoulder to cry on and a constant support. I'd take my fate ten times over if it meant he was out of harm's way. Losing Dante almost killed me; losing Gio as well would destroy my soul.

Utterly exhausted, my legs begin to shake with the effort of standing. I don't have the energy to make it to my bed, opting to sink down the wall into a heap on the floor.

Out of hope and all out of fight, I let the cool floor try to tame down the heat in my cheek, wishing the floor would open and consume me.

It's almost worse that Leo's left me here for another three weeks rather than taking me away now. He's left me with nothing but time to sit and dwell on everything that I'm about to lose. How am I supposed to carry on and enjoy all the little things I've come to love?

I suppose this is his final trick before the grand finale. Maybe he's secretly hoping that I will try to end my suffering before our 'big day'. It would mean an easy out for him. But the bigger picture is that I can't do that.

Now, to just remind myself of that as my clock runs out.

22

Dima

Everything is going to shit.

Things were going well; we had Camilla to ourselves, getting close to us, sharing experiences, and the sex was fantastic.

Was being the keyword.

She blew off our plans for a movie night a week ago, making up some excuse about being sick when Abram went to pick her up. That alone isn't that suspicious, but it was every day following that. She's locked herself in her dorm, only coming out to go to the gym with Gio accompanying her, acting like her bodyguard. She's skipped class, therapy, everything. And she won't open the door for any of us.

We're all racking our brains for what could have happened, but we're coming up blank.

Abram thinks we should give her some space, let her come to us if and when she's ready. I, on the other hand, don't share the same sentiment. That's why I'm standing outside of her dorm, checking the hallway for any students before I work on picking the lock.

Since she started skipping classes, I've been trying to keep an eye on her. I watched from across the quad as she headed to the gym with Gio a half hour ago, which means I have about another half hour before she's back.

I don't want to invade her privacy, but with her ignoring us, our options are limited. So, I'm taking it upon myself to snoop around and see if there's anything I can find to try and figure out what the fuck is going on.

Picking the lock is child's play; taking a look around her dorm room, it's very plain. She doesn't have many things, leaving the room very bare. The only personal items she seems to have, aside from her clothes strewn about the bed and floor, are a knitted blue blanket and a sketch pinned to the wall. Upon closer inspection, the sketch is of her, complete with a note at the bottom, addressing her as "Future Mrs. Marino", telling me it's from Lev.

The dorms here aren't huge by any means, but they're roomy enough. Plenty of space for a full-sized bed, a futon, and a small kitchenette area in the corner. She has a small stack of books by her bed, all romance books based on the cheesy covers, but other than that, there's not much. No TV, no computer, no tablet. What does she do in her free time?

Feeling deflated with nothing to go on, I dig through her backpack, looking for anything at this point. Her bag is filled with various papers from all her classes, notes, assignments, and enrollment forms from earlier in the semester. I find a stack of documents for our joint project, reminding me that she's been blowing off our planning sessions, flaring my irritation again.

Just as I'm putting everything back in the bag, a thick slip of paper falls from the stack onto the floor. Curious, I pick it up. My blood begins to boil as I process what I'm seeing. A fucking wedding invitation clutched between my fingers, becoming wrinkled from my increasingly tense grip. The wedding isn't a surprise, that much we knew already, even if she wouldn't give us details. The date is a bit of a shock; we didn't think it'd be happening this soon since she spoke so highly of going to college. We thought she'd finish school before the wedding. What truly has my blood boiling is the name of her intended husband, listed in the mockingly elegant script.

Leonardo Ivanni

One of the most deranged up-and-coming heads of the Italian mafia. He's been shadowing his father for years now, murdered his brother to ensure that he was the only heir, and is a power-hungry son of a bitch. Their family's legacy isn't one built on morals; it's built on greed and power.

This isn't good.

Camilla can't be tied to a monster like him. I'm not sure that she'd survive that. Even if she did manage to hold her own, the only fate with a man like him is a shallow grave. She's likely going to be used to give him an heir, and once that purpose is served, she'll either be disposed of or sold off to one of their trafficking rings to make him a quick buck.

Why wouldn't she tell us this? We could help her, or at least get her away from here, hide her away where that sick fuck couldn't find her. Instead, she cut us off; it doesn't make sense.

She admitted that she knew we were in the Bratva. I'm betting she doesn't know the depth of that statement. We ran the fucking Bratva; our families combined were the most powerful thing the Bratva's seen in years. No one could come close to overthrowing us, and we were well respected all over. Years back, our families had a war with her elders, one that the Bratva wasn't well equipped for at the time, which resulted in us leaving what would now be her father's territory. Our elders went back home to build and grow their own empire, spanning their reach all across Europe, while silently sneaking into her father's territory to build business and develop a small network of allies, so when the time came again for a war, we had no shot of losing.

Unbeknownst to Camilla, she might just be the catalyst for that war.

We may have only known her for a short time, but that doesn't change our feelings for her. She is *ours*. She was Dante's flesh and blood, but beyond that, she's wrapped herself through us like a winding vine; it would kill us all to let her go. And to see her taken away by a monster to be used and abused rather than wined and dined for the rest of her time on Earth, we won't stand for it. Her eyes hold shadows of sadness and pain that we want to wipe away, replace with light and happiness. We won't have that ruined by someone like Leonardo Ivanni.

Out of time, I shove the invite in my pocket, putting all the papers back into the bag relatively as I found them. Looking around, I make sure I didn't disturb anything else and slip out, checking that I lock the door behind me before heading home.

I get back to the house the same time Roman is pulling in the drive, most likely from watching Camilla at the gym as he usually does, though she doesn't know he's doing now, since officially she banned him from joining her after she cut us off. He hasn't stopped; he's just gone back to more creative, borderline stalker tactics.

"Where have you been?" He asks, swinging his leg over his bike and pocketing his keys.

The drive home allowed my brain to wander, only building my frustration and anger back up. I'm on edge and desperate for a solution to this whole mess that Camilla's landed in.

Ignoring his question, I rush towards the door. "Where are the others?" I ask over my shoulder.

"Abram was in his office when I left, and Lev was headed in there so they could look over some of the details Charlotte sent from the file on Franklin's computer."

I don't need to tell him to follow; he falls in step behind me as I rush through the house and slam the door to his office open.

They both sit hunched over a phone in the center of the desk, their startled expressions looking up in synchrony. I hear Charlotte's voice filtering through the other end of the phone, but Abram must notice my urgency and Roman's appearance behind me.

"Charlotte, we'll have to call you back." He cuts her off, ending the call without waiting for a response. "What's wrong?"

"I was just at Camilla's," I start, immediately interrupted.

"I thought we agreed to give her space," He sighs, rubbing the bridge of his nose between two fingers.

"*You* suggested that, *we* never agreed to it."

"But you should give her space. If she's upset about something, then I'm sure she'll come to us about it." He tries to reason, but it must sound weak even to his own ears. His expression is unsure, but hopeful, like he's trying to make himself believe what he's saying.

Tossing the invitation onto the desk, I let them all have a look. "Well, we're on a time crunch, it seems."

They all look at it with furrowed brows.

"She's getting married in three weeks?" Lev looks up with wide eyes. "I didn't think it was happening that fast."

"That's not the only issue."

Nodding to the invitation, they drop their heads to study it closely.

"Shit." Roman hisses, at the same time, Lev's face drains of all color.

Abram remains oddly silent, staring a hole through the desk.

"The fucking Ivanni's? Why the fuck would she not tell us this?" Lev starts to pace behind the desk, pulling his hair by the roots.

"Fuck that, why didn't she tell us she only had three fucking weeks left!" Roman explodes next to me. "I know she said this was all just fun while she was here, but I thought that meant longer than a few weeks."

"Maybe she didn't know." Abram finally speaks, sounding worlds away.

Lev stops in place, spinning to stare at him, "It's an *arranged* marriage, how the fuck would she not know?"

"Because it's Leo fucking Ivanni!" He snaps out of whatever trance he's been in, jumping out of his chair, knocking it to the floor behind him to stand with his hands braced on the desk. "You know the world that he comes from, you've heard the same stories I have about the bastard."

"You think he sprung this on her?" I clarify, having the same gut feeling myself.

"I think Camilla is good at holding her cards close to her chest, but something tells me she would've thrown herself into school as much as she did and jump into this fling with us if she knew it was only going to last a couple of weeks."

He has a point there. Since we found her, she's been bright-eyed and eager about trying new things and excited even over the boring classes she's enrolled in. It doesn't make sense for her to be that excited over such mundane things if she knew she'd only have the opportunity to experience them for a couple of weeks at most.

It just doesn't make sense why she's shutting us out. Why wouldn't she come to us with this? I know she made it clear that this was just a fling, a little bit of fun, but surely she knows she can trust us.

"Well, what are we going to do about it? She's not even talking to us right now. Are we supposed to just let her get walked down the aisle to that psycho and move on? 'Hey, your pussy is to die for, you seem to be in some deep shit though. Have a nice life," Lev stands with arms wide open, looking between the three of us with raised brows.

"Obviously not." Roman snaps.

Abram rights his chair, settling into it to rest his head in his hands.

"I might have an idea," He trails off, leaving Lev's impatience to fill the silence.

"Well, feel free to share with the class, we're on a tight schedule here."

Cryptic as ever, he starts throwing out instructions. "Lev, get with Charlotte and see if she can find any details for the venue listed on here. Layout, guest list, even the fucking caterers, anything she can find." Passing off the instructions, he looks to Roman, "You're with me, there are some documents we need to comb through, and we need to figure out what the Ivanni's have worked out with her father with this deal."

Lev rushes out, already dialing his phone to get started on his task, while Roman drags a chair over to the desk to get comfortable, leaving me.

"And me?" I ask.

As he looks up from the desk, he has a new, determined glint in his eyes, our fearless leader fully back in place.

"Keep an eye on her, make sure you know where she's at. When we get everything sorted out here, I'll let you know."

I'm not one to complain about watching Camilla; I've done it enough, and it's really no hardship. Knowing where she's at eases my nerves more than blindly going through each day, wondering if she's going to disappear on us again. But I'm not sure where Abram is going with this plan. I trust him with my life, but it doesn't mean I love being in the dark.

"And then?" I ask, needing more direction than just playing stalker.

His mouth ticks up into a crooked grin, "Then you bring her here." He says. And just like that, I don't care what the rest of the plan is; all I care about is that I get to bring her back to us.

We made a promise to Dante, and we've all decided beyond that promise that we want to keep her.

She can hide all she wants, but she's not getting away.

23

Camilla

What do you do when your life is ending before your very eyes? You blow off classes, go out, and get wasted.

Seems simple enough.

What else do I have to do with my time?

Going to class is laughable at this point; there's no reason to it if I'm not going to be here past the first semester. Fucking the guys is only going to lead to endless painful memories while I'm suffering in my new life, plus I fear that if I see any of them now that I know my time is up, that I'll break down and tell them in some convoluted hope that they can save me.

The only person I've allowed myself to see since Leo's visit is Gio. It may be selfish, but I want to spend time with him and make up for all the time we lost. On a deeper level, I know that I'm staying close to him because I'm fearful that someone is going to come and take him away, even though it was a threat to keep me in line; I can't stand thinking about anything happening to him if Leo feels that I'm not staying in line.

I'm lucky that he's such a great friend; he knows something is up, but hasn't pushed me on it. I'm too much of a coward to tell him about my new deadline; I'd rather his last few days with me be happy instead of brooding and depressed. Plus, he'd spend all our time trying to find me a way out of this, and it would only make it harder for him when he realizes that nothing will work. Not to mention that he'd potentially be signing his own life away by doing so.

I've kept it pretty tame throughout the week, skipping classes to sulk in my room by myself and inviting Gio over to drink and binge-watch movies at night. But tonight was finally the weekend, so I didn't feel as bad about convincing him that we should go out to party tonight.

"You really think this is a good idea?" He asks for the fifteenth time while I finish applying eyeliner.

"No," I cap the pen, turning to grin at him over my shoulder. "I think it's a *great* idea."

Gio's boyfriend came over with him one night this week and let it slip that there was a fight night going on with two of the frats tonight. Free booze, eye candy, and entertainment, naturally, I jumped on the opportunity to tag along.

Gio was worried; he thought it was too violent for me to be around.

Joke's on him, this might be a glimpse into my new life based on the backhand Leo delivered the other morning.

Gio tried to insist that we go back to the club I danced at a few weeks ago instead, but it's now tainted with memories of Lev and Roman, so I quickly shut that down.

Slipping into my mini black dress, I toss on a cropped leather jacket with some Chucks. Ignoring the fact that it's near freezing outside, I grab my phone and some cash into my pocket before ushering him out the door.

Walking to the car, I feel the hairs on the back of my neck stand up, instantly putting me on edge. The feeling of being watched sobers me up from the shots I took while getting ready, replacing it with fear. Leo said he wouldn't send Michael for another two weeks. At this point, I wouldn't be surprised if he brought him for his little visit and left him to keep watch this whole time.

Well fuck him.

If he wants to hear about me going out and getting drunk off my ass, then so be it. I'm not breaking any of his rules by living out my freedom for a couple more days.

The drive is quick, only taking about twenty minutes before we're pulling up to an abandoned skating rink. People linger in the parking lot, coolers full of drinks and stereos blasting music.

Inside the rink is not as run-down as it looked from the outside. Bars are set up in various spots on the outskirts of the room, spotlights are set up over a ring in the center of the room, complete with a cage surrounding the outside to keep spectators from entering. Music blares from various speakers, making the floor rattle beneath our feet. There are no spectator seats; it looks to be standing room only, with a few raised platforms, roped off with loose ropes like the ring in the center of the room, that seem to be first-come, first-served.

Obviously, that's where I want to be, grabbing Gio's hand, I drag him behind me as I shuffle through the crowd, making it to one of the platforms without much issue and climbing up. Gio follows right behind me, giving me a look before shaking his head.

"Never one to do anything casually, are you?"

Shrugging innocently, I turn to take in the surroundings now that we're elevated above the crowd.

"I'll just ask Derek to bring us some drinks up here." He types away on his phone, but I'm distracted by the eye candy that is some of the fighters off to the far end of the room, warming up and getting taped.

They're all shredded, all muscles on display, and low-slung gray sweats settled on their hips. Most of them have headphones on, lost in their own minds, while others are talking to whoever I assume are their coaches. It's like an all-you-can-eat buffet, the way they're all just laid out in front of us to devour with our eyes.

I wish I weren't still hung up on the guys. I feel like a victory celebration with one of the night's winners could be fun. Just as quickly as the idea comes to mind, I feel nauseous, flickers of Abram, Dima, Lev, and Roman's faces flashing before my eyes at once, imagining their disappointment.

"Hey," Derek pulls me out of my thoughts, shaking me. I take the drink he offers, giving him a weak smile in return. Discreetly, he grabs Gio's hand, giving it a quick squeeze before releasing it.

Gio finally admitted that he was dating Derek about a week ago, not that I was surprised. But he did tell me that while they were happy together so far, they weren't ready to be open about it out in public. It made me sad to think they felt they had to hide who they were, but I got it. Coming from the life that I do, I know how intense families like Gio's and mine could be, plus it wasn't my place to tell them what they should do. As long as they were happy together, that's all that mattered; the chance to openly share that happiness would come eventually.

"Camilla, are you bringing any of your boy toys tonight?" Derek asks, earning a look from Gio.

"I told you that was done." He hisses at him, looking at me to gauge my reaction.

I didn't tell Gio about Leo's visit or anything he said about the guys or his threats. He thinks that things just fizzled out, and we all agreed to go our separate ways. How much of that does he actually believe? I'm not sure, but he hasn't made a big deal about it.

I shoot Gio a smile, silently letting him know it's fine.

"Not my boys, so no, they won't be here," I tell Derek.

His pout is adorable, "Why? I saw three of you together at my party; you guys were hot. And I've seen you around campus since then. It looked like all four of you were getting cozy."

"It was just some fun, nothing more." I throw back my drink, hoping the conversation comes to an end. Luckily, he lets it go, sidling up next to Gio as the announcer comes over the mic to announce the first fight.

The fights are fast and ruthless, all the fighters look like they have some vendetta against their opponent, and no one is willing to go down easily. Unlike fights that I've seen on TV before, this is more like a street fight, no gloves, and seemingly no rules. It seems pretty straightforward: go in the cage and win, or get your ass knocked out. We're only three fights in, and the amount of blood that's been shed already should be sickening. But something in me loves the ruthlessness of it, cheering them on like gladiators fighting in ancient times.

One of Derek's friends from the frat made his way over, talking to him over the divider that separates us from the rest of the crowd. I didn't think anything of it, but now, seeing the way Gio's tensed all over and shaking his head, I'm curious what it's about.

I would ask, but I'm buzzing off the many drinks Gio and Derek have supplied me with and am not willing to kill the buzz.

"Just ask her." I hear the guy tell them over the music.

Buzz be damned, my curiosity is now at the forefront of my mind. "Ask who, what?" Slipping between the two of them, I look from them to the random guy who walked up, waiting for someone to answer.

"James is president of one of the frats hosting tonight," Derek is the one to answer. "They always have ring girls for the headliners, but the girl who was supposed to do it got in a fight with her boyfriend earlier, one of the fighters, and now is refusing to do it."

Okay, I would have thought there was a much bigger issue than lacking a ring girl, given Gio's body language during this whole exchange. I'm not seeing the big problem here.

"Okay, so what?"

"So I was asking Derek if you'd be interested?" The guy speaks to me this time, "I know you danced at his party, it was hot as fuck. And you get free drinks on the house."

"You want me to be a ring girl?" I clarify.

"Camilla, you don't have to. We just came out to have fun." Gio interjects.

We did come out to have fun, and dancing around the ring between fights, having a front-row seat to all the sweaty muscles and action, sounds like a fantastic time.

"Sounds like a blast," I tell Gio, turning to James to add, "I'm in."

Gio reluctantly agrees, telling me that he'll meet me after the fight back out front. I would feel bad about ditching him if he didn't have Derek with him, but honestly, tonight has just made me feel like a third wheel. I'm happy for them, but hanging out and watching their secret glances and stolen touches reminds me of my own loneliness.

I decided to have fun and drown my sorrows, so that's what I'm going to do.

In a flash, James leads me to a storage room in the back that acts as a dressing room of sorts. One of the sorority girls helping out shoves an outfit in my hands and pushes me behind a curtain to change.

Within minutes, I'm following James back through the crowd towards the cage, dressed in a latex black and red two-piece outfit that leaves little to the imagination. The combination of the alcohol in my system and the dim lighting of the rink helps ease my concerns about my scars being visible.

He gives me a quick rundown, but it's not rocket science. Grab the card, walk the ring, get out of the cage, repeat.

The crowd gets something slutty to look at, and I get drunk. Everybody wins.

Watching the fights from the ring side is much different, more intense. I may be a bit blood thirsty, because I'm loving it.

As the bell rings to signal the end of another round, I down the last of my drink, jumping to my feet. The room sways around me, but I manage to steady myself fast as the two bloodied fighters retreat to their own corners.

One of the refs holds the ropes open as I slip in, grabbing the number plaque.

Strutting from one side of the ring to the other, I feel absolutely full of myself, on display with the roaring sounds of the crowd blending into a muted buzz. All of the faces are just blurs in a dark sea faded behind the spotlights shining on the ring, which is probably why I don't feel any nerves even though I know there are a couple of hundred eyes on me right now.

Stepping out of the ring, I manage to catch a glimpse of Gio still on the platform across the room. I expected him to look relaxed and like he was having fun, but instead, he's waving his hands at me, looking frantic and trying to tell me something, but he's too far away to read his lips.

I can't understand what he'd be on edge about and trying to tell me, nothing out of the norm is going on within the ring compared to the last hour.

I don't have any time to figure out what he was trying to tell me, as soon as the door is opened to the cage and I step out, I'm snatched up. A shoulder digs into my stomach as I come face-to-face with a broad back cloaked in a dark t-shirt.

The floor blurs beneath us as my captor weaves through the crowd. I can see feet shuffling out of the way as they make a path to carry me effortlessly out of the rink and into the crisp night air.

My instincts kick in, and I start to fight. Raining punches down on the broad back under me that I'm positive hurt me worse than them. I manage to get one kick in before an arm bands over both legs, locking them in place a split second before a heavy hand delivers a stinging slap to my left ass cheek.

Stunned for a moment, my fear is muted as my brain tries to catch up to what the fuck just happened.

Another slap to the other cheek makes my anger flare, and I'm thoroughly annoyed by the situation now. Reigniting my fight, I double down my efforts, slapping and punching anywhere I can reach, squirming from left to right, trying to dislodge their grasp.

"Put me down, you big bastard!" I yell in hopes that someone out here will hear and help me.

Of course, there's no such luck as they continue through the lot without a single soul stopping us.

The shoulder in my stomach vibrates with laughter, causing my whole body to shake.

"Oh, kitten." Dima's rich velvety voice filters through the blood pounding in my ears as I still. "Your time to hide is up."

I'm so fucked.

24

Camilla

Dima drives with ease, whistling along with the radio without a care in the world, while I stew in my anger and try my best to ignore his presence.

After carrying me through the parking lot like a sack of potatoes over his shoulder, he ungracefully dumped me in the passenger seat, making sure to engage the child locks before jumping behind the wheel, which leads us to now.

I don't need to ask where he's taking me, recognizing the drive towards their house just off campus.

Figures, just as I was out and having fun, clearing my mind of all the bullshit going on around me, one of the four men I'm desperately trying to forget shows up to steal me away - literally.

I spend the entire drive thinking of how I can slip away from him before he drags me inside the house, because he will have to drag me. I know as soon as I go inside and see all four of them that I'm at risk of spilling all my secrets in a desperate attempt at being saved. But I can't do that to them; none of this is their issue, and the bottom line is I still barely know them.

There's also the seed of doubt still ringing in my mind about what Leo said, about them being responsible for Dante.

I've looked at it from every angle in all of my alone time, and it just doesn't add up. Dante told me about his friends from time to time, and I'd heard some of them in the background when he'd call to check up on me. I'd recognize their names, or their voices, right?

Nothing about any of them was familiar in my mind. That's not something that I would just forget. I had three years at Briarwood to rethink every text, every phone conversation. I would have remembered them.

Dante pulls up to the house, and I'm no closer to having a plan. Seems I'll just have to wing it.

Without a word, he exits the car, rounding the front to come to the passenger side. He barely has the door open a crack when I kick out, knocking the door open and him back a couple of steps in the process. I take my opening, slipping out of the car and sprinting down the driveway.

Suddenly, I'm so grateful that I decided to wear Chucks tonight.

Once I get to the end of the drive, I don't take a second to think, turning right to head back towards campus. I only make it about fifteen feet before a hand tugs a chunk of my hair, wrenching my head back as I'm tackled from behind. Dima tucks his body around mine to take the brunt of the fall as we land in a heap in the grass. Scrambling to get up is no hope; he has me pinned under him in seconds, slamming my hands to the grass up by my head, staring down at me like a predator.

"Oh, kitten, you thought you could run from me? That's cute."
His head tilts as he studies me hungrily. Leaning down, he
slides his nose up the side of my neck, inhaling deeply before
whispering in my ear. "But you should know that I love to
chase." His teeth sink into my earlobe, making me hiss as my
body comes alive for the first time in over a week.

He stands, dragging me up by my wrists and tossing me over
his shoulder once again, only laughing when my fists start
beating on his back again.

Another slap to my ass has him laughing. "You can fight all
you want, but I'm not letting you go, and I have the perfect
opening for retribution." He makes his point by slapping the
other cheek.

I don't let up, raining hits and kicks anywhere I can land them
as he steps over the threshold and into the house.

"Let me down, you ape!"

"Why are you holding her like that?" I can hear Lev ask from
somewhere.

"What the fuck is she wearing?" Abram's voice rings out at the
same time.

Dima stops in the middle of the living room, making me dizzy
as he spins to face them.

"Kitten decided to run, so I got to chase and didn't want to let
her slip away again. That was after I found her playing ring
girl at the frat fight night."

"Just put her down already." Roman finally chimes in with something productive.

Dima does just that, dropping me onto the couch without any grace. Pushing my hair out of my face, I go to roll to the right, but am quickly blocked by Roman, sitting on the couch and blocking my path. Turning the other way, I'm met with Lev as he takes the other side, leaving Dima to sit on the coffee table in front of me, effectively boxing me in.

Defeated and exhausted already, I throw myself against the back cushions, waiting for whatever it is they brought me here for.

"Hey, wifey." Lev stretches out beside me, tossing an arm over the back of the couch. "Haven't seen you in a minute."

"Would've been longer if I weren't kidnapped and brought here against my will."

Dima rolls his eyes. "Kidnapped is such a strong word."

"Oh, really? Is it? What would you call it then?"

Tilting his head, he scratches his chin, "Assisted motivation and transportation."

"Motivation for what, exactly?"

Abram answers this time, from where he stands in front of the mantle, "To sit down and talk to us."

"I don't think we have anything to talk about, so if that's all, I think I'll see myself out." I go to stand from the couch, only to be brought back down by Roman's hand on my shoulder.

The look on his face tells me they're not letting me out of here without saying their piece.

"What do you want to talk about?" I look back to Abram, standing stoic with his arms crossed.

"I think we deserve some explanation. You ditched us out of nowhere, and now you've been ignoring us."

"I don't owe you anything," I argue, annoyed that this is the argument he wants to start with.

"No? You sleep with all of us for weeks, start to get close to us, and let us catch real feelings for you, and then cut us off without a word?"

I look at each of them, waiting for someone else to see how ridiculous this is, but all of them look back with expectant stares, waiting.

"I told all of you from the start that this was a temporary thing. This was never going to be serious or long-term. It's not my fault you didn't listen." Throwing my hands up in the air, I add, "I'm getting married! You knew this wasn't going anywhere."

He laughs without humor, "Funny you mention that."

I don't see why that would be funny to him. It was a valid point, one that I made before we all hooked up in that hot tub weeks ago. Gio made hooking up sound easygoing; he never warned me that the hookups would come back, demanding answers for why it was called off.

"How so?"

"Because you made it seem like you would be around a lot longer than three weeks before you'd be walking down the aisle." Lev offers.

"How did you-"

"How did we know?" Abram cuts me off. "Don't worry about that." He begins to pace in front of the mantle. "Did Leo find out about us? Is that why you cut things off so soon? Because you didn't seem so eager for your wedding before when all of this started."

First, they know about the wedding being moved up, and now they know about my demented fiancé? Where the fuck are they getting all this information from?

Here's my chance, I could easily tell them everything now, lay it all out on the table, and hope for a miracle in their abilities to save me from this marriage and save themselves and Gio from harm as well.

This could be my out. So why can't I open my mouth and let the words come out? Why can't I tell them everything?

Leo's stupid words are what happened. His words planted a seed of doubt in my mind about the four men sitting around me, and I'm too much of a coward to ask them about Dante because I'm afraid of what their answer will be. I'm so scared that they'll prove Leo right.

I'd rather live in denial than live feeling betrayed. Because for a short time with them, I felt loved, and I felt trust in them to keep me sane, at least for a little while.

"What he thinks doesn't matter. I had my fun and I got over it, that's all there is to it." I shut down my emotions, trying to sound as disconnected as possible while feeding them more lies. "I didn't know I needed to hold a group meeting to discuss it; I thought your egos could handle it."

"Sorry for thinking that we all meant more to you than a simple fuck." Roman growls out, full of disgust.

Their hurt is hard to ignore in all their faces. I look down at my clasped hands in my lap before they break me with their devastation, before delivering what I hope will be the final blow.

"I never promised you anything else. If you thought there was more, then that's on you." The words taste like ash in my mouth. The silence in the room is deafening. If I focus hard enough, it's almost as if I can taste their disappointment, a stale and bitter taste.

Roman scoffs, standing up and storming from the room without another word. Dima keeps his head bowed before me, and one look at Lev shows me he's trying to look anywhere but at me.

Abram, though, stands straight ahead, staring me down, refusing to look away. He looks like he's trying to peel back all my layers, to find all the secrets I keep burying.

"You're just on board for the wedding now? No objections? This is really what you want?" His words are like steel, direct and to the point, and devoid of any emotions.

I make sure I look him in the eyes, putting all my effort into keeping my voice steady so as not to give anything away. Not to give them any reason to think that my words aren't true.

"What I want doesn't matter. This is how it is. I have a duty to my family, and I'll fulfill it in two weeks. Whatever this was is done."

That sends Dima and Lev stalking from the room without a backward glance, leaving Abram and me in a silent standoff.

"We can *help* you, you just have to say the word and we'll do what we can. We can get you out of this." He's almost desperate now, nearly as desperate as I am to trust his words and take the offer. But I hold steady.

"You can't help. This is how it has to be."

He releases a heavy sigh, shaking his head as he moves to the table off to the side of the couch, grabbing a sheet of paper and a pen. He sits down in front of me on the coffee table.

"If that's what you want, then the least you can do is sign this form for Dima." He nods towards the paper, hovering over me with his arms crossed again, detached. "Since you abandoned your joint project, he needs to turn in a statement that you're withdrawing so he doesn't fail because of you."

The project is the last thing I thought he'd ask me about. Granted, I haven't worried about any of my classes since I stopped showing up, but I didn't know my dropping out could affect Dima in any way. It makes sense, the more I think about it.

All in all, my bullshit isn't any reason to cause him trouble with the stupid class. So I grab the pen, scribbling my signature across the bottom line, not even reading whatever statement he wrote.

Offering him the page, he takes it with enough force to wrinkle it, revealing a glimpse of his emotions.

Pushing up from the couch, I stand toe to toe with him. Using the last of my dwindling energy to keep up a brave face.

"Anything else?" I ask, arching a brow.

He takes a step closer, his chest brushing against mine. His head tilts down towards mine, and for a brief moment, I think he might lean in for a kiss.

He stops with his lips a breath away from mine.

"Good luck with your new husband, *Mrs. Ivanni.*" Pulling back abruptly, he moves to leave the room. "You can see yourself out," He adds over his shoulder before disappearing.

Once he leaves the room and I'm left all alone, I feel my heart start to splinter, threatening to shatter and take me down with it. The weight of my lies and all my secrets sits heavily on my chest, making it hard to breathe. I can already feel the burning of unshed tears in my eyes; the dam is ready to burst.

I run from the house, all the way down the drive and out to the corner before I let the first tear fall. My hands brace on my knees as the pieces start to crack, the dam begins to crumble, and I fight to pull air into my lungs.

Letting them go is the right thing to do, I know that. So why does it hurt so fucking much to walk away?

25

Camilla

Time has a sick way of messing with your mind.

It's been almost two weeks since I walked out on the guys, but it may as well have been two years with the way the time drags on. Hours feel like days, seconds feel like hours, and I can do nothing more than lie here, alone, in my dorm and wallow in my own self-pity.

I've resorted to just watching the time pass by. I've lost interest in trying to live out my last days of freedom; there's no point when all it's going to do is remind me of what I'm losing.

I've even stopped letting Gio come around, having said a silent goodbye to him the last time I invited him over. I know he doesn't believe me when I say nothing's going on, so I ended up sharing some hard truth: I'm sad about leaving the guys behind. It was just the right amount of truth for him not to push me any further in asking what's wrong. I know he wants to come around, that he has to know that my sudden isolation is about more than just the guys, but I can't bring myself to tell him.

Since leaving the guy's house, it's been crickets. I haven't heard from them or of them since, other than the rogue question from Gio trying to find out what happened. I can't be surprised by that. I told them I was done, and they listened. That small part deep inside of me was still holding onto hope that they'd see past all the bullshit and come to the rescue. That part of me withers away more and more with each passing day.

The sun finally sets, calling an end to another meaningless day filled with nothing but staring at the same four walls. Unanswered texts and calls flood my phone. Gio is still trying to reach out to me, to get me to talk. My time is almost out. I can't let him back in now; a clean break is going to be the easiest for him to face, the most familiar to him.

The end of another day means nothing to me, just another grain of sand slipping through the hourglass.

I go through the mundane tasks of showering and changing clothes before flipping out the light, sealing the room in darkness with only the small slivers of moonlight slipping in. I shouldn't be tired, but a bone-deep exhaustion weighs me down into my mattress. I feel like I'm back at Briarwood. I've become a shell of a person; the light inside me is being slowly smothered, just like the light in the room.

Another night filled with restless sleep leaves me tossing and turning, the same as every other night for as long as I can remember. In that light space between consciousness and sleep, I hear a sound across the room, like footsteps moving by the door.

I will my body to open my eyes, to check the room, but sleep drags me under as the room falls silent again.

I'm startled from sleep, this time fully awake, when I feel a heavy weight settling over my hips, pushing me down. Panic flares instantly, and I try to pull my hands forward to push at the weight on top of me, coming up short as my hands are trapped. Something binds my wrist, keeping it tethered to the headboard with only a couple of inches of space to move it back and forth.

The moonlight that filtered into the room before I went to sleep has vanished, cloaking the room in total darkness. I can't see what's binding my hands, but more importantly, I don't know what's holding me down.

Panic claws at my throat, and I fight to get air into my lungs as it builds.

My thoughts start to spiral. Did I miscount my days? Is my time up? Why does Michael have me tied down if he's here to collect me? Is this Leo fucking with me again?

Whoever is pinning my legs down leans forward, resting more of their weight on me as they do, only making my fight for air double down.

Through my panic, I catch a whiff of a familiar cologne. Scents of whiskey and teak wood infiltrate my senses, momentarily calming me as I remember where I've smelled it before.

Dima.

I only have a second between my brain registering his cologne before his voice is in my ear, startling me when his cheek brushes against mine.

"Did you miss me, kitten?" His voice is rich and deep, like honey washing over me. With my vision gone, all of my senses are heightened; his words and intoxicating scent have my core clenching in response.

"Like one misses an STD." I buck to try and throw him off my hips, but he doesn't budge. "I thought I told you all I was done."

He nuzzles one side of my face, following my jawline around to the other side.

"Hmm, maybe you did. Doesn't mean I agreed to listen." He bites his way down my jaw and further down my neck, pushing my shirt aside to follow the line of my collarbone.

"Well, you should," I gasp when he hits a particularly sensitive spot, shaking my head to keep my mind on track, and not on his erection currently digging into my stomach. "This isn't going anywhere, so it's a waste of time. It's only going to lead to disappointment."

He stops his ministrations with his tongue, hovering his face over mine so close that I feel his breath brushing my lips.

"Oh, so you are disappointed with your *choice* to let us go?"

"I meant disappointment on your end. You showing up here already proves that point."

His body vibrates with silent laughter.

"You really expect me to believe that you don't want this? Not even one night, a last farewell?"

"I don't," I mutter the lie through gritted teeth, holding back the parts of me begging and screaming at the other parts to shut the hell up and take whatever he's willing to give.

"Let's see, shall we?"

His hands land on my chest, squeezing and kneading them both until my nipples are hardened points beneath the thin sleep shirt.

I know he wants to hear me moan, to hear that he's affecting me, but I won't give him the pleasure. My teeth sink into my bottom lip, and the metallic tang of blood fills my mouth from the pressure while I fight for my life to stay quiet.

The sleep shirt is just a minor roadblock in his explorations. Yanking it up, he pulls it up my arms to rest on top of my bound wrists. The cold air from the room raises goosebumps all over my heated skin as his mouth trails around both breasts. He hovers over each, blowing cool air onto both to make me squirm and arch my back to get him where I want him. He teases me, moving back and forth, but never settling on either of them.

He takes one of his hands, trailing his finger down the center of my stomach, over my hip, and down to the outside of my thigh. He hikes my leg up over his side, the new angle causing me to feel his entire length through the thin panties I put on under my sleep shirt.

I startle as I feel his fingers slide into my waistband, sliding back and forth, teasing.

A protest lies on the tip of my tongue, knowing that as soon as he moves his hand, he'll find the evidence he's looking for to move further.

His hand slips past the waistband, and his fingers dive instantly into my hot, soaking core.

Any protests I had die right there in that moment, feeling his fingers stretching me, stroking that spot inside of me to make that fire rage, building into a roaring inferno while the bite of pain from the stretch keeps me there.

"Lying again, I see." I can hear the smirk in his voice.

"I'm not." My words trail off into a moan as he adds another finger, hitting even deeper than before.

"Tell that your wet cunt, currently squeezing the life out of my fingers." He emphasizes his point by hitching them forward, hitting my G spot. The motion sends a jolt through my core, followed by another embarrassing moan that I can't keep contained. "You thought I was going to listen to your bullshit lies about being done with us and just go on my merry way?"

He picks up the pace with his fingers, ramping up the heat in my core, spreading it through my veins, and pushing me to the edge. Dipping down, his mouth captures one of my nipples, biting and sucking on the hardened point.

The pain and pleasure blend seamlessly, making my head spin. I'm not bothered about my lack of sight; it ramps up the feelings, and right now, the feelings are setting every single nerve ending in my body alight.

"Tell me to stop right now, and I'll leave." He moves to the other breast and delivers another sharp bite.

I can do nothing more than hiss at the sting. Try as I might to force the words from my mouth, to tell him this is a horrible idea and to get out, they won't come.

"That's what I thought." A sharp cry escapes me as he bites down even harder this time, pulling back before releasing with an audible pop.

His mouth latches onto my neck, right at my pulse point, sending my orgasm crashing into me like a wave, pulling me under the surface.

Giving me no time to recover, as the aftershocks still have my legs twitching, he rips my panties straight off of me. The fabric bites my skin as it stretches, then snaps into pieces.

He's sheathed inside me in one single thrust, throwing me into a second orgasm. He stills inside me, feeling my core clenching down on him, groaning in approval, sealing his lips to mine for a kiss.

His tongue fights for entrance, which I allow easily, as our breaths mingle and our tongues war with one another, he begins to move, keeping me firmly rooted in a sea of pleasure, all the sensations blocking out any other thoughts from permeating my brain.

His thrusts are rough, pushing me up the bed so I have to brace my hands against the headboard to keep from bashing my head. My arms shake from the strain of his unrelenting pace.

"You take me so well, kitten. The way your body begs me for more, even as you cry." He switches the pace, going from fast and hard to slow and methodical, pulling all the way out to slam back in. "Admit that you want this, that you want *us*."

I don't take the bait, refusing to give in all the while hooking my feet behind his pack to force him back where I need him.

He doesn't seem to want to play that game, abruptly pulling out, sitting back on his knees. The whine escapes me before I can pull it back.

Grabbing both my hips, he flips me onto my stomach, pushing me up to my knees and entering me from behind. The new position puts a strain on my arms, now crossed over one another with the way they're tied.

The new position has him hitting an entirely different angle, much deeper than before, feeling like he's going to split me in half.

My head is wrenched back to face the ceiling by his hand in my hair, his other hand coming around to rest on my throat while he continues to pound into me.

"If you won't admit that you want us, then how about you admit that you don't want this bullshit marriage." His hand releases my hair before a slap lands on my ass, causing me to cry out in surprise as he smooths the sting with his hand. "Tell me you don't want this and we'll make it go away."

"Why, so you can feel good about yourselves? Feel like saviors?" It's hard to push the words out through the tight grasp he holds on my throat, but I push through. I walked away already. I did the hard part, and I've been dwelling on it for two weeks. I won't fall into his trap that easily, even if the dick is that good. "If I needed your help, I would've *asked* for it."

He delivers another slap, the heat from his slaps radiating across my entire ass now.

"See, I don't think that's true." Another slap, making my core clench around him as his hips keep the same pace. "I think you're scared and backed into a corner. That makes you act irrationally and make poor decisions." Another slap. "Maybe you think that sacrificing yourself is the best option, or you're just too prideful to admit that you need help." Another slap.

He has to project his voice to be heard over my screams with each slap of his hand and each pulse of his hips, hitting spots deep within me that have never been touched before, sending star bursts exploding in my eyes.

"Admit it," He growls, delivering two more slaps while picking up the pace. My arms burn from the strain of pushing back against him and keeping my face from hitting the headboard. I bite my lip, refusing to answer him anymore, or be backed into a corner.

Another slap and I feel my body tense, ramping higher and higher as his intensity increases.

"Admit it," He sounds animalistic now, his hips beginning to stutter as he approaches his peak.

Ignoring him, I angle my hips, bringing him back down to that spot that threatens to make my legs give out, pushing back with my arms to sacrifice my body to him, begging for release.

His hand tightens even further around my neck, stealing my air with it. One more slap and my entire body convulses. I fight the bindings around my wrists, and I fight for air while riding out the waves of pleasure.

I fall limp as the wave recedes, his hand releases my throat, allowing me to gasp in lungfuls of air while he grabs both hips, unleashing all of his pent-up frustration until he finally stills in my with one last, brutal thrust. His hot breath washes over my neck as I feel him spilling inside me, twitching and pulsing until he finally stills.

Our mingled pants fill the silence of the room while we both come back down to Earth. Pulling out roughly, he shushes my whine of discomfort, gently rolling me onto my side while he steps off the bed.

I drift off in the few moments he's away, startling when he pushes me onto my back, spreading my legs, and sliding a damp washcloth between my legs. The dark cover of the room hides the embarrassment washing over me and the heat rushing to my cheeks.

Finally, he pulls the sleep shirt back down my arms, giving me the comfort of a cover as it brushes back down to my thighs while he works on releasing my wrists. Hissing at the pull and strain on my arms as they're finally free, he lies down beside me, kneading and rubbing them to get the blood flowing again.

Without a word, he pulls me to his chest, pulling the blanket over us both and rubbing gentle circles on my back.

He needs to leave. I can't lie here with him and let him lull me into that safe space of comfort that I've come to feel around all of them. Knowing it's only going to be ripped away again in a matter of days. Even knowing that, my body softens into him, soaking up the warmth.

"Just be real with me for a second," He starts, scaring me from falling back under the cover of unconsciousness. "Do you honestly want to go through with this marriage?" He tries to mask his desperation, but I still catch it through his words.

He's silently begging me to give him the answer that he wants, what he plans to do if my answer changes, I don't know, but I can't afford to find out. There's too much on the line and too much still unknown.

"I told you, this is what I have to do. That won't change, regardless of what I might want."

"Just let us help you, don't go through with something you'll regret," He pleads.

"Why do you care so much? You just met me weeks ago, and we fucked. Your concern for me doesn't match up, and it's honestly a little concerning." I feel my frustration mounting. I'm tired of having this discussion with them and tearing myself up inside every time I have to remind myself of what I'm giving up.

His frustration seems to be matching mine, his tone hardening, "We care about you. Is it so far-fetched to you that this is about more than just sex?"

Leaning over, he flips on the lamp next to the bed, casting the room in a soft, warm light and revealing his hardened expression. "We can see you, Camilla. We see the parts of yourself that you hide from the rest of the world. We can see your sadness and your pain, but we also see the light in you that shines brighter with every new thing you try, every new experience you embark on." Tears prick at the corners of my eyes as his words hit me. I never wanted them to see me, but they've brought out the side of me that I've kept repressed for years for my own survival. "We see something special in you, something that we want to explore more. We see that you're vulnerable, and we just want a chance to be with you, but we can't do that if you won't let us help."

He seems genuine, but Leo's words still haunt me, leaving the seed of doubt in my mind. I can't ask them for help because I can't trust them. Gio's life, their lives, and my future all rest on what could be one big lie. I don't want to ask because I know it could bring the whole illusion I've built around them crashing down, but I can't walk away without knowing the truth.

"Did you guys find me by coincidence?" My voice sounds strained to my own ears. As soon as the words are out, I want to take them back, but I know I need to push forward to figure out how to move on.

His brows pull together while he mulls over the question. "What do you mean?"

"I mean, did you all come here to go to school and stumble upon me by chance of fate, or did something bring you here, specifically to me?"

"What would have brought us here to you?" He shakes his head, lost in the conversation.

"Guilt, maybe?"

"Guilt over what?"

"Dante."

I watch the color drain from his face, and his confusion turns to a haunted look. His eyes become unfocused as he becomes lost in his own mind.

"Who?" He chokes out, trying to recover. But I've already seen the recognition in his eyes at the mention of him. The damage is already done.

"Dante, my older brother." I spit out, my anger coming in at full force now, at the realization that Leo's words weren't just a front to ruin my life even more than it already has been. "Did you all come here because of some sick, twisted form of guilt after you killed my brother?"

"What? No. Camilla, we didn't kill Dante." He scrambles, looking for something else to say, but I can't ignore my disgust.

Jumping over him, I pace the floor, feeling my emotions start to spiral as they begin to consume me. Memories flash through my mind, Dante smiling and laughing, enjoying life. Morphing into images of his lifeless body, ashen skin with the life sucked out of him, that I've conjured up by my own imagination. Thoughts of him calling out to me for help, begging for his life, all at the hands of the man sitting in my bed.

Shaking the morbid thoughts, I face Dima, letting him see all the hatred and disgust I've been keeping locked away.

"You knew him. You won't admit you killed him? *Fine*. But you knew him for years, and then you came here to what?

319

Make yourselves feel better after, like fucking his little sister was supposed to free you from your guilt?"

Standing, he holds his hands before him, like approaching a wounded animal and trying to show he's not a threat. He takes a slow step towards me, stopping in his tracks when I match him with two steps back.

"Camilla, please. That's not how it is." He begs.

"Did you know him?" I growl out, needing him to admit it.

Releasing a heavy sigh, he nods.

Ice washes over me, diminishing all of my anger and fight, leaving me utterly numb.

"Get out." The words are barely audible.

He tries to take a step closer, "Please, just let me-"

"I said, get out!" My voice cracks at the strain of yelling.

Resigned, he pulls on his clothes, looking dejected and lost as I stand frozen in the center of the room, not daring to move, following him with my eyes as he stalks towards the door.

Once he has it open, I hold my breath, trying like hell to keep all my pieces together for just a few more seconds. He turns to face me, one more time, but I stop him as he opens his mouth to speak.

"Get the *fuck* out of my life."

One more heartbroken glance and he spins on his heel, slamming the door behind him.

I stagger across the room on shaky legs, like a newborn deer, flipping the lock on the door and bracing my back against it as I collapse. Pulling my legs to my chest, I wrap my arms around them, fighting to keep myself together. But as the pressure on my lungs threatens to suffocate me, and my mind begins to whirl with all of the suppressed memories and suppressed emotions since that day three years ago, come rushing in.

I'm powerless to stop it, the last of my fight stolen away with the final confirmation that my life as I know it is a lie, orchestrated by those around me.

Sobs rip from my chest as the pain consumes me. Acceptance of my fate to relive every tortured moment and memory with the only hope that it will kill me. I shatter like a broken mirror, spilling across the floor into a thousand jagged pieces, begging darkness to come and capture me, drag me down to the depths of hell because that's always been my only fate.

This is it.

The dam has been broken, and now all my demons are coming out to play.

26

Camilla

There are always things that are worse than death.
People always speak about it as if it's the scariest thing in the world; most people fear it more than anything else in the world. I wasn't one of those people.

Death is peaceful, a freeing moment when your soul is released from the shackles that bound it in the mortal world, able to take any form imaginable and move freely. At least, that's how I perceive it.

I crave death as I stand here, dressed up in white lace and satin, like a doll being dressed up. Makeup weighs heavily on my face, making me itch to scratch my skin and peel it off my body. It's a new mask than the one I usually wear, only this one is much more fake. This mask isn't for my own benefit; it's for everyone around me. Hours of effort put in to hide the dark circles painted under my eyes, to add color back to my cheeks. All of the effort in vain, because as much as they paint my face and try to mask my pain, there's nothing that can hide the fact that I'm a broken shell of a human, simply existing through the motions.

Michael came to collect me right on schedule, scooping me off the floor like my world wasn't shattered around me, dragging me back home into a whirlwind of wedding preparation activities.

No one seemed to care that I wasn't fully present; they carried on, preening over me like a show dog.

I've luckily been spared the torture of seeing Leo since getting here. One look at me and I'm sure he'll see just how much he's broken me already. A knock at the door almost has me laughing at the cruel irony of the world, just as I acknowledge my luck, he comes to snuff it out.

Rather than Leo, though, shock slams into me as Gio steps over the threshold into the room.

His face is a mask of pain, and I can see his red-rimmed eyes holding back more tears. Stopping a foot before me, he gives me a once-over, cringing at the monstrosity of a wedding dress that was chosen for me. It was meant to put me on display and make me uncomfortable, I'm sure. The tight-fitted satin clings to my skin, the train lined with lace that's long enough almost certainly to ensure that I'll trip when trying to walk. My arms and the top of my back are left bare, and most of my chest with the indecent neckline that plunges deeply between my breasts.

"What are you doing here?" I force the words through my lips, my throat stinging from the recent crying and misuse.

Wiping a hand down his face, he tries to hide his tears. For his sake, I pretend I don't notice.

"I couldn't let you do this alone," Glancing down at the dress again, he visibly shudders. "Love the dress, by the way." He forces a laugh that I can't force myself to join.

"How did you find out?" Through the fog in my mind, it finally registers that he shouldn't know this is happening today. I purposely didn't tell him so that he could have a clean break; that and he'd be as far away from Leo as possible without revealing anything to him.

He has the sense to look slightly ashamed. "When you stopped answering the door and ignored all my calls, I went to see your guys."

"They're *not* my guys; they stopped being mine the moment I found out they killed Dante," I argue vehemently.

Momentarily stunned at the venom in my words, he carries on. "Well, I went to talk to the four mysterious men, who are most certainly not yours, and asked them if they had heard from you. They were surprised that you didn't tell me yourself, and I have to say, I'm a little hurt that you didn't. And I know that you think they hurt Dante, but I'm telling you, there's more to the story than you think."

I focus on his tie, refusing to meet his eyes and see the hurt that stares back at me. I intended to keep him safe, not make him feel abandoned.

"When did you find out that the wedding was moved up? Or was this always when it was meant to be, and you just lied to me when you told me about it that day?" His words shift from hurt to pissed, slowly growing in volume as he speaks. "Because I'd like to think that my best friend wouldn't lie to me about that. But here we are, standing in a dressing room while you prepare to walk down the aisle, and you don't seem very shocked, Camilla. And the Dima told me he found the wedding invite in your bag, two weeks ago, so why from then to now did you not say anything?"

"Because it doesn't matter, Gio!" I snap.

"It's your fucking life, Camilla! It matters!"

This is what I wanted to avoid, this whole conversation right here. As much as getting ripped away from him before hurt, it was a clean break; there were no discussions, no arguing that we could've come up with a plan to save the day. None of the unnecessary heartbreak was a part of this last time; plenty of pain, but it was easier to swallow without having to see his emotions.

"My life was over the day Dante died, and I got shipped away to a mental institution for trying to follow him! Everyone around me got to carry on, grieve in their own way, while I was beaten and starved into submission for showing any emotion because I'd already tried to take my own life. You were better off thinking I fell off the face of the Earth; I should've just stayed that way." I fight to hold back my own tears, my newly resurfaced emotions not taking long to overtake me. "You say my life matters, but it doesn't. It doesn't matter more than your life, or Dima, Abram, Roman, or Lev's life. Because I *love* you all and I refuse to live in a world where you all suffer because of me! Even if I get shipped back to Briarwood, I'd gladly suffer through that torture if it means that you all get to live your lives and not be dragged down by all of my bullshit."

325

My chest heaves now, the exertion from my emotional outburst draining my sleep-deprived and mentally wrung-out mind.

One thing I know is that before I mutter the words 'I do,' I need to try to rebuild those walls I once had cemented in my mind, because that will be Leo's first point of attack to shut me down truly.

He steps towards me, enveloping me in his arms while I fight the sobs racking at my chest, swallowing them down as best I can.

"That's not your choice to make. You're not responsible for all of our lives, and you should know that the guys and I wouldn't have hesitated to do anything we could to find you a way out of this, whether you wanted us to or not. But any consequences of that would've been on us, because it's the choice *we* made."

"I already lost Dante, I can't stand it if I lose someone else," I argue weakly, knowing he's not going to give it a rest.

Pulling back so he can see me, he settles both hands on my shoulders, "Losing people is a part of life, Cam. It doesn't mean you can avoid anyone who might mean something to you to prevent yourself from feeling that hurt. A life alone, without love, is a long, miserable existence. You're going to lose people, but knowing that is what makes the time you get together so special. And the pain, and the fear, remind you to cherish it before it's gone."

Just like the straw that broke the camel's back, his words are the final blow to crack my resolve. The tears break free, flowing down my cheeks and probably ruining the makeup that had been caked on earlier this morning, not that I give a shit.

Throwing my arms around his neck, I nearly strangle him as the tears continue to fall.

"I'm sorry," I choke out the words. "I was just trying to keep everyone safe. I didn't want anyone to get hurt."

"I know," he smooths a hand over my hair, being careful not to disrupt the carefully crafted, slicked-back updo. "But I've already lost you once, and it would kill me to go through that again. You can't just disappear on me and expect me to just move on."

The door swings open, revealing Leo's cocky smirk while he observes the tears on my face and revels in my weakness. I stiffen at the sight of him, my entire body becoming rigid and ready for a fight. Gio squeezes me one more time, bringing his lips to my cheek in a soft kiss. I keep my eyes on Leo, watching to make sure he doesn't try to make a move, but he stands casually, leaning up against the door jamb.

Just before he pulls away, Gio whispers under his breath, "We'll figure this out. Just trust us."

It takes all my effort not to show any emotion on my face at his words, not with Leo watching like a hawk.

That glimmer of hope rears its ugly head, deep in my core. He said 'us', who is us? He mentioned going to talk to the guys. Did that mean that they were here too? If they are, do I let myself hope that they have any chance at stopping this? Or am I only setting myself up for another tremendous heartbreak?

Gio steps away, smiling reassuringly before sliding past Leo and out of sight, leaving me with the monster before me.

He takes slow and measured steps towards me, stopping just close enough that I have to tip my head to meet his eyes.

"Did you like your gift?" His head tilts to the side, amusement flickering in his eyes.

"Why did you let him come?"

"I thought you'd enjoy a chance to say goodbye properly. Besides, today is such a big day, I figured you'd like to have a *friend* here to witness our beautiful union." He brushes a thumb along my cheek, catching a tear off my chin. Bringing it up to his mouth, he licks it, closing his eyes and savoring the taste. "Your tears are delectable, I'll be sure to get more every day for the rest of our lives."

Digging down deep, I try to channel that false bravado that I know is in there, refusing to let him see me cry.

"If that's going to be the most exciting part of your day for the rest of your life, then that's pretty pathetic."

The vein in his forehead pulses, hinting that my words hit a soft spot, but he keeps his smile locked in place. Stepping around me, he trails a finger along my neck.

"Keep up that spirit," Behind me now, he leans forward to hiss in my ear. "It will be all the more fun to break you if you've still got some fight in you."

His hands move in my peripheral, and something cold wraps around my neck, choking me as it presses into my trachea.

Bringing both my hands up, I try to loosen it, but he pulls it tighter.

"In another act of kindness, I've brought you another gift." I hear a soft click, and the pressure on my neck loosens, marginally. My legs threaten to give out beneath me while I cough through the pain in my throat, swallowing as much air as I can take.

Stepping back in front of me, he admires the new piece of jewelry.

"Perfect, every *bitch* needs a collar." Reaching up, I can feel a smooth metal choker. Pulling and tugging at it, it doesn't loosen. The back of it, where I should find a clasp, is just a smooth slot that must be opened with a key. Stepping into me again, his hand locks around my jaw, sending pain shooting up the back of my neck as he pushes my head back to meet his stare. "Now, are you going to walk yourself down the aisle like a good little bitch? Or do I need to get you a leash?"

His eyes darken as his head tilts, waiting for an answer. His hand tightens even further when I take too long to respond.

"I'll walk," I manage to rasp out.

"Good, pet." Patting my cheek, he finally releases me. "You have five minutes, don't keep me waiting."

The door slams behind him, leaving me in a blissful silence. Stumbling over to the mirror, I take in my new *accessory*. Smooth black metal, joined with a red ruby in the center, stands out starkly against my pale skin. The black metal has small silver indents. Leaning closer, I notice they're words.

Property of Leonardo Ivanni reads along both sides of the ruby, labeling me as a pet for as long as he deems.

I swallow back the bile creeping up my throat. I refuse to break down anymore because of this prick.

I've survived much worse than being labeled a pet—broken bones, beatings, starvation, medication, trauma therapy, all of that worse than a collar.

I refuse to break.

Wiping my tears, I smooth myself over, heading to the front of the church to wait before the closed doors will take me to Leo.

Muffled voices and chatter filter through the doors, but my mind is busy replaying Gio's words.

He said, 'Trust us,' and I can only assume he means the guys. With every fiber of my being, I grab onto the final shred of hope left in me, clinging to it for dear life. He wouldn't have said those words on an empty promise; they have to be here. Even if they're not here, they have to be coming, refusing to believe my lies the same way Gio did. If they do, I might even be able to find it in myself to return the favor and give them the chance to explain their situation to my brother, rather than write them off again.

All the days spent with them replay in my mind, and I welcome the memories, relieved to have something other than pain and sadness filling my mind for the first time in weeks.

Even if they aren't here, I'll have the memories to keep me sane. A reminder that life isn't all pain and misery.

The doors begin to swing open, and the wedding march begins to play.

Taking a breath, I take the first step into the unknown, ready to face whatever comes my way.

I can feel the eyes on me from every side, a sea of strangers' faces watching my every move. Leo stands at the end of the aisle, looking like Lucifer himself in all his glory, standing over all of his disciples.

My father stands to the right of the aisle, next to Leo's father, looking more aged and weaker than the last time I saw him. His face is tight with tension, and he watches me like a hawk, no doubt looking for any signs of rebellion.

To the left of the aisle, I find Gio's comforting smile, standing tall, he watches me with ease, instantly relaxing me.

I keep my eyes trained on him as I count the steps down the never-ending aisle. Somehow, I make it to the end without tripping over the ridiculous heels shoved on my feet, and Gio is quick to offer a hand up the three steps leading to the altar.

With a final reassuring squeeze to my arm, he passes me off to Leo, retreating back to his seat, and everyone is instructed to sit.

Casting a glance over the attendees, I don't find any recognizable faces, and Leo's crushing grip on my hand pulls my attention back to him and his menacing stare.

The priest begins to read his script, droning on in scripture and words of love and union.

"At this time, if there is anyone who objects to this union, you are asked to speak now, or forever hold your peace." He calls.

A pin drop could be heard in the silence that follows. As no one comes forward, he begins to speak again, preparing us to recite our vows. I release a breath I didn't realize I was holding, feeling slightly deflated but masking it quickly, not to draw Leo's attention.

As the priest asks me to repeat after him, I swallow the lump in my throat, resigned to my fate and ready to recite the words that will be the final nail in my coffin.

"I, Camilla Russo, take Leo-" A loud crash sounds, echoing through the church and stopping my words mid-sentence.

Looking back down the aisle, towards the front of the church, my heart stops beating.

Abram stands in the church, looking like a fallen angel, a golden light radiating behind him as he stands tall in his perfectly pressed suit, assertive and commanding in the face of a room full of enemies.

Sweeping his eyes over the guests, he looks unimpressed, until his eyes finally land on me. From across the room, I can see the spark of heat light up his eyes, taking in the dress and darkening once they land on my hand clasped in Leo's.

His eyes shoot back up, finding Leo, as a smirk pulls at his lips.

"Sorry, I'm late. Don't tell me you started without me?"

27

Abram

The slamming of a door startles me awake, sitting up, I groan at the kink in my neck from falling asleep in the living room once again, my laptop open on my lap, but the battery is long dead now. Another endless night of combing through the files Charlotte sent over on the Ivanni's and the Russo's.

We'd spent days looking for everything we could find on both families, learning the ins and outs of the deal struck when Camilla was sold to Leo.

After she sat here in front of us, spewing lies of being willing to go through with the wedding and needing to fulfill her duty to her father, we'd all been hurt. Still, many discussions later, we were looking for anything that might show she had an ulterior motive for going through with this, not believing that she was in this on her own free will.

Believing that she didn't want this didn't make her rejection sting any less. We couldn't figure out what happened to make her turn on a dime the way she did.

Dima barrels into the living room, looking disheveled with his clothes wrinkled and panic etched across his face, yelling for Roman and Lev.

"What happened?" I ask, shuffling to move my laptop and stretch my body to relieve some of the tension. I need caffeine and aspirin if I'm going to get through another one of his tantrums over Camilla. He was taking this the hardest of any of us, constantly on a roller coaster with his emotions, swinging from anger to depression, to hope, and back again. He grew up with a family that was constantly coming and going in and out of his life, so it was no surprise that any signs of abandonment put him on edge.

Roman and Lev step into the room, looking half asleep still.

"What is it now?" Lev yawns, and we all watch Dima as he paces in front of the mantle.

"She knows, she fucking knows!"

The three of us share a look, trying to decipher what the fuck he's talking about.

"Who?" Lev asks.

Pulling at his hair, he doesn't cease his pacing. "Camilla! She fucking knows!"

"For fucks sake," Roman quickly loses his temper. Stepping in front of him to block his path, he grabs his shoulders. "What does she know?"

"When did you see her?" Lev asks, ignoring the death glare I send his way, silently telling him to shut up.

"Last night, I needed to talk to her," Dima shakes his head, ignoring our combined protests. We all agreed to leave her alone while we worked out the details of the plan we were piecing together. It seems we should've kept a closer watch on him. "She knows about Dante, or that we knew him."

"Shit,"

"Fuck,"

"How?"

Our words overlap as we take in the implications of her knowing that we lied. How would she even come across that information to know about our relationship with him?

"That's not the worst part," Dima admits, leaving us on edge and flaring my irritation as he keeps us waiting.

Roman shakes him again, forcing the words to spill out.

"She thinks we killed him." I watch his face crumple at the thought. He's no doubt reliving that night, the same as the rest of us, feeling the pain of waking up and finding Dante the way we did.

"Why would she think that?" Lev joins in with Dima's pacing; they both start to wear a hole in the carpet as they stalk back and forth.

"Where would she even get an idea like -" The doorbell ringing stops Lev mid-sentence. All of us glance towards the door, hesitating only a moment before falling over each other to answer it, clinging to a hope that it's Camilla on the other side.

Swinging it open, I'm shocked yet again, coming face to face with Gio, standing rigidly on the front step with his hands stuffed in his pockets.

"What the fuck do you want?" Roman all but growls beside me.

Looking between the four of us, Gio licks his lips, shuffling from foot to foot.

"We need to talk."

Dima moves to protest, but I put a hand on his chest, pushing him back and nodding for Gio to step inside.

Settling in the living room, we all take separate sides of the couch, boxing Gio in on the center of the sofa with Dima at the head of the room.

"We're listening, talk." Roman stares at Gio, not masking his irritation.

"I need to know if you've seen Camilla?"

"Not since she stormed out of here two weeks ago, telling us that she wanted nothing to do with us," I answer, watching his reactions.

His jaw flexes, muttering a curse, and he fidgets with his hands.

"Why are you asking?"

"She's barely let me see her since fight night when he dragged her out of the rink." Nodding his chin towards Dima, he continues, "She was brushing me off for days, saying she was

336

sick, but now she won't answer my texts, won't answer the door, nothing."

"And you think we did something to her?" Lev's tone takes on a defensive edge, completely unlike his usually carefree demeanor.

Snorting, Gio brushes off his tone, not the least bit concerned. "No, I know she loves you guys. And I know she's reluctant to those types of feelings, so if she shuts me out and she shuts you out, then something else has to be going on."

He does have a point. Camilla can brush us off all she wants; most likely, she is terrified of her own feelings. And being engaged was really a valid reason to call it quits if she was starting to develop genuine feelings for us all. But she wouldn't shut Gio out if that were the case. She's been glued to his side since we found her. If she wasn't with us, then she was with him; she hated to be alone.

"Well, there's the fact that she thinks we killed her brother. We were just wondering where she got that idea from," I toss out. "Any ideas on that one?"

Ignoring the three glares set on me, I watch him. Now's the time for answers, not to tiptoe around this shit anymore. We're running out of time. If he hasn't turned his back on her by now, he isn't going to.

He doesn't try to mask his shock; he tries to piece the information together.

"Dante? Why would she think that? How do you even know about him? She refuses to mention his name if she can help it."

Sharing a look with the guys, we have a silent conversation, agreeing to fill him. He can only help us if he knows how we got here.

"We knew Dante pretty well, actually." Lev starts.

"He joined the academy we were all at in our third year. We clicked from the start, and he fit into our group seamlessly." Roman picks up where he left off.

"He used to talk about Camilla all the time, sharing stories, you could see how much he loved her. It felt like we knew her before we ever met her." I add.

"A drunken night with too many feelings spilled, he made us all promise to look after her if anything ever happened to him. We didn't think it would ever come to that, but then the accident happened, and we lost him." Dima adds, "We were coming to look for her after the accident, but she was gone. There was no trace of her. Years later, we found a match, and that led us here."

"So, you were friends." Gio clarifies, "Why does she think you killed him?"

"That's what we'd like to know." Roman turns to face him with a murderous glare.

"You think I told her that shit?"

Tipping his head, Lev adds, "It's a possibility."

"I didn't even know you knew Dante until two seconds ago. Why would I ever tell her that you killed him?"

Suddenly, it clicks. "Leo," I mutter his name like a curse.

"Fucking bastard," He scoffs under his breath.

"You think so?" Dima asks.

Mulling it over, the likelihood is high. "It would make the most sense. He finds out that she's hooking up with us, gets pissed, moves the wedding up as a punishment, and finds a way to turn her against us in the process."

"Hold on, move the wedding up? To when?"

"Saturday," Roman spits out.

Gio's face drains of color; jumping from the couch, he, too, starts to pace the room.

"No, she can't get married this weekend! She was supposed to have a year; I was going to find a way out of this for her. I can't let her get married to that asshole. I was supposed to have more time!" He spirals before my eyes, crumbling further with every pass across the room.

The pieces all fall into place, the puzzle coming together to paint a whole picture. We've been played from all sides, it seems.

Our time might be running out, but we still have a trick up our sleeve. If we're going to do this, then we need her to trust us, to know that we're on her side.

Stepping in front of him, I stop his pacing.

"We don't have time, but we do have a plan. We need to know if you're with us for the long haul. Because it won't be pretty and it's most likely going to start a war, you need to pick your side now, because once you do, there's no going back."

He doesn't hesitate, showing his true alliance to Camilla.

"Whatever you need, I'm in." He swears, looking me in the eyes, showing me all the love that he shares for the girl who captured our hearts. "You can't let her go through with this."

I can see why Camilla trusts him; his loyalty shines through him, an unmistakable force that can't be swayed. If Camilla trusts him, then that's good enough for me.

Nodding, I offer a hand, shaking his with a firm grip.

"Alright, here's what we're going to do."

Present Day

There's one thing about weddings that I've never understood.

The white dress, fancy food, endless toasts, all of that, I get. But I've never understood the script.

Why stand in front of everyone and willingly give someone a chance to object?

It's foolish.

If you love something, you keep it by your side forever, daring someone to test the bond you've formed with it; you don't offer it up on a silver platter for anyone to swoop in and steal.

Although at this moment, I can see the cosmic irony in Leo, including that particular line, which gives me my opening for a grand entrance.

Straightening my suit, I wait for my cue. I have to make a good impression, after all.

As the silence rings through the church, no one offering any objections, I take that as my cue. Pushing the door open, I give it an extra shove for flair, making sure it hits the wall with a crash.

The ceremony comes to a halt, Camilla breaking off her vows, swinging her gaze to me, startling like she's seen a ghost.

Looks of shock stare back at me, while Leo looks back with murderous rage. My eyes can only focus on the beauty that is Camilla. Dressed in all white, the satin dress hugs every curve of her delicious body. The way her hair is swept up leaves her neck and shoulders on display, looking flawless, except for the monstrosity of a collar wrapped around her neck.

I feel my teeth grind at the thought of him collaring her like a dog.

We'll have to deal with that later.

"Sorry I'm late. Don't tell me you started without me?" I relish the sight of Leo visibly shaking with rage, not likely having expected anyone to rain on his parade.

"I'm afraid we did, we thought the trash had been taken out before the ceremony."

Laughing at his poor excuse of an insult, I dig the invitation from my pocket.

"Oh, but I was invited. Do you always invite trash to your intimate gatherings?" Arching a brow, I hold the paper high, allowing it to be seen in all its glory.

"Ah, an oversight then. Someone will be getting fired for that." He's dumber than he looks if he can't figure out where I got the stolen invite. That or he's really trying to keep his composure up on that altar.

"Well, no worries. It seems I arrived just in time. I hate to do this to you, but I'm afraid I have to object."

Gasps ring out through the crowd. Whispers fill the church, but my focus stays locked on Camilla. She hasn't taken her eyes off me since I stepped in. Her wide eyes lock onto my every word, willing them to be true.

She winces in pain, and I notice Leo's white knuckled grip on her hand. Tamping down my anger at him inflicting any pain on her, I maintain my composure.

"I'm afraid the time for objections has passed," the old priest says behind them, and Leo vibrates with anger.

Letting the tension build, I wait.

And three, two, one.

Dima's arm locks around the priest's neck from behind, pulling him back from Camilla and Leo. "I don't think it has, after all, the rings haven't even been placed."

Leo and Camilla's heads both whip around, staggering at the sudden appearance.

Camilla and Leo's fathers both stand, pulling guns from their waistbands to aim at Dima's head. In the same moment, Lev and Roman appear on either side, their own guns in hand, aimed and ready.

"I brought some guests, I hope that's okay." Leo spins back around at the sound of my voice. "The invite didn't have a limit for plus ones."

"Whatever you think you're doing, I suggest you drop it now. Drop your weapons and leave before every gun in this building is aimed at your heads."

"Don't be hasty," I hold my hands up. "I just came here to put a stop to this charade you have going on."

He drops Camilla's hand, taking a step towards me. "There's no charade; this is a beautiful occasion that you're tainting with your childish antics. Tell me, what do you hope to achieve here?"

I stroll down the aisle, ignoring the death stares sent my way, unconcerned with any illusion of danger pointed my way.

"I've just come to collect what's mine." I reach the end of the aisle, keeping my eyes on him, from the bottom of the steps.

He's fighting to keep his calm facade, but the cracks are starting to show. He's slowly unraveling.

"And dare I ask, what do you think is yours?" He asks through clenched teeth, flexing his hands at his sides.

I can't hide my smile as he falls for the trap, hook, line, and sinker.

"Camilla, of course." Her gasp is the only one I hear this time, chancing a glance her way, I admire her beautifully confused expression. She begins to shake, her eyes darting between Gio and me, the wheels in her mind turning.

Leo's laughter rings through the church, echoing off the walls. The whispers behind us grow louder and more frantic.

"Camilla is not, and will never be *yours*." He draws his own gun, aiming for my head. "Now cut the shit, and get the fuck out, before I paint the floor with your blood."

"It sure seemed like she was ours, while she was choking on my cock five nights a week." Dima drawls, looking bored, still holding onto the trembling priest.

"Or when she was begging for more. Jumping from one of us to another, never getting enough." Lev agrees, digging his gun into the side of Leo's father's head.

"And when she was swallowing my dick while bouncing off yours," Roman glances at me, a wicked grin on his face. "That sure did feel like she was ours."

Camilla's father shudders with disgust.

For a moment, I feel bad, seeing the crimson shade rushing to Camilla's cheeks, but a closer look shows her thighs clenching together beneath her dress, and I know she's getting turned on at the thought of it. And she thought she could convince us that she didn't want us.

That seems to be enough to light the fuse, pushing Leo over the edge.

"Just because my wife is a *whore*, doesn't mean she belongs to you. She'll be punished accordingly for her digressions, but you don't have any claim over her because of where you stuck your dicks."

"I suppose he has a point," I look to the guys, feigning contemplation. "Sex doesn't mean ownership." They nod along, playing my game.

Leo narrows his eyes, flipping the safety on his gun, still aimed to take a shot.

"But I do have this," Reaching into my suit pocket, I pull out the holy grail.

Walking up two steps, I stand within reach and wait for him to take the bait. As expected, he does.

"What is it?" He growls, snatching the paper from my hand, he fumbles to unfold the document while I explain.

"That would be a marriage license, showing that Camilla and I have been happily married for about a month now." Silence falls over the church once again.

Leo's hands wrinkle the page as his eyes scan over it.

Camilla stumbles on her feet, clutching at her chest.

His face hardens into stone, glaring a hole through the page.

"I know, it seems a bit fast. But when it's true love, you can't stand to wait." I continue, "The biggest shock was the support from Camilla's father, but once we explained the depths of our feelings, he surprised us both; he even witnessed the marriage for us."

Aurelio sputters, trying to deny it, but Roman, not missing his cue, is quick to slap a hand over his mouth, keeping the gun pressed against his forehead and giving Leo time to find the witness signature.

Tossing the paper to the ground, Leo's hand shoots out, grabbing Camilla by the throat and dragging her to his chest.

"You think this means anything? You're mine. I don't give a fuck what some piece of paper says, I paid for you, and I'm not letting you go because of some half cocked plan to get out of this." She tries to speak, but the words are muffled by his hand squeezing her jaw. Tears spill from the corner of his eyes, and he tosses her to the floor, staring down at her with disgust, where she lands in a heap of silk and lace.

"Get. The. Fuck. Out." He yells, turning the gun on me yet again.

"Gladly, just as soon as I have what I came for, we'll happily get out of your hair."

"Over my dead body,"

Sighing, I look to Dima behind the priest, then glance at Roman and Lev and back again.

"I suppose that can be arranged." No sooner are the words out of my mouth than chaos ensues.

Grabbing his gun, I shove it up and back, dislodging it from his hands and tossing it aside. Stepping forward, I take advantage of his shock, landing a blow to the side of his jaw.

At the same time, Dima slams the butt of his gun against the priest's head, sending him to the ground and pulling Camilla up off the floor. Gio rushes past me to help pick her up, the three of them shuffling towards the back of the church.

Trusting them to get her out of here, I focus back on Leo, narrowly dodging his fist as it flies towards my face.

The crowd of guests breaks out in panic, screams ring out all around, some people running while others stay back, drawing their own weapons.

I can see the moment Leo realizes not all the men here are aiming at us. What he doesn't know is that they're not all his allies; we have our own network of friends spread throughout the bunch.

Doubling down his efforts, he gets wild with his hits. Swinging aimlessly, we go blow for blow, some of his landing, most of them missing.

The crack of a gun sounds out just behind me. Turning my head, I catch sight of Aurelio falling to the ground, a pool of blood spreading rapidly beneath him. Leo's father follows with another gunshot, freeing up Lev and Roman to fend off two of Leo's men rushing them.

The distraction leaves and opens the way for Leo to get a hit in; his fist cracks against my jaw, followed by another hit to my nose. I hear the sickening crunch of bones breaking, and the blood starts pouring.

He's not a weak opponent by any means, but I trust my abilities and the fact that I have a lot more to fight for than he does.

I finally get him pinned on the ground, locking him down with my knees on his shoulder, pulling my gun to point it at his head while he bucks beneath me.

Before I can pull the trigger, a shot rings out from the back of the church, followed by a blood-curdling scream. Gio's voice follows, screaming Camilla's name. My blood turns to ice.

Leo's laugh draws my attention, his blood-soaked teeth shining up at me as he smiles.

"If I can't have the whore, no one can." He laughs as my mind reels, quickly turning into coughing as he chokes on blood.

I slam the gun into his face, knocking him out and scrambling off of him, rushing towards where they took Camilla.

We had a plan, and everything was going perfectly.

She's just scared, I tell myself, not believing that anything could happen to her. We got her out, we had her covered.

She's fine.

I keep repeating it to myself, pushing through the door and into the back alley.

The sight before me brings me to my knees.

This wasn't a part of the plan.

28

Camilla

Chaos erupts, filling the church.

I'm still trying to catch my breath, my mind still working to keep up.

Abram and I are married?

That can't be possible. But I saw it, my signature was on the bottom of that marriage license.

Nothing is adding up. One moment, I'm saying my vows, and the next, the men that I was begging in my mind to show up appeared. Like white knights, they all appeared in the church.

I've been pulled in twenty different directions in the last half hour, my emotions running through the whole spectrum, leaving me exhausted and confused.

Abram tosses Leo's gun, advancing on him and landing punch after punch into his face. I'm stuck feeling that same bloodthirsty emotion as I did on fight night, but heightened now that it's Abram throwing the punches.

I'm content to sit and watch him beat the crap out of Leo, to give him what he deserves, but Dima's hands grab my shoulders from behind, pulling me off the floor. I struggle to get my feet underneath me, but Gio appears in front of me, steadying me with his hands on my waist.

"I told you to trust us," He winks, and I can't fight my smile, shaking my head and kicking off the stupid heels so I can stand without fear of falling over.

"Come on, kitten. Let's get out of here." Dima throws an arm over my shoulders, tucking me between the two of them as they usher me towards the back door.

Entering the back hall, the sounds from the church instantly become muffled.

They continue to push me forward, but I struggle in their hold, trying to turn back from where we came.

"What about them?"

"They'll be right behind us," Dima assures me, keeping us moving forward.

We make it to another door, this one leading out into an alleyway, littered with trash, and a car waiting at the end.

The exhaustion washes over me again, now that the danger is out of sight. Slowing down, they're practically dragging me towards the car now.

"Just a little further, you're almost there." Gio coaxes me.

Passing over a set of keys, Dima tells him to go ahead and start the car. He takes on more of my weight as Gio runs towards the car.

A couple of hundred feet from the car, a sharp pain stabs the bottom of my foot, faltering my steps.

"Shit!" I hiss, looking down to find a shard of glass from a broken bottle lodged in my heel.

"Fuck, hold still." Dima crouches down to get a closer look, gently trying to pull the glass out.

Out of nowhere, a gunshot rings through the alley. I look up in time to see a man in a suit stand just before the car, his gun still pointed at Gio as he crashes to the ground.

The scream pours out of me before I can stop it, fear seizing me at the sight of him, lifeless on the ground.

Dima's on his feet before I can blink, taking aim at the attacker and rushing towards him when he starts to retreat around the car. Staggering on one foot, I try to shuffle towards Gio, needing to see that he's okay.

I make it about two steps before an arm bands around my neck from behind. I forget about the pain in my foot, and I fight and thrash to get free, pulling at the arm around my neck to no avail.

Dark spots start to cloud my vision, and my fight grows weaker with each passing second.

"Rot in hell with your father, *whore*." I recognize Michael's voice a second before a sharp pain radiates from my stomach.

Warmth rushes down my stomach as his arm releases me, my body instantly falling to the pavement. Rolling onto my back sends fire through my stomach, radiating through to my back.

I should be able to breathe now, without his arm around me, but still I struggle for air, gasping like a fish out of water.

Looking around, Michael's nowhere to be found. Deep crimson spreads across the front of my dress, tainting the blindingly white satin.

My head falls back to the pavement, the effort of keeping it up too much, as the darkness conquers more of my sight.

I fight to not slip into the darkness, not to give in, but it's relentless with its efforts, not letting me go as it takes me further and further away.

Then, like a switch, the pain morphs into something softer, warmer.

The fear and panic give way to a feeling of peace.

I can hear the sounds of footsteps around me, and frantic shouts briefly register in my mind.

"Kitten, open your eyes!" Pressure weighs down on my stomach, intensifying the warmth. "You're going to be fine, just look at me."

"What happened?"

"Go check Gio!"

The name stirs my mind for a moment.

What's wrong with Gio?

"- stabbed her!"

Who got stabbed?

"Tell them to hurry the fuck up! Keep pressure!"

Why is everyone so angry?

"I can't find a pulse!"

Why is everyone so worried? I feel so warm, I just want to sleep.

The darkness closes in, filling my ears and silencing all the voices.

And then, peace.

29

Epilogue

Ringing fills my ears, a blinding light breaks through my eyelids, disrupting the peace that I was savoring.

I fight to find it again, the warmth and the darkness, but the ringing intensifies, making it impossible to relax.

"Cami," The muffled voice sounds far away. I brush it off, hoping they'll let me sleep. "Cami, wake up!"

The voice grows louder, more persistent.

"Camilla! Wake up!"

Groaning, I slap the air, hoping to hit whoever is bothering me. "Shut up!"

"Wake up!" The voice is louder than before, startling me awake, the harsh light blinding me.

Blinking to adjust my eyes, I finally manage to keep them open. Looking around, I'm in an empty room, nothing but four walls and a bed. Something about it seems oddly familiar.

The voice continues to echo around me, coming from outside the room.

Pushing to my feet, I take a moment to steady myself, getting my shaking legs stable beneath me.

How did I get here?

The last thing I can remember is the wedding. Standing at the altar with Leo, seeing Abram walk through the doors, and then, nothing.

Where is everyone?

Making it to the door, I push it open, stepping through the threshold.

The door leads me into the church, and suddenly I'm back at the end of the aisle, facing the altar. The pews are empty, all the guests gone—all but one.

A man sits in the front pew, facing the altar.

One foot in front of the other, I make my way down the aisle again, my footsteps silent beneath me.

As I get closer to the pew, my heart starts to pump faster, a feeling of panic building with each step.

I'm not sure where the panic is coming from, and I yearn to stop and turn around to go back to the room and fall back into sleep. No matter how much I want to turn back, my body refuses to listen, pushing me forward with an urgency to see who's waiting.

I'm almost hyperventilating as I reach the final pew, panic clawing at every nerve in my body.

Despite the panic, I watch my hand reach out towards the man before me.

A mere inch from touching his shoulder, he turns.

My heart stops beating.

Sobs fight their way up my throat, and I choke on air, my lungs refusing to accept.

I manage to pull in a small breath, like breathing through a straw as they watch me struggle.

Staring at them, my mind fights to register what I'm seeing.

Patiently, they wait until I manage to utter just one word.

"Dante."

To be continued…

Afterword

I love a cliffhanger, but man, that was brutal.

This story was so much fun to write, and it helped me when I needed a distraction from the different things going on in my own life. The most significant change is the loss of my soul dog, Pebbles, after 16 years. Being able to channel my emotions into a character experiencing her own form of grief and seeing how she handled it was a helpful outlet for me.

I genuinely love the group of guys who join Camilla on her journey, and I had a blast coming up with them. As it is only the second book that I've ever published, I'm still getting the hang of things, but I am immensely proud of the progress I can see myself making.

I hope you enjoyed Honored Oaths and Tangled Truths, and that you're just as eager as I am to see where the story takes us from here.

Please feel free to leave me a review, tell me what you liked and what you hated about the book. Please give me all your feedback so these stories can continue to grow and take you into another world for an escape.

Thank you so much for taking the time to join me as we follow Camilla. I hope you'll come back to see what happens next!

About the Author

B. Lynn Hedge is wife and 9-5 worker by day, and a writer by night. She runs on diet coke, energy drinks and power naps.

Born and raised in Florida, she still resides there with her husband and fur babies.

She published her first book at 26 and has quickly followed up with a second book, now at 27.

Her extensive book collection showcases her favorite genre, romance and has everything from YA to the darkest of dark romances.

More about B. Lynn Hedge and her upcoming works can be found on social media!

Instagram

TikTok

Facebook Group

www.ingramcontent.com/pod-product-compliance
Lightning Source LLC
Chambersburg PA
CBHW021522250626
47154CB00006BA/1938